Love and Lockdown

Also by Alyce Caswell

The Galactic Pantheon Series

The Tortured Wind

The Twisted Vine

*The Flickering Flame**

*The Shifting Ice**

*The Whispering Grass**

*The Creeping Moss**

*The Galactic Pantheon Novellas***

*The Adventures of Grace Pendergast, Galactic Reporter***
(TBR 2021)

*novella

**collection

Love and Lockdown

Alyce Caswell

ISBN: 978 0 6485444 6 3 (EPUB)

ISBN: 978 0 6485444 7 0 (Paperback)

Cover artwork © KPPWC/Shutterstock.com

For Ben and Dot
together again

1

'It's not like you're asking him to *marry* you. Baby steps, Ange. It might be the twenty-first century, but men still think we have to wait around for them to deign us worthy enough to get on bended knee. So we have to be subtle. Play the long game. Pretend it was their idea all along. Anyway, what choice do you have? Really? Look, this isn't why I called. I need to tell you about all the weird stuff my roommate has been doing lately…'

Angela Tweedie stopped dead on the front stoop, her phone tucked under her chin and her spare elbow braced against the heavy glass door as she debated whether or not she should hold it open.

On the one hand, her neighbour was approaching with his hands full of groceries and his mouth full of wallet. On the other hand, technically she wasn't allowed within two metres of him. Her body might be tensing to do the polite thing—'the done thing' as her mother would say—but they were in the middle of a global pandemic.

Not that she needed the Prime Minister to tell her to keep clear of Colin Cooper.

Even if he wasn't infectious, there was his annoying habit of checking his assigned letterbox after midnight, when she intended on doing the same thing so as to avoid any carriers of the contagion (there must be thousands of them nearby, given the shortage of masks at the shops). Then there was the fact that, aside from the aforementioned mail run, Colin only left his two-bedder (directly on top of her studio, unfortunately) to go to the supermarket—and that was before grocery shopping became one of the few legal reasons to be out and about.

Worse still, he often made strange, erratic thumping noises that reverberated through the poorly soundproofed floor.

Everything about him annoyed her, from his sun-kissed complexion (good genes, obviously, since he rarely went anywhere) to the messy brown hair that somehow defied gravity—and how could she forget those deep green eyes that watched her calmly and unflinchingly, no matter how grumpy she was when they encountered each other.

Colin always seemed so unaffected by her presence. It made her want to strangle him and she wasn't even sure why.

'Ange?' her best friend, Emily, prompted from half a world away.

Angela stepped away from the door. It made a satisfying clunk when it hit the frame.

Colin slowed too late, clearly expecting her to hold it open for him, and he ended up so close to her she could smell his cedar-scented aftershave. God knows what else she was inhaling off him right now, thanks to his complete and utter lack of social distancing. Sure, she was wearing a mask that she'd made last night (aka a sock that had seen a pair of scissors), but it wasn't surgical grade and he wasn't wearing anything across his face *at all*. Wallets stuffed into mouths definitely didn't count.

There was a reason they were supposed to keep two metres away from each other. It was even enforceable by law.

Angela kicked up an eyebrow at him and he dutifully shuffled back a pace.

Head held high, she sidestepped onto the shorn grass (twenty square metres of greenery, along with a matching paint job on the exterior, had apparently been enough for the block of flats to earn the name 'Grace Park') and left a yawning gap between them that would have fit three people obeying social distancing rules. And maybe a dog.

Colin paused on the stoop and turned towards her. The wallet bobbed in his mouth, as if he was about to say something. Uh oh. He wasn't going to let this go, like he usually did.

Panic flushed through Angela, hot and cold like one of her mother's 'tropical moments' (menopause had arrived late for Janet Tweedie and she liked to broadcast how much of a bother it was). It was *waaay* easier to be silently passive aggressive than to defend one's non-neighbourly behaviour. Let him think it was because she'd decided he was plague-ridden.

So what if it wasn't 'the done thing'. He'd live. Maybe. That was no longer a given.

'The long game, right,' Angela said hurriedly and raced towards the footpath on the side of the road. Not a backwards glance at Colin Cooper, not at all. She focused on enunciating her words so that they wouldn't be mangled by her DIY mask. 'Em, has that long game ever worked out for you?'

Emily sighed, clearly exasperated. 'You weren't even listening to me, were you? Like always. Fine, yeah. I get your point. I've given up on the whole dating thing.'

'Too dangerous in the current climate,' Angela agreed as she stamped her way down the hill. She was *exercising*. Definitely not on her way to visit her boyfriend so she could ask him something that would put them on the path to a lifetime of commitment.

Yes, exercising. Of course she was. It was still allowed, just like shopping for essentials was, even if she was using that reason as a cover for a social visit (which was a big no-no). An uncomfortable grey area, but she wouldn't be in it for long if all went according to plan.

'*Nooo*, not that,' Emily said. She was definitely rolling her eyes, Angela was sure. 'Dating in another country is *so* much effort. You meet these guys online, you go see them at a hipster café because no one does pubs anymore, they show you around because the tourist thing is an icebreaker, and then they get bored of you when you stop being new and exciting. All that wasted time and for what? Zip. I should start using Tinder. Much less hassle. It's better if they look pretty and don't say a word.'

Angela yanked the phone away from her ear and stared at it, appalled. 'Social distancing, Em!'

Emily's tone became distinctly disgruntled. 'I'm not doing it *now*, okay? I am seriously climbing the walls here, Ange! And I'm running out of time. God, I'll have to freeze my eggs or something.'

'You're only thirty-one,' Angela assured her.

'And you'll be *only* thirty-one next month, Ange! Practically out to pasture. At least you have a boyfriend. You're a step ahead, you lucky bitch.'

Angela worried her lips together. 'You don't think twelve months is too soon to be asking this?'

'Oh no you don't!' Emily exclaimed, horror etched into every word. 'You can't back out now. Get this boy nailed down ASAP or you'll start eyeing up your daggy surfer roommate. Like I've been doing lately. Anyone starts to look good at my ripe old age.'

Angela thought of Colin Cooper and shuddered.

'I'm not *that* desperate,' she muttered. 'And neither of us is over the hill, Em. Plenty of older women get dates. Just ask my mum.'

'Yes, but she's a classic beauty, isn't she? And her child-bearing days are over. She has forever. We need to act *now*.'

Angela swallowed. Her stomach began twisting itself into knots.

So what if her hourglass figure was a little fuller than average? So what if Emily was about two-thirds her size and had rail-thin shoulders that even coat hangers were envious of? Angela had a hot boyfriend and soon she was going to be able to see his chiselled jaw every single day. Maybe even for the rest of her life.

'Baby steps,' Angela muttered under her breath.

'What was that, Ange? I missed it.'

Angela cleared her throat. 'Wish me luck.'

'Oh, you're going to need a lot more than luck. I've gotta go. Laters.'

The call disconnected. Angela left out a sigh of relief that battered her mask and forced condensation up across the lenses of her glasses.

Sometimes she forgot why she'd been happy to wave her best friend off at Heathrow.

***

'Ho ho ho, special delivery,' Colin Cooper announced, dumping several bags full of groceries on the floor for the third week in a row.

Hands finally free again, he grabbed the wallet that he'd just spat out of his mouth. Right, he'd need to sanitise that before he went out again. The teeth marks were a little obvious. He really ought to have shoved it into his jeans before grabbing the bags, but he'd often used his mouth to hold things when he was busy. It had the added bonus of warding off anyone who might try to say hello to him.

But this weird old habit might actually get him killed if his hands transferred the virus from shelf to wallet to mouth…

'Wonderful!' Loraine White said once the door had opened, revealing spotless beige carpet that clashed with the tired, greying version filling the corridor. 'We are so blessed, Bernard! The Lord has been kind to us this year.'

'Sounds like the Lord has indeed blessed us with bog roll in our time of need,' her husband said flatly, the door now open wide enough to show him ensconced on his favourite armchair in front of a dark television set. Bernard White had declared last week that there was no point tuning into the morning news if there were no longer any cricket test scores to catch up on.

Sport, having gone the same way as casual physical contact, was something Colin missed—but not because he'd ever participated in it himself. Bernard had spent many an afternoon directing colourful language at the Australian batsmen, so loud that he could be heard in Colin's flat, which was two whole flights of stairs away. Loraine would usually follow up Bernard's cursing with pleas for the Lord to forgive her husband, growing more frantic in her prayers while Bernard continued to rile her up in that bored-sounding monotone of his.

Listening to them bicker had been the highlight of Colin's day before he'd actually come down and introduced himself to the couple living in Number Three. Now he knew their names, the names of their children, the names of their grandchildren, and the names of all four dogs they'd once owned.

He really wished he had knocked on their door a lot sooner.

In their eighties and inhabiting a ground-level studio with a gated patio, they were like the grandparents he'd always wanted—as opposed to the stingy ones he had left (Colin had adored his mother's father, but Grandad had been a wonderful exception so of course he'd been the first of them to pass away). If Colin had met Loraine and Bernard before all this started, he'd feel like less of a pillock. The guilt sometimes made him feel physically ill.

At least they didn't know the real reason he'd made their acquaintance.

'I'll leave your groceries out here,' Colin said, already backing away from the reusable cloth bags that he'd run through a washer/dryer the previous night. 'Wait until I'm down the hall before you come all the way out.'

Loraine sighed. 'It's not right, this. It's not natural.'

'It's necessary,' Colin reminded her. One more step. Two.

'But for how long?' She wasn't arguing. She just looked sad. Households were forbidden from having visitors, which meant that she was now unable to see any of her five daughters (one of the many reasons he mentally referred to them as 'The Bennets' in his head instead of 'The Whites', awkward political correctness notwithstanding).

'Until it's safe,' Colin said with a small, apologetic smile. The measures that had been taken to slow the spread of the pandemic could be quite isolating.

'Got to do our bit for the cause,' Bernard added. 'Sitting on my arse is the easiest way I've ever served my country.'

'Bernard!' Loraine gasped.

It was difficult to tell what part of his comment had offended her the most.

Colin hastily forced the laugh back down his throat. 'Drop your next shopping list into my mailbox, okay? Number Twenty-Two. Best do it before Thursday, since the Easter long weekend is coming up. Not sure anyone's dense enough to open up on Good Friday.'

'There are plenty who are dense enough to open their doors to the masses in order to turn a profit, even if these times,' Bernard said. 'And there are plenty more dense enough to shop. No one's got anything better to do. They can't even visit their families. At least at the supermarket they can see a friendly face at the register.'

Some of Colin's annoyance with the crowd at the shops faded away. Bernard was right.

Colin nodded and turned to go. After he'd gone about four metres, he looked back over his shoulder and saw Loraine struggling to pick up the bags. He winced, wishing he could do more than leave them in the hallway. No doubt he wouldn't get into trouble for walking inside and setting the groceries on the counter, with social distancing rules still in effect, but he'd agonise over it for longer than was healthy. Like most people in Newfield, he didn't own a mask (not for lack of trying, mind—you'd only find them in fairy tales now).

What if he brought the virus into The Bennets' cramped studio and killed them? He couldn't be responsible for that. Definitely time to stop eating his wallet.

'Oh cripes!' Loraine exclaimed as she dropped a two-pack of paper towels.

Colin hesitated, considering his options, but Bernard was already asking, 'Did you just take the Lord's name in vain, Loraine dear?'

'I said "cripes", you heard me!' Loraine snapped at her husband.

'Didn't sound like it. What will the Lord think of you now?'

'Make yourself useful and bring the groceries in! You have the better set of hips.'

'Yes, but yours make a nicer view from the sofa,' Bernard said idly.

Her response was sharp, but anyone who knew her could hear the undercurrent of loving exasperation. 'Bernard! Get these bags inside *now*!'

Smiling to himself, Colin climbed the stairs up to his second-floor flat. He stopped briefly on the first floor and darted a look down the corridor, half expecting to see Angela Tweedie from Number Twelve glowering at him from behind a crack in her door.

He only knew her name because the postman kept putting her letters into his box by mistake. He hadn't expected anything so grand for hand-delivering them pre-pandemic ('pre- and post-pandemic' was how he viewed the world and he wondered if The Bennets had thought something similar while growing up during World War Two). A simple 'thank you' would have been enough, but Angela had always recoiled from him as if he was some sort of deadly snake.

And then there were the snide comments she liked to pepper him with, such as 'I'm only awake because *some people* can't stop making weird noises at all hours' or 'I thought I'd get some peace and quiet out here, not unwanted company, but oh *well*'.

Too bad she was such a grump—he might have asked her out otherwise. She was on the short side, but she seemed to have a wardrobe full of clothes that were designed to mask her height. The pleated black skirt was his favourite; it flattered her figure and complemented her dark brown eyes and darker chin-length bob. The look suited her.

The attitude didn't. It also didn't suit him.

Oh well. Not everyone could tick the attractive *and* pleasant boxes.

2

The sun had finished slinking behind a cloud by the time Angela descended the hill to the nearest café. A huddle of twenty-somethings were already queuing up outside, all of them perfectly spaced apart, all of their shoulders conspicuously vacant of straps belonging to satchels and laptop bags. The Bean and Gone was popular with Newfield's Millennials because tourists never made it up the hill from the Dover foreshore and the WiFi was impressively fast compared to the stingy connection to be found at the nearby McDonald's.

The barista on duty today was a bit of an artist—if you desired a Charizard or Harry Potter's glasses paired with a lightning bolt on the top of your froth, then he could deliver it with a smile and your name caressed by a Scottish accent. But opening your eyes would put an end to the fantasy almost instantly.

He definitely wasn't a Jamie. Or a Gerard, or even a Ewan. He looked more like an awkward gangly teenager who'd just had his cheeks cleaned by a mother wielding a spit-sodden hanky.

Angela stood at the back of the queue, trying not to judge her fellow Millennials. Everyone had their vices and coffee was a lot more harmless than some of them. You had to take your pleasures where you could, especially when there weren't many excuses for someone to be out and about these days, fetching takeaway being one of them.

A coffee run kept the freelancers sane. Best to avoid *The Purge* breaking out in Newfield.

Angela envied the freelancers their adaptable lifestyle: remote working, no long commute to London, no boring days spent answering phones. The gig economy had allowed them to make jobs for themselves, so they hadn't lost the ones that someone else had given them. Her queue buddies were used to uncertainty. But even they'd be reduced to eating mushy peas when people with 'normal' jobs stopped being able to pay them the paltry freelance rates they survived on. So many households were losing their main sources of income. The lockdown had closed down many businesses and not every job could be done remotely.

Angela was sure she shouldn't feel so relieved at having lost her normal job before all this started. But it did keep her from breathing in germs on the train.

'Hey! You saved me a spot.'

Angela turned towards Ben, her lips already forming the kiss before she remembered that she shouldn't be doing that. But he wasn't so careful. He closed the two-metre gap, ripped the damp sock off her face as he ensnared her, and then sucked her lips into a kiss that would have earned them both a right proper fine.

Angela extracted herself after about five seconds and flung a guilty smile at the nearby customers. They were all side-eyeing her, she was sure of it, and she really couldn't blame them. She probably looked like one of those people who flouts the rules, infects a busload of people, and then lives to tell the tale while pensioners drop dead around her.

'Two metres, Ben,' Angela muttered, hunching her shoulders and shoving her sorry excuse for a mask into her handbag.

He rolled his eyes, but dutifully retreated until he was standing where the law permitted him to be. And there he needed to stay. Well, for now. They wouldn't need to put that much distance between them after she finally asked him The Question. She was looking forward to waking up beside him every day. She'd even open the front door for him.

Because Ben Littleton was the complete opposite of Colin Cooper.

Ben had perfectly short sandy hair, dark eyes that matched Angela's own (she could admit to liking the aesthetics of that), and an actual job. And he was *built*. He had to be—his body was his brand and his business. Ben was a personal trainer at one of the many gyms lying in the shadow of Dover Castle.

Good God, he was nice to look at.

Ben smirked, clearly enjoying her admiring appraisal. 'Okay, have your two metres. Don't think that'll last long, given your lack of restraint.'

Yes, he was smug. But that kind of confidence was attractive, right? It meant he was going places, because no one could refuse him. He'd never be out of work. Unlike her.

Fifteen minutes later, both of them armed with herbal tea and maintaining the legally-required distance (despite Ben poking fun at her about it, as always), they began looping around the local park. Angela eyed the birds twitting about on the weathered benches with envy; at least they were allowed to stop and take in the sunshine. She'd rather stay here in this treeless (and admittedly quite barren) park, smiling up at the sky instead of reading and re-reading the doom and gloom on her social media feeds. This pastime was so widespread that it even had a name: doomscrolling.

'I'm beat,' Ben said. 'Early training sesh this morning. Let's sit down a sec.'

Angela drew in a hasty breath. '*Ben.* You know we can't.'

'Why not?' he challenged as he perched himself on a bench.

Angela flung a frantic look around the park, but she didn't see any policemen hiding behind the drooping bush of hydrangeas.

'We can't—we have to be exercising, not sitting,' Angela whispered. 'It's the rules.'

Ben flicked his fingers between the two of them. 'What's the difference between us walking and sitting two meters apart?'

Well, he did have a point. Angela gingerly sat down, her heart thumping.

'You're such a goody two-shoes,' Ben said. 'We were swapping spit just last week, so chances are we've already infected each other.'

Angela managed to keep herself from explaining (yet again) that repeated contact might make matters worse for them, because she didn't feel like defending herself just now. And she really didn't want to ask if his 'early training sesh' had involved a client. He'd think she was being paranoid. Not about him being tempted by a bit of fluff—nope, he would correctly guess that she was worried he'd caught the virus from flecks of sweat hitting his skin.

Anyway, she had more important fish to fry. Or maybe she should bury this particular fish underneath a pile of brown sauce to make it a little more palatable. Ew, what sort of metaphor was that? It was a good thing she only read books and didn't try to write them.

'Ben, we don't know how long this pandemic will go on for,' Angela began.

'It'll be over soon enough,' he said cheerily. 'You and your worst-case scenarios.'

Angela shook her head. 'No. I don't think it'll be over soon. We can't spend time in the same room anymore, because we're not in the same household. This is bad enough. We're not really exercising and if someone sees us here on the bench—'

'They can't stop everyone,' Ben chortled.

'I can't afford the fine if I get caught!' Angela said. 'It's a lot of money.'

Ben went quiet for a moment. '*Sooo*...you won't come by anymore?'

Angela closed her eyes briefly, trying to channel the confidence that Emily carried around with her, the same confidence that had seen her move to Sydney to take a job as a yoga instructor—along with about three other jobs that seemed to serve the gig economy better than they did Emily Benson. Okay, maybe there was something to be said for a normal job. At least those treacherously long days resulted in a steady salary. Something Angela didn't have at present, which was why she'd agreed to meet Ben this morning.

Angela surged ahead with The Plan. 'Well, that's what I want to talk about.'

'Oh?' Ben appeared interested, at least.

'You know what the papers said,' she continued, deliberately not looking at him. Maybe it was 'the done thing' to meet a person's eyes when you were asking for something (and she should never stoop to begging, obviously), but she'd lose her nerve if she saw any derision on his face. 'There's three options: we live with the distance for as many months as this takes to blow over, bite the bullet and break up—or we move in together.'

Silence. A nearby Border Collie had stopped sniffing the grass and was now rigid as though rigor mortis had set in, tiny eyes pinned on the only two humans in the park. The wind, however, decided it wasn't going to stick around to watch the fallout and promptly departed.

'Your flat's a studio, though,' Ben said. 'It'd be too small for the two of us.'

Relief swept through Angela. It wasn't a no. He was being practical.

She raced onto the next step of The Plan, concocted over the phone with Emily and well after midnight, when Angela should have been sleeping or searching for non-existent jobs on the Internet. Differing time zones were not entirely to blame for her being up so late (would it kill Emily to stay up for just one call so that Angela didn't have to do it for once?). No, the two bottles of supposedly sedate Moscato had done most of the damage, to be honest.

Angela vaguely remembered stumbling downstairs to check her mail and saying something waspish to Colin Cooper. The details were a little fuzzy.

Angela cleared her throat a couple of times. 'You have a lot more space.'

'Yeah, I do,' Ben agreed.

'Well…I should move in with you, then.'

His eyes went owlishly wide. Not a good sign.

'My parents wouldn't like us sleeping in the same room,' Ben said slowly. 'You know they're Catholic. And old. They're set in their ways.'

It was true. His parents had ended up having him quite late in life, making him a Millennial instead of a Gen X-er like his brother. They were very prim and proper. Angela knew it was too dangerous to mention that a marriage would make her presence much more agreeable in the eyes of Mr and Mrs Littleton.

'They let you use your brother's old bedroom as well, don't they?' she pressed.

'That's my home gym,' Ben said.

'Oh. I forgot.'

Ben needed that room for his work. He recorded daily workout videos for his YouTube subscribers. Thousands of complete strangers paid a surprising amount of money on Patreon to watch bonus footage of him flexing shirtless.

'I can't ask you to give up that income stream,' Angela sighed. 'Especially since the gyms are all shut down.'

'Yeah, I need to save up for a place that doesn't belong to my parents. Sorry, Ange.'

Angela frowned at the clouds for a good long while, wondering why she had been so worried about getting caught on the bench and fined. This outcome was far worse.

'We could get a place together,' she suggested.

'Could we find a decent enough place right now?' he asked dubiously. 'I don't want to get locked into a crummy lease. Things will settle down in a few months anyway.'

'But...' Angela trailed off.

She very nearly told him. But she couldn't. He looked down on people who didn't have a plan B for when they lost their job, who relied on benefits instead of hustle to get by. She did have a parent she could run to for help, but her mother was brimming with judgement and expectations that her eldest daughter could never meet. And Angela would have to choose between her old room, still kitted out in pink with matching curtains that featured a prancing unicorn pattern, or the room that had belonged to her sister, aka The Lawyer.

Phyllis Tweedie worked for a financial trading company in London. Her bed still bore the perfect hospital corners she'd put there during her last visit (none of these visits coincided with invitations for Angela to come by the house and she could take a hint). No long commute for Phyllis; she rented an apartment much closer to the city. Phyllis was The Favourite. And their mother would never dare harangue a twenty-six-year-old lawyer for not having children just yet.

'But what?' Ben prompted. He was frowning now. Clearly she'd been spaced out for too long if he'd noticed something was up.

'But it's going to be a long time before we can touch each other again,' Angela murmured.

He smiled and patted her on the shoulder, apparently not noticing that Angela had tried to lean away from him. 'Cheer up. It's not like it was when that Spanish Flu was going around. We'll still see each other. We've got the Internet now. And apps.'

'Hooray for apps,' Angela said dully.

'Hooray for Zoom!' Ben added, his expression eager. 'We can strip for each other and do naughty things on camera. It'll be fun. And really sexy.'

The thought of hurling images of her naked body across the Internet sent a shudder racing through Angela. She'd always believed that more data existed than MI5 could ever sort through, but there was always a chance she'd somehow attracted their attention and they'd chosen this specific month to check her webcam.

But Ben just looked so *excited*. She couldn't let him down. She'd already done that enough by not keeping up with the exercise regime he'd mapped out for her.

Angela forced her lips to cut through her cheeks, performing the smile that he no doubt expected from her. 'Sure! That sounds great.'

What it really sounded like was a disaster waiting to happen. How was she supposed to have Zoom sex under her mother's roof? It'd actually be less embarrassing if she was caught sneaking a Tinder date out the front door.

Angela accepted another of Ben's illicit kisses and watched him sprint off.

The Border Collie waddled its way over to her.

'Looks like it's just us now,' Angela said gloomily.

That was of course the moment the dog chose to bolt, leaving her alone on the bench.

Oh well. It wasn't like she was unused to her own company. At least this way she could watch whatever she wanted to on Netflix—finding the one thing they could agree on was exhausting.

3

'You'll have to do better than that, Colin. A lot better.'

A few weeks ago, Colin would have rolled his eyes to the heavens and made obscene gestures, maybe even muted his phone and mocked his boss' disapproving voice, all while miming the use of a walking stick. Leo always sounded paternal, despite being planted firmly in his early twenties—though he'd probably have a stern word with God about his birth year when the time came.

An unplanned phone call from Leo used to be short, painless, and verbal only. Colin knew he wasn't the only one who liked to parody Leo, because he was friendly with the handful of DJs who also worked weekday shifts at Radio SPLATZAPP!, an Internet radio 'station' with no fixed address, its employees scattered all over the country. Thanks to the popularity of podcasts, radio had been coming back into fashion even before the pandemic hit. People were figuring out just how much junk they could listen to while doing other stuff.

Now, unfortunately, Colin had to behave while talking to Leo.

Because The Time of the Killer Virus was also The Time of Zoom. And if you ignored those multiple Zoom meeting invitations, then the person who was trying to contact you would then opt for a direct video call. The government's restrictions had somehow led to everyone deciding that they needed to remain in constant visual contact, never mind how much time they'd actually spent looking at each other beforehand.

Sure, it was nice to finally see the DJs he conversed with on a private Discord server that Leo knew nothing about, but Colin had suffered through enough hours of faces being plastered all over his phone in recent times. His relatives liked to tell him that he should break the silence and speak to his mother and/or father again. He liked to pretend that he didn't have parents who thought he should be applying himself to more lucrative endeavours or learning to run the family businesses.

Before the Zoom Boom, the entire lot of them had left him well enough alone.

'How can I do better?' Colin asked his boss wearily, sinking onto the battered sofa he'd rescued from a friend a few months back. The torn fabric and uneven feet made it look like it had come from a halfway house, but the cushions still had some comfort to offer. 'I'm delivering groceries to two vulnerable people downstairs. That has to count for something. I can run with that again, if you like.'

'Oh yes, the geriatric couple.' Leo waved his spare hand dismissively. 'Old news. The segment is called "Daily Inspo". Your listeners want you to *inspire* them. Everyone has an old granny they can take groceries to. They're already doing it because people will side-eye them if they don't.'

Colin swallowed the bile creeping up his throat. It was a good thing The Bennets only listened to AM radio and didn't know how to find his show on the Internet. They'd be disgusted if they knew he'd only helped them because his boss had told him to do good deeds, so that he could boast about them to his listeners.

'Leo, I can't inspire people all by myself,' Colin argued. 'And trying to fill a whole segment with minutiae like opening doors and smiling at people? Forget it. Snoozeville. Why can't I keep talking about the inspiring stuff other people are doing?'

The pitch of Leo's voice climbed a notch. 'The *stuff* you find on Twitter?'

'Yeah. That. I did a great piece on that guy who's dressing up as Santa and delivering toilet paper to a bunch of care homes. I cracked quite a few jokes during that segment, even included some our listeners suggested. They loved it. Toilet humour never goes out of style.'

'I refuse to discuss the so-called merits of toilet humour,' Leo said, his eyes narrowing until they were glacial blue strips. 'I will admit that I was pleasantly surprised by your uncharacteristic willingness to do research for this segment. But anyone can find a Tweet, Colin. Our listeners can scroll their social media feeds for free all they want—we need enough listeners to justify the fees we charge our sponsors. Enough of borrowing other people's good deeds. Time to invent more of your own.'

Colin looked out the window, desperately searching for something to give Leo. It was a good thing he hadn't cleaned the glass in a while. No reflection and no panicked expression. There was no 'inspo' out there either. But the street wasn't deserted.

He saw Number Twelve dawdling along the footpath, maskless and downcast. Her usual thunder seemed to have been replaced by a miserable raincloud.

Odd, he kind of missed the thunder.

Her thick, white-rimmed glasses added to the severity of the expression she used on him for breathing too loudly after midnight or whatever else he'd done to annoy her. Last night, his greatest crime had been his ability to always look like he'd been holidaying in Cornwall. He had learned that she was done with suffering because of her constant pastiness, that she was fed up with not being able to tan, always burning as red as lobster.

Angela had been weaving on her feet and clutching an empty bottle of wine during her rant, so he'd thought it safer to retreat. He probably should have asked if something was bothering her. It was unusual of her to be roaming the halls while drunk.

Nope, she'd probably have tried to tear strips off him.

'Colin, it's impolite not to look at the person you're speaking to,' Leo chided.

'Yeah, my mother told me that,' Colin said with a snort. 'When I was *four*.'

He belatedly winced. This was his boss he was talking to, not some interfering aunt (of which he had many). And there weren't enough jobs going right now that he could jump straight into another one. Colin admittedly didn't need much money, but the radio show had given his life purpose. Something that was his and his alone.

Leo didn't fire Colin on the spot, but he suddenly sounded a good deal less cordial. 'I do not care about your mother's opinion, unless she too has built and run her own radio station. I need something better. So find it. And do it before your dismal listener numbers force me to make an unpleasant decision about your show.'

Leo ended the call without so much as a farewell. He wasn't into pleasantries or discussing the weather. A relief, actually. Colin had had far too many of those conversations lately. That was the problem when one of the few real-life conversations you were allowed to have was with the person running your groceries over a scanner.

Number Twelve visibly drew a large breath and sank down onto the grass just inside the gate of Grace Park. And then she started sobbing.

Colin watched her, wondering if he should open the window and shout down to see if she was okay. Nope. Best to leave her to it. She'd stop crying at some point. Eventually. Any minute now.

I need something better, Leo's voice threatened inside his head. *So find it.*

Colin was racing down the stairs before he even knew what he was doing.

***

It said a lot about Number Twelve's mental state that she didn't unleash her tongue on Colin, run away screaming, or leave two car lengths between them like she had that morning. She looked up at him, sighed, then took off her glasses and wiped them on her peach-coloured jumper—only to curse softly when the lenses smudged even further. She used her skirt instead, which was less fuzzy and seemingly more effective. Her eyes were half-mast and weary behind her glasses when she slid them back on.

Right. He should say something instead of just staring at her from two metres away.

'Are you okay, Angela?' he asked. She really wasn't herself.

Angela rubbed her temples. 'Well, yes. I'm not ill. No one I know is in the ICU.'

'But...' Colin prompted.

'I lost my job,' she said. 'So I can't make rent.'

Colin squashed the first idea that popped into his head. He wasn't a bottomless pit of money. But he could call up his parents…no, definitely not. They'd demand more contact in return and that price was far too steep. He'd used his trust fund to buy a flat half a country away from them for a reason. He'd gladly go broke (not that he would, having saved the rest) if it meant never talking to them again.

Colin pressed his lips together. Leo wanted an impressive good deed out of him and Angela's situation showed promise, but he felt slimy at the thought of taking advantage of her. He settled for saying, 'Have a chat to your landlord. See if they'll give you a discount. Losing your job because of the pandemic has got to make them sympathetic.'

A watery laugh burbled out of Angela. 'I lost my job last year. I had something in London, but I was so tired from the commute I kept making too many mistakes. That stint in admin was just supposed to last until I found a job in my field, you know? I've got a master's in librarianship. I finished it years ago, except I've never been able to land a position. So I'm months behind on my rent and I received an eviction letter before the pandemic actually hit. Sorry. You probably don't want to hear this. I've never been exactly friendly, have I?'

'I hadn't noticed,' Colin said airily and was rewarded with a small smile, something he'd never expected to see her direct at him. The smile exposed cute dimples. He wished he'd seen them sooner. 'I assumed you were just peeved because you had the same idea about checking your letterbox after midnight, when no infectious neighbours are about.'

Her smile grew. The dimples deepened. 'I thought you were doing that just to annoy me.'

'Oh, no. I'm really lazy. I can't be bothered to think up ways to annoy people.'

'A natural gift, then?'

Colin barked out a laugh. She must feel better already if she was taking potshots at him. He should just walk away now, avoid sticking his foot in it—and blow this perfect opportunity.

'Oh God, I'm in trouble,' Angela muttered.

I don't have to use it in my segment, I'll find some other way to make Leo happy, Colin told himself. But he knew that was a lie. Leo was like a Staffy with a knotted rope in its mouth. He'd never let this failure go. If Colin didn't outright lose his job, he'd have to suffer through endless reminders about how badly he'd disappointed Leo.

And the sponsors, of course.

Colin cleared his throat. 'Do you have someplace to stay?'

'Yes. My mother's.'

Oh, he knew that look. 'A nightmare, is she?'

Angela set her chin in the palm of her hand, deep creases spiralling across her forehead. 'Mum's always comparing me to my sister. She's a lawyer. And she's *sooo* successful, with *sooo* much direction in life. I really can't bear the thought of spending months in lockdown with my mother, having to hear her harp on about my life choices and how she had two kids and a thriving career at my age. She'd usually have a busy social life to distract her from me, but right now she can't go out and I'd be the only thing keeping her occupied. No *way*.'

Colin shuddered in sympathy.

'Oh God.' Angela's hands fisted in her skirt. 'I have to hire movers, but what if they won't come? And I don't want strangers touching my things! How long can this virus last on surfaces anyway? Three days?'

Ah, Colin thought. There was the opening he needed.

'I can help there,' he said. 'I know how to dismantle beds and I've got a mate, Rob, who can help me shift sofas. Used to help him move all the time. He had rotten luck with landing a permanent rental until recently.'

'You don't own a van or even a car,' Angela accused.

And there was the scowl, back where it belonged. Colin was strangely relieved to see it.

'I don't need a car to move your stuff upstairs,' he said.

Angela's lips were stitched into a firm line. She didn't dare ask him to clarify what he meant. But she badly wanted to. He could tell.

Colin rolled his eyes. 'I won't charge you rent until the nationwide lockdown is over, okay? I'm going mad without company upstairs. I'm not going to talk your ear off or anything, I promise. It'd just be nice to see someone who isn't my own reflection. I'm really not fond of heading out, but I'll try to keep out of your way.'

She hesitated.

'Only one of us needs to check the mail if we live in the same place,' he baited.

Angela's gaze drifted away from him. Colin felt the sweat gathering between his shoulder blades. He needed her to say yes. So he tried again. 'I'll even stick a thermometer in my armpit to prove to you that I don't have a fever.'

Finally, another smile. An incredulous one. 'You could be asymptomatic.'

'So could you,' Colin pointed out with a smile of his own. He didn't have dimples, but Rob had always grumbled about his floppy, curly hair. Said it made Colin look like he belonged in a boy band, an unfair advantage apparently. 'Guess I have to bring out the big guns, since you're being so stubborn.'

'The big guns?' Angela repeated.

Colin puffed out his chest in an exaggerated fashion. 'Yep. I have toilet paper. It's what makes me so *Charmin*.'

Angela snorted. That was a good sign. And she didn't look like she was about to openly judge him for his preferred brand of toilet paper, which was an even better sign.

She couldn't hate him that much, then.

'Why are you offering?' she asked. 'I don't buy that you're lonely and need company. You could ask anyone to move in with you.'

Colin shrugged. 'Sure. But you need help and I've got a soft spot for people who hate my guts. My spare room is empty right now. All you have to do is help out with the cooking sometimes, because I'm crap at it and I've exhausted all the local Uber Eats options. Lol.'

'Did you just say "lol" out loud?'

'Is that a deal-breaker?' Colin asked with a smirk.

Angela shook her head. 'No. It's fine. I'll move in tomorrow, if that's okay. You don't need your mate to help you. I don't have much stuff.'

'Sounds good. I'll knock on your door at eight.'

A loaded silence followed, long enough to make him nervous. She studied the grass in front of his feet, her cheeks flushed. 'I'm sorry I didn't open the door for you earlier.'

'It's fine, I get it,' Colin assured her. 'Social distancing and all that. I managed.'

He turned and walked away, mulling over the fact that soon he'd be able to stand a lot closer to her than two metres—and he'd be the only person in the country allowed to do so.

Colin shook his head. 'Now *that* is a weird thought.'

At least she'd have no excuse not to open the door for him next time.

4

'Is that it?' Colin asked, his words bouncing off the bare walls of her studio—correction, her landlord's studio. It was already rented out to the next person. The realtor had done a virtual inspection by awkwardly angling their phone about during a brief FaceTime call, but it seemed to have done the trick.

Angela couldn't see why Colin had insisted on one last sweep, just in case they'd missing something. Her mattress and medium-sized suitcase had already been moved upstairs and, aside from those larger items, she'd only owned a kettle and a microwave (both in very poor condition and now headed for landfill). She'd be using Colin's appliances from now on.

Wills, her beloved stuffed bat, usually had pride of place at the head of her mattress, but she would probably need to find a safer place to stash him (and his little tuxedo, which she only put on him for special occasions). No one needed to know about her soft toys or her childhood crushes—least of all Colin Cooper, who she'd never seen dressed smartly. He was constantly roaming the halls in torn jeans and loose band shirts.

But he admittedly had a much nicer crop of hair than the aforementioned Wills.

Angela's gaze landed on the kitchenette, now a lot less cluttered without her colourful tins of loose-leaf tea. Had she forgotten anything? 'Oh! The router. I'll just unplug it.' Then, realising they hadn't discussed utilities, she blurted, 'You do have Internet, don't you? Can I have the WiFi password? I'll let you use my Netflix in return. Unless you want me to pay half of your Internet bill instead…'

Colin shook his head, still looking bemused. 'Oh, no. I'm more than happy to barter for Netflix. What I meant is, there's nothing in here. You slept on a mattress? I'm not judging the lack of TV—who has one of those anymore—but this is kind of Spartan.'

Angela felt her cheeks burn. 'I sold most of my things on eBay.'

But obviously not Wills (*never* Wills). Or her coveted collection of second-hand Highlander romances, which always lived inside her supposedly empty suitcase so that Ben wouldn't see them and make fun of the covers. She'd parted with the *Game of Thrones* Pop! Vinyls, though. That was a pain she could endure. Especially after *that* ending.

'You sold your furniture to cover rent?' Colin swept the room with his eyes again, as if a chest of drawers might be hiding somewhere. 'Can't imagine you got much for it.'

'No, but selling nearly everything kept me away from Mum for an extra month.'

Colin laughed. 'She that bad?'

'The worst,' Angela said, then quickly backpedalled. 'She's not abusive or anything. Just…you know.'

His expression became unreadable. 'Yeah. I do. Let's get this router upstairs.'

Angela trailed after him, wondering what she'd said to make him shut down like that. It occurred to her that his mother might be just as bad as hers (or worse). Appalled by her sudden and burning curiosity, she kept her mouth shut as he carefully arranged the useless router beside her mattress in his spare room. Her suitcase was standing in the corner, looking lost and lonely. Angela glanced at the built-in wardrobe, a pair of mirrored doors that clearly showed the soy sauce stain on the sleeve of her jumper.

Colin's reflection was standing barely two metres from hers. If he took one more step towards her...it would still be legal. And neither of them were wearing masks. It was moot when they were going to be sharing the same space for so long.

'There's one condition I forgot to mention,' Colin announced.

Well, wasn't that convenient? He only remembered this so-called condition when she was all moved in. It better not be something dirty or exploitative. She stared at him, letting her raised eyebrows speak for her.

Now he looked as embarrassed as she felt. 'Don't open the wardrobe. I mean it. I'm deadly serious.'

The words '*why so serious?*' popped into her head before she could stop them.

Angela nodded in what she hoped was a reassuring way. 'That's fine. I don't have enough clothes to fill it anyway.'

'Right,' Colin said, though it was impossible to tell what he meant by that. His lovely green eyes were hooded. Ugh, no. Not lovely. Just green. 'Okay. I'm going to work now. You make yourself at home. I think there's some green tea bags left in the cupboard.'

Colin abruptly stalked off, putting an admirable distance between them in an instant. He slithered through the gap between his bedroom door and its frame, offering Angela a tantalising glimpse of metallic surfaces, and then he was gone, sealed away and doing God-knows-what. She stood very still, listening intently. She couldn't hear anything, so either he worked in silence or his walls had better soundproofing than the ones she'd had downstairs.

The walls in his living room were a lot less boring as well. Instead of footprints left behind by a previous tenant (Angela still wondered how someone had managed to reach the ceiling), they were covered in framed band posters. The Duran Duran one caught her eye, especially since it was from one of their more recent albums. Only real fans liked those.

Maybe they had more in common than she thought.

Angela shook her head and retreated to her new room. The window stuck when she tried to lift it at first, then screeched with annoyance as she finally succeeded. She winced. Clearly Colin didn't use this room very often. Except to store something in the wardrobe.

She eyed its mirrored doors.

As forbidden as an apple in the Garden of Eden. As tempting as a cronut after a long run along the White Cliffs. Well, okay, she didn't run. It was more like a shuffle-and-puff while Ben darted backwards and forwards, telling her to keep pushing until she felt the *burn*.

'Nope, nope, nope,' Angela told herself, backing away from the wardrobe and the guilty expression her reflection was wearing.

She fired up her laptop, ignoring the persistent and worrying whine that came from inside the dented case, and started looking for work in the nearby area. She even broadened her search to include retail positions. There had to be something, *anything*. Nope. There was nothing in Newfield or Dover. London might be ninety-plus minutes away by train, but it had jobs—and a noticeably higher rate of infections than in small towns like hers. But jobs!

U busy? Emily texted, interrupting her.

Oh that's right you don't have a job anymore

Going to call u in a sec ok?

Angela was considering how best to respond when Emily rang her instead of waiting for the go-ahead. Just typical. Angela never dared to ring her best friend without obtaining permission first—she'd end up on voicemail for a week or she'd get texts about how busy Emily suddenly was, which might be true or it might be some polite form of punishment. Emily could only be reached on *her* schedule.

Yes, okay, perhaps their friendship could be a bit lopsided sometimes.

But Angela didn't exactly have her pick of best friends these days.

Two seconds later, despite the gnawing ache in her stomach, she was on the phone to Emily. 'Hi, Em. What's up? Is that wind I hear?'

'Yes, you caught me,' Emily said, sounding breathless. 'I'm out doing exercise.'

'But, Em—you *never* exercise outdoors. You don't like nature.'

'Yes, I do! I always have. Where did you get that idea?'

Angela quickly sorted through her memories. She was pretty sure that was the excuse Emily had used whenever Angela had wanted to go for a walk somewhere. But maybe Emily had changed in the year since they'd seen each other face-to-face.

That was a better conclusion than the alternative.

'I'm going mad inside that apartment,' Emily went on. 'Absolutely mad. And I have to keep fit or I'll end up wearing those maternity jeans I bought for my fat days!'

'Nothing wrong with wearing jeans that don't give you an uncalled-for muffin top,' Angela said, who owned a pair herself. They were comfy. 'Why can't all jeans have stretchy fabric from the hips up? Wait, never mind. I've got something to tell you.'

'Uh oh,' Emily said.

'It's not bad, I promise,' Angela rushed out. 'It's actually quite good.'

'Then spill. And do it fast. I'm only running to the train station and back. I don't have time for an audiobook of your life story.'

Angela gritted her teeth. *If you have nothing polite to say...*

Emily's extended absence had been a good thing, in more ways than one. It had sent Angela to a nearby gym in search of new friends, though it turned out that no one wanted to talk to strangers at the gym—unless they were a personal trainer looking for potential clients, that is.

That was how she'd met Ben. He had been new to the area, so she'd shown him the best chippy and the only café that had decent herbal tea. It wasn't long before she had run out of money for his sessions. But he'd wanted to keep seeing her, miracle of miracles.

She had fallen for him within weeks. Who had the patience for someone like her? Someone who didn't have a filter and always woke up on the wrong side of the bed? Ben had laughingly told her that she was lucky he didn't mind as much as most guys would. He was right. She *was* lucky to have him.

'Hurry up, Ange,' Emily said. 'I can see my apartment complex.'

'I moved out of my studio,' Angela said, deciding not to remind Emily that she had never been fond of 'Ange' as a nickname. Ben was having a lot of trouble remembering that as well.

Emily loudly gasped for air, then wheezed out her next few words. 'Well done, you. I take it Ben convinced his prudish parents to deal with it.'

'Uh...' Angela hesitated.

'I bet they've realised this is the only chance they'll ever have of marrying their son off,' Emily continued, her voice slowly steadying.

'He's quite in love with his own reflection—that's not a bad thing, Ange. He won't get that middle-age spread. I'm so proud of you!'

That supposed pride sounded a lot like envy. Angela couldn't help but smile.

'Yeah, I guess I've done pretty well for myself,' she chirped back at her best friend.

'Well, I'm home now, Ange. Laters!'

'Laters,' Angela echoed, a boulder of dread hanging heavy in her stomach.

Great, now she was going to have to unearth some ancient photos of her hanging out in Ben's bedroom and upload them to Facebook so Emily would think that Ben had said yes.

Angela dropped her forehead into her palms. 'Idiot!'

She had no idea how she was going to pull this off. But if she did, and if Ben finally relented in the next few weeks (absence made the heart grow fonder, didn't it?), then Emily would never know. He might even pop a question of his own! He had to be planning it by now, surely.

'He *will* ask,' Angela muttered.

She stood up and closed the door. It was better to bring out the romance novels in a safe spot where no one could walk past and see her reading them. Ben always laughed when he caught her at it.

She shuddered to think what Colin Cooper might have to say about her habit.

5

'For those of you just joining us after your first disastrous attempt at making sourdough—hi, by the way—I'm DJ Coop, your host for the next three hours. And don't forget, the name of the show is The Late Morning Rambles. It's sunny down here near Dover—yes, it's sunny, no complaints from this Englishman today—and I'd wager you can see all the way to the white cliffs of Calais. Funny, I never could be bothered to walk along our *own* white cliffs before all this mess started. That's my Post-Pandemic Resolution. I'll ditch the car in exchange for fresh air and a view. So yeah, you know I'll never actually do it.'

Colin swallowed quickly, but didn't dare let that second of silence devolve into dead air, a DJ's worst enemy. 'Is it wrong to admit that I'm doing fine? Not getting cabin fever at all? I'm an introvert and hate bumping into people. You lot are alright, because I don't have to talk to you, just at you.'

Another pause, this one a bit longer. Time to get into the Daily Inspo segment. Leo was listening—along with about six thousand bored people on the Internet, according to the numbers. That wasn't bad, but it needed to get better. A lot better.

'I know it's crazy out there—cats and dogs living together, mass hysteria, that sort of thing,' Colin said, his eyes roving around the soundproofing he'd plastered over the walls a couple of years back. He could easily remove the section covering the window, but right now it was blocking out the sunlight and helping to create his own personal Cave of Wonders.

The muted ceiling lights did nothing to hide the ugly, stained curtains that he'd pinned on top of the soundproofing. He'd gone for beige, to match the walls underneath his DIY job, but the fabric had been second-hand, another casualty of Rob's last flat, and the colour was more like the distilled essence of snot. Sure, Colin could have slept in the less depressing spare room (when it *had* been spare), but he'd squished his bed in here during the awkward 'We're Broken Up but One of Us is Still Looking for A Place to Live' phase he'd gone through with his last girlfriend. He'd been too lazy to move the bed back out.

'But maybe, just this once,' Colin went on, selecting the next song with a deft click of his mouse, 'instead of side-eyeing anyone whose shadow falls over our Instagrammed coffees, we should think about how we can help others during this time. No, don't congratulate yourself for social distancing. That's the bare minimum. No brownie points for that. And for the record, baking your own brownies doesn't give you any points.'

Colin laughed shortly, making sure he didn't puff any extra air into the microphone. Feedback wasn't his friend any more than his new roommate was. Speaking of which…

'So what about *my* brownie points?' he mused. 'I'm no hypocrite, thanks for asking, user79089.' He rolled his eyes at the social media posts displayed to his left; he was following the radio station's dedicated hashtag on his second monitor. 'Well, let me tell you a story. I moved into this flat a couple of years ago and the first thing I noticed was my downstairs neighbour, aka Number Twelve. Every time she saw me, it was like my mere presence offended her. When the pandemic hit, I decided to make sure I scheduled my trips to the letterbox so I'd never run into anyone. You know I don't like people. I mean, who in their right mind does? Especially if a single sneeze of theirs might kill you? Anyway, Number Twelve didn't get the memo that this was *my* time and she just kept showing up.'

Colin wet his lips. What he wouldn't give for a drink right now, but he couldn't touch his bottle of water—he didn't want his listeners hearing him take a slurp. The mute button he had at his command was never to be used in the middle of a segment.

He had to ration his pauses. His boss counted every single one of them.

'Look, I'm not going to begrudge someone for getting the same *brilliant* idea as me,' Colin assured his listeners. 'But instead of smiling and remarking on the weather, like any decent neighbour would, she demanded to know what I was doing. Now, I'm no creep, but I thought it would be funny to joke about it. Creeping about like a creep at midnight, when all of our neighbours are in bed. Yeah, it was kind of stupid. I was tired, okay? Then she said only a creep would joke about being a creep and I should pick another time to check my mail. I mean, *wow*. I did mess up, but that was uncalled for. Right?'

His listeners were split on whether or not he'd deserved that. Fair enough.

'I did my best, folks, I tried to avoid Number Twelve like the plague—' Colin abruptly broke off and chuckled. 'Let's just forget I said that, okay? So we kept running into each other and she kept giving me the best passive-aggressive stare. I mean, this stare is *legendary*. I'm usually the king of this sort of thing, but she's got me beat. And as for those snarky comments? *Oof*.

'Now, you're probably wondering when I'll get to the Daily Inspo. Well, I found Number Twelve in a bit of a state yesterday. I'm not cold-hearted—I asked her what was wrong. Turns out this pandemic hasn't just robbed her of a job, it's robbed her of the savings that were keeping a roof over her head.'

Okay, slight exaggeration. But this segment was called 'Daily Inspo', not 'How I Helped Someone Avoid Spending Time with Their Dear Old Mum'.

He had to milk it for all it was worth. Leo was always listening.

Colin stowed the grimace—not that anyone could see it. 'So I have a spare room. Yeah, a whole extra room to myself. We have this thing called space outside the big cities. *Shocking*, I know. Anyway, I offered the room to Number Twelve yesterday. Not because I'm a decent sort, but because my boss says I need to impress you lot during this segment.'

His Twitter feed filled with amused comments. His listeners liked his honesty.

'I now have a roommate and it's all your fault, folks!' Colin told them. 'Here's hoping that our mutual dislike still keeps us two meters apart.'

He swallowed, but his throat remained dry and grated painfully. 'Coming up after the ad break is a B-side from a 1980s record, a soundtrack from a movie, actually. My boss hates it when I play something this old. In my defence, it's pretty good. But don't take my word for it. Have a listen and go vote in the poll running on my Twitter profile. I'll be checking those results in just a few minutes, so get a move on! We'll soon know if my taste in music really is crap—instead of charmingly eccentric. *Goooo!*'

He pressed the 'play' button on his panel, which was like a clunky old keyboard but even bigger—and covered in buttons and dials that would have looked completely alien to an outsider. The most basic (and most important) feature was the level meter. If his audio output didn't remain steady, it would force his listeners to adjust the volume on their end. They might start the show straining their ears to hear him—and then nearly go deaf when a loud song blasted on.

Leo would be very, very unhappy if he heard complaints about this.

The queued song immediately started playing, thanks to Colin's panel being plugged into his desktop computer. A quick stab of another button muted his microphone and switched his computer's audio from his headphones to the speakers. Now his listeners would hear three minutes of ads, followed by fourish-minutes of music. All the files he used for his show were MP3s, linked together by specialised software. He wouldn't need to lift a finger for seven whole minutes.

Colin doffed his headphones and leaned back in his chair, pleased, but the smile slipped right off his face when the fitness tracker on his arm buzzed angrily at him.

Time to get those steps in.

'Yeah, yeah, yeah,' Colin grumbled. He remembered the Tumblr post that had been popular a few months ago, the one joking that fitness trackers were like Tamogotchis from the 1990s, except the animal you were trying to keep alive was yourself. The fudging thing was even more demanding than Leo sometimes.

Colin kicked off his slippers and jumped out of his chair, making a beeline for the kitchen. The kettle was still hot from a pre-show boil, so he threw the water over a tea bag and began pounding the carpet in the living room while he waited for it to steep to an appropriately bitter level.

Around the sofa he went, again and again and *again*.

Music crept out of his bedroom, the B side he'd promised his listeners. He checked his phone and laughed. The poll definitely wasn't working out in favour of poor old Harold Faltermeyer, his favourite retro composer. Colin's audience skewed young (they were in their early twenties and he had a whole decade on them), but age was no excuse. They really needed to develop more sophisticated musical tastes.

His phone buzzed with a message. It was from Leo, a stern order for Colin to put on something his listeners actually wanted to hear. Something *decent*. Like Sam Smith or Billie Eilish.

Colin walked even faster, stomping his heels into the floor.

'Oh my God, what is that noise!?' someone exclaimed.

Colin jolted and slammed his thigh against the sofa. *Fudge!* Just what he needed. Another bruise at armrest level. And of course it lined up with the hole in his favourite pair of black jeans.

He'd forgotten about Number Twelve—or rather, the newest Number Twenty-Two. Quite the achievement, considering he'd just been talking about her to the entire world (well, anyone who happened to be listening to Radio SPLATZAPP!—the supposedly 'hip' name Leo had chosen in an attempt to draw in younger listeners). Running the show through his speakers while he was out of the room had always let Colin know if he needed to go back in because a file had failed to play. But now someone *else* could hear it.

Colin hesitated. He didn't have time to defend Harold Faltermeyer to his new roommate.

He raced back towards his room, nearly tripping over the sofa in the process, and made it inside just as he heard Angela's door open. *Whew*. Colin performed a victorious fist pump.

Then he realised he'd left his mug of tea on the kitchen bench.

'Double fudge,' he muttered.

Colin waited out the rest of the song in his chair and unmuted the mic to deliver his intro again, a necessary waste of breath that reminded everyone they were listening to The Late Morning Rambles and should make a racket about it on social media. That done, he said, 'So I see that the song requests are piling up on my feed. Don't you guys have Spotify? Nope, pretend I didn't say that. We're not promoting another service. No way.'

Colin frowned as he adjusted his chair, slowly enough to avoid an audible squeak. 'Am I getting trolled, folks? Eurovision songs? I thought no one in this country took that stuff seriously. I mean, we sent Humperdinck one year! You philistines. Look, have some Billie Eilish. Apparently I need to play something *decent* for you.'

The show wound up at midday and he handed the reins over to Graveyard Danika, who was based in The Mumbles. She was a vintage 1990s Goth and never shied away from discussing the subculture. Some of her listeners argued on Twitter that she was a poser; other listeners called out the first batch for being sexist, because they were invariably male. Danika had far too much toying with both sides of the argument during her two daily shows. She covered some of the afternoon and a five-hour stint late at night.

And yet she never seemed tired in the Zoom meetings that Leo insisted on holding every day at 6am—*sharp*.

Yawning, Colin shut down his computer. He'd had a late night. Yes, he probably should have spent some of that time writing for his show, but he'd never been a fan of prep work. He preferred to wing it. Leo didn't like that, but Colin had yet to mess up a segment.

The common area in his flat was mercifully empty when he scurried out of his room at lunchtime. Colin considered explaining his job and the potential noise pollution to his roommate, but decided against it. He wasn't in the mood to sit through any snarky comments Angela might have to say about his chosen career. He'd heard enough of those from his family to last a lifetime.

Nope, his bedroom door would just have to stay firmly sealed during his stints on Radio SPLATZAPP!. He would even shut it in Angela's face if he had to.

A little karma might do her some good.

6

She'd nearly caught him yesterday.

She'd nearly caught him doing...whatever it was that made the mysterious thumping noise in the living room. It was only a matter of time before she succeeded.

Angela had camped out on the abominable sofa last night with a blanket spread between her and the ratty cushions, because she wasn't sure whose bum had been on them and what that bum had or had not been wearing. But her patience had not been rewarded. Colin hadn't made the noise. And nor had he gone to the bathroom.

That annoyed her most, since she had the smallest bladder this side of London and she'd needed to go multiple times during the wee hours.

Colin emerged at exactly six-thirty, pairing yet another band shirt with yet another harried expression, and stumbled his way into the kitchen. That cramped room wouldn't have bothered her (she made a point of staying well away when he was in there), except that in order to enter she had to pass through a ridiculous set of saloon doors. Someone had put effort into those—they were stained the same brown as the skirting boards. But they still stood out. And not in a good way.

Colin dawdled through the kitchen's saloon doors, cradling a bowl of cereal that was obnoxiously colourful and sugary. He gave a start when he noticed her on the sofa and nearly dropped his bowl. Angela glowered at him.

'What did I do this time?' Colin demanded. 'It's perfectly reasonable to let the sink fill up with dishes until after dinner. And I've tried not to breathe too loudly, in case that's what's offending you, but I won't stop breathing entirely. I kind of need to keep doing it.'

'What!' Angela threw her eyes up to the ceiling and back. 'Don't be silly. Of course you can breathe. For goodness' sake.'

'Are you sure?' he asked with an infuriating grin that he had no business sporting.

Angela curled her lip. 'Yes, I'm sure. It's the doors I have a problem with.'

Colin blinked. 'What?'

'The *saloon* doors!'

'Oh.' He looked over his shoulder. 'Hey, they are saloon doors.'

'Oh?' she repeated. 'Did you misplace your eyes along with any taste in interior design?'

A wince twisted Angela's cheeks when the words had finished exploding out of her. She could be snarky, but that had sounded downright mean. She quickly prepared an apology.

Colin, however, was smirking. 'I won't claim to have any taste in interior design, but at least those were here when I bought the place. I did notice the doors, by the way. I'd just forgotten the name for them. It was driving me and Rob mad! We'd started calling them washboard doors.'

'One of you could have googled it.'

Colin laughed. 'Sure. But it's been keeping us occupied. We spend a good five minutes on the phone every day joking about it.' He pursed his lips for a moment. 'They are a bit 1970s, aren't they? The realtor assured me this building was less than ten years old.'

'It is. Which means someone deliberately installed them in the last decade.' Angela shook her head, amazed. 'Wow. I'm glad it wasn't you.'

'Why's that?'

Angela waved at the bowl in his hands. 'I can live with someone who eats pure sugar for breakfast.' He clutched his bowl tighter to his chest, like a treasured child. 'But I couldn't live with someone who thinks saloon doors are a good idea. I'd have to move out. It's safer living with my mother than that sort of psychopath.'

'Got it, I'll keep pretending they weren't my idea,' Colin said cheerfully.

Angela looked down at her lap. Shit, the romance novel she'd been reading. She hurriedly slid it back underneath the blanket. She might have worried that he'd seen it if there wasn't something more concerning going on here.

Had she just *smiled* at Colin Cooper? His joke hadn't been that funny.

The lockdown must really be getting to her.

'Well, if that's the only problem we're going to address in this absolutely vital roommate meeting...' Colin trailed off, but before she could jump at the opening he'd given her, he zapped himself back into his room and the door banged shut behind him.

Angela grumbled under her breath. She hadn't been able to ask him about the mysterious thumping noise.

Right. She needed a stiff drink. Something *really* strong.

***

Angela perused her beloved tins of tea, now lined up against the wall of Colin's spare room, then extracted a thistle-and-heather blend she'd ordered from a small Skye-based company. Ordinary black tea served as the base, so the brew shouldn't be more potent than any other of its kind, but for some reason it kept her going for a solid eight hours. Best avoided after the sun went down. Or after midday, really.

Cupping a mug of the stout stuff (especially bitter today because Colin Cooper's existence made it necessary) and taking in the view of Newfield she had from the living room window, Angela tried not to feel listless.

It was kind of hard when she had nowhere to be and nothing to do.

She was terrible at baking so she couldn't pass the time by attacking the oven—and her skills with the cooktop were basic at best. Colin hadn't complained about the stir fry she'd made last night, but he'd probably been too polite to say anything.

Angela sighed. Even her own boyfriend couldn't sit through one of her dinners. Ben had insisted on preparing all of their meals after the first time she'd made him the infamous stir fry. She didn't mind Ben's food all that much, but he was obsessed with trying a new diet every other week. It was exhausting trying to remember what food she was supposed to lie about eating during the day. Almost as exhausting as remembering to hide the romance novels when he came over. Not that there was any danger of that happening just now…

Angela made herself comfortable on the battered sofa and placed her mug of tea on a tissue she'd folded up on the coffee table. Colin didn't seem to possess any coasters. His dismissive attitude towards his furniture grated on her, but she was trying (operative word: trying) not to complain about every little thing, especially since he'd rescued her from her mother's clutches.

But there was no way she'd stop mocking those saloon doors.

Smiling, Angela let her book fall open along the well-worn crease in the spine. Clearly the previous owner had enjoyed this particular sex scene. The spunky heroine wasn't sure if her tartan-bedecked hero would ever feel love along with the lust. Angela was pretty sure the heroine needn't worry.

She enjoyed the formula in romance novels. Predictable and safe. Unlike a certain pandemic that refused to die out and instead kept circling like a vulture.

Angela's backside buzzed. She duly fished her phone out from underneath her.

Watched my latest video? Ben's text asked, complete with a smiling emoji.

'Shit, shit, shit!' Angela said, frantically scrolling through her subscriptions on YouTube. She could indulge in smut later. Right now she had to support her boyfriend.

Her phone started ringing before she could click play.

Angela cleared her throat, preparing herself. She wanted to sound sultry, but not too sultry. Cheerful, but not too cheerful. She was missing Ben already. She just couldn't let on how much. She wasn't *desperate*.

He would want to be showered with a bit of attention, though.

Don't sound too eager, Ange! Emily's phantom voice cautioned her.

'Hey,' Angela said, then tried to take a sip from her mug. The scalding liquid exploded back out of her, hitting the pages of her book. 'Shit!'

'"Hey, shit"?' Ben repeated. He didn't sound impressed.

Angela managed not to reflexively toss her mug onto the floor—the carpet wouldn't break it, but she'd rather not bend down and use her last bottle of hand sanitiser on the stain in case Colin came out and caught her. Hand sanitiser could erase a lot of ills on fabric. What it couldn't erase was the original insult. She had to *live* with this guy. Putting a stain on his carpet would be like a slap to the face. Very poor guest etiquette.

Even if the carpet looked like it hadn't been cleaned since he'd bought the place.

'No, I didn't mean that!' Angela cried. 'Hey, Ben. I just had some very hot tea.'

'Caffeinated?' he demanded.

'Oh. No. Herbal. It has, um, natural ingredients.'

Angela set her mug down on the coffee table and pushed it as far away as she could without leaving the sofa. Ben's view on caffeine was eerily similar to his parents' view on premarital sex. It must not be indulged in. Ever.

But thistle, heather, and tea leaves *were* natural. So there.

'Did you watch it?' Ben asked.

'It?'

Annoyance punctuated his words. 'The video!'

'Oh yes. It's very good.' Angela hastily put Ben on speaker and muted her YouTube app, then clicked halfway along in his video. 'I didn't know you could use gas bottles as kettlebells in a pinch. Using whatever's on hand while the gyms are all shut. Very clever.'

'It is, isn't it?' She could easily envision him preening.

'Wait a minute,' Angela said. 'Shouldn't we be doing a video call?'

'Not a good time, babe,' Ben replied, sounding suitably remorseful. 'I'm hot and sweaty right now. I look a mess. Maybe after I get out of the shower?'

'Too bad I can't join you. And too bad you can't take your phone in with you!'

'Yeah. I'll talk to you in a bit.'

Angela resumed drinking her tea, perplexed. Since when had he brushed off the sexy comments he was always asking her to make? And when had he started calling her 'babe'? It was a good thing that Ben had many desirable attributes. Unlike someone else she could mention.

Someone who was now standing outside his room, empty bowl in hand.

'You can get waterproof cases, you know,' Colin offered.

Angela wanted to evaporate on the spot.

'That was a quick call,' he went on, breezing his way back into the kitchen. 'Is your boyfriend working from home?'

'Yes,' Angela muttered. 'He'll call me back later.'

Colin leaned casually against one of those saloon doors in a way that made his shirt gape open and expose a smooth sliver of skin. Angela flicked her eyes back up to his face. She mentally cursed the surge of adrenaline her phone call with Ben had caused. Her heart was beating erratically.

'What's wrong?' Colin asked, either genuinely concerned or at least having the decency to look like he was.

'I accidentally called him "shit",' Angela said and explained what had happened. She tripped over every second word and then somehow ended up giving him a long-winded history of her tea and some of the strange things she'd done while drinking it in the past.

Colin's laugh didn't settle her heartbeat. In fact, it did quite the opposite.

'Can I have some of that tea?' Colin asked. 'If it's as potent as you say it is, I'll definitely need some for my work today. If you don't mind sharing?'

'Oh, sure. No problem.'

Angela shot off the sofa, then paused halfway across the room—she hadn't hidden the romance novel. Uh oh. But she couldn't go back now. She'd only draw attention to it. Seemingly unaware of her dilemma, Colin took a step to the side and allowed her into the kitchen. The chrome kettle had already started steaming before she realised that Colin was standing barely a metre away. He didn't seem to notice. Or care.

'I just wanted to thank you,' she said.

Colin smirked. 'For what? Not judging you for calling your boyfriend something unpleasant? I'm sure you've said worse about *me*.'

'No! You know what I mean. You let me in move in. For free.'

The smirk dropped.

'These are crappy, uncertain times,' Colin said, watching the kettle intently. He seemed to be checking out his reflection in its shiny surface—was it because of vanity or was he simply avoiding eye contact? She had no idea. 'We should be nice to each other. Not because we're supposed to. But because it will make it easier for all of us to get through this.'

Angela side-eyed him. He did sound sincere.

Colin glanced at his phone and his mouth dropped open. 'Crap! Fudge! You know what? Just give us a yell when the tea's done. Gotta go!'

He all but sprinted into his room, leaving Angela to stare at the space he'd vacated.

'Just when I think I'm starting to like you…' she muttered.

Colin stuck his head back out. 'What was that?'

'Nothing! I said nothing.'

'Okay, well, if it's nothing…can I quickly get at the wardrobe in your room?'

Angela performed an elaborate shrug and dropped a small tea strainer into his mug. But she kept an eye on her room's closed door. And she watched *verrry* closely when he emerged with a rubbish bag wrapped around something bulky.

'Your tea's ready,' she informed him.

'Oh good,' he said distractedly and took it from her with his spare hand before promptly disappearing again.

She found it increasingly difficult to focus on her book after that and instead sat in the corner of her room, definitely not staring at the built-in wardrobe and definitely not wondering what was in it.

Finally, with a sigh, she picked up her phone and distracted herself by watching some of Ben's latest videos. Angela laughed when she saw how many peach and eggplant emojis Ben's viewers had left in the comments. She really couldn't blame them.

Her smile faded within moments.

Right now he was as untouchable to her as he was to his fans.

7

'Just for the record, none of my girlfriends have ever called *me* "crap",' Colin said, deftly avoiding the profanity he wasn't allowed to spout on radio.

We're not some free podcast, we have conservative advertisers to appease, Leo always said whenever one of his DJs brought up their burning need to use one of George Carlin's seven dirty words. Colin had made sure to switch out those words for harmless substitutes when he'd started working for Leo. He wasn't sure he even knew how to curse properly anymore.

Colin glanced over the chatter scrolling down on his left-hand screen and laughed. 'Hey, I can see your Tweets, Jellyfish1996. You should ditch the official Radio SPLATZAPP! hashtag or make your account private. Or maybe say nothing if you can't say something nice! Until I hear otherwise, I'll assume that I'm not crap and nor will anyone address me as such. My roommate is too biased to ask her opinion. She's hated my guts ever since I took up too much space on the stairs while I was moving in.'

He could almost picture Leo impatiently twirling his hand in the 'wrap it up' gesture. Colin might have done just that, if the hashtag wasn't so crowded.

He'd never seen his listeners this active before.

'But I will say this,' Colin said, adopting a thoughtful tone. 'She does have great taste in tea—and she made it strong enough that I could tolerate even you lot today. I think I'll pay her back with a waterproof phone case. That'll be my next contribution to Daily Inspo, alright? Never let a lockdown get in the way of a good time. Or sexy times, rather.'

Colin frowned as several more Tweets with the designated hashtag appeared. 'Wait, you guys are *shipping* me with Number Twelve? For anyone out there who isn't a Zoomer, Millennial, or Gen X-er, the term "shipping" is generally used by fans of TV shows, films, and books. It's what you do when you want to see Character A and Character B hook up. No way. I am *not* hooking up with Character B. The only thing I'm doing is being nice to her. And drinking her tea.'

That's how Mum & Dad hooked up, one listener twittered. *He was the postie & she kept inviting him in for tea. The tea wasn't that great tho haha #splatzapp*

forced proximity is a trope you guys!!!! #splatzapp, someone else added.

No way it's totally enemies to lovers #splatzapp, was another listener's input.

'This isn't fanfiction! Or a romance novel—it's real life!' Colin exclaimed. 'I will not be having this debate. Not now, not ever. It's over. It's done. No more Daily Inspo for you. Here's a song I queued up earlier, but I've forgotten all the witty things I wanted to say about it. Sure, I should have written those witty things down—like a responsible radio host, I know—except I never have a problem coming up with stuff on the spot. Or at least I *did*.

'Fudge! You know what? I blame all of you.'

Colin frantically lined up three generic pop songs, all of them from the past year (that should keep Leo from completely exploding), then slammed the mute button. He managed to kick his chair over as he stood up and was grateful that no one could actually see his attempt to storm off. Talk about undignified. Especially since he managed to clip his shoulder on the doorframe, which led to him spinning around like a drunkard auditioning for the Russian ballet.

When he finally rightened himself, he noticed Angela peering out of her room, her brown eyes wide and a book hanging from two fingers.

'Co-workers,' was all he said.

'You're going to have to see them again at some point,' Angela pointed out in that patented tone of superiority he'd come to expect—even looked forward to hearing—from her. Wait, where had that thought come from?

'Happily, no,' Colin responded. 'I've always worked remotely.'

'Lucky. I hated commuting to London.'

Colin's phone buzzed and he dug through his pocket for it. The text message wasn't a surprise. Nor was its origin. Colin felt the blood drain right out of his face and drip down into his toes. He looked back at Angela.

'What's wrong?' she asked.

'My boss wants to talk. *Now*.'

Angela grinned. 'Uh oh.'

'You could at least pretend to feel bad for me,' Colin complained.

'Is it my fault you went off at your co-workers? I'm assuming that's what you did.'

Yes! Colin wanted to shout at her. *Yes, it is your fault! If I hadn't seen you crying outside, if I hadn't invited you to move in, if I hadn't mentioned you on my show…if you hadn't been born…*

Colin screeched to a halt with that train of thought when he realised the words had taken on the voice of his father. He knew the divorce wasn't his fault, that he'd been a failed attempt to solve a broken marriage, that two wealthy families needed more to unite them than common investment goals—but he still felt about two inches tall whenever he thought about his parents. While Maisie Linton-Cooper would rather ignore her son, Jonathan Cooper had seen fit to lay blame on anyone but himself. Constantly. And somehow always when Colin was finally feeling okay about himself for once.

'I'd better go see what the boss wants,' Colin said distantly and retreated into his room.

'Good luck!' Angela shouted after him.

The angry vibrations coming from the phone in Colin's hand indicated that Leo had tired of waiting for him to respond to the growing number of texts and was now directly video-calling him. This wasn't going to be pretty.

'Colin!' Leo barked as soon as Colin answered. 'Scrap the Daily Inspo segment. Your listeners are hooked on what you just gave them, so we need more of that. Close your mouth! You look like a goldfish. I hope your memory lasts a little longer than three seconds or you *will* have to start writing your segments down, like you promised you would.'

Colin stared at the miniature version of Leo he was holding.

'You're not firing me for going off at my listeners?' he chanced.

Leo's stern frown morphed into bewilderment—that or he was constipated. 'Why would I do that? Haven't you ever heard of talkback radio? The "sheeple" out there love to be insulted and lectured and told how they should be feeling about things. And they need a bit of outrage or they'd never get out of bed in the morning!'

'I'm not a shock jock,' Colin said testily.

Leo waved a hand. 'Irrelevant. You're not panelling a drive programme. Commuters don't listen in to your show—not that there's many of them listening to Sunshine's or Danger's shows at the moment. No, you were meant to be providing entertainment. Which you did. But that's over with. You, DJ Coop, are now *entertainment itself*.'

Colin wondered if an explanation was about to make an appearance.

He didn't have to wait long.

'We've had a spike in listeners,' Leo revealed. 'They're all discussing you and Number Twelve. Seems they want a bit of *romance*. They need a distraction in these uncertain times, something familiar, something that gives them the warm and fuzzies. You do realise that your share of female listeners is abysmal compared to the late morning shows our rivals run? You know the ones I mean. The ones that talk about *Game of Thrones* and *Outlander*. Something you never do, by the way. I think you're the only person on both sides of the pond who hasn't seen an episode of either.'

White-hot panic blasted through Colin.

'What do you want me to do?' he demanded. 'Ask her out? Find some way to fall in love with her? Is that what I'm supposed to do now?'

'Don't be ridiculous, Colin. Just make it up as you go, like you always do.'

'Make it up as I go,' Colin muttered, unconvinced.

Leo began moving through his apartment, the camera on his

phone revealing a kitchen with granite benches and a very odd rangehood that seemed to be held up by a skeleton statue. You could blink and miss it—and Colin wasn't game enough to ask for another look to confirm its existence.

Leo didn't miss a beat. 'It doesn't have to be real. Just pretend. A fictional love story starring you and your roommate. Your listeners won't know the difference.'

'*A fictional love story?* I'm not a novelist, Leo!'

'Do you have bad reception over there, Colin? I seem to be hearing an echo. And I don't need a novelist. I need a radio host. You are one of those, aren't you?'

Colin grimaced. 'So what are you expecting from me, then? A monologue about our supposed time together? A full-cast radio drama with sound effects? Leo, I don't write fiction and I never have. And *romance*? Forget it. I won't do it.'

'You will if you want to keep your job,' Leo said airily.

Colin bit back another retort. Leo could approach any number of eager podcasters in a single day, just like he had done on the ordinary Thursday he'd chosen to create a 'stable' of DJs for his forthcoming radio station. A paid gig during a pandemic was a mouth-watering opportunity. It wouldn't take long for Leo to find a DJ who was a lot better than a Millennial obsessed with 1980s music and bitter tea.

'This lockdown isn't exactly sexy or exciting,' Colin said, grasping for an excuse—any excuse, really. 'And surely there's already enough stories about roommates falling in love. There must be *thousands* of them.'

'That doesn't mean people are tired of hearing about it,' Leo said, now standing near a large window that allowed light into his fancy open-plan apartment (complete with exposed beams). 'Tropes exist for a reason, Colin. Everyone wants to know what they're signing up for and it's comforting to know that things will turn out alright in the end. People love that. As an aside, "*and they were roommates!*" is one of my favourite tropes.'

'Not you too,' Colin groaned.

'Think about the amount of interest this will generate!' Leo went on, completely ignoring him. 'We can offer our listeners a romance that unfolds in real time. They'll be able to have their say on each new development, maybe even influence those developments. I'd like to see our rivals top *that*.'

Colin was already shaking his head. 'This sort of thing just doesn't happen in real life. No one will buy it. Did you ever fall in love with one of your roommates, huh?'

Leo tilted his phone to the side, revealing a bespectacled young man working at the mahogany desk behind him. 'I did. And I married him. Get it done, Colin, or consider yourself expendable. I expect an update during tomorrow's meeting.'

Colin stared at Leo's husband, bemused by what he was seeing. Curry-stained shirt, an alarming amount of bed hair, and a colourful tattoo sleeve. Definitely not who he'd expected for Leo. Forget marriage—how had they even survived each other as roommates?

Leo's carnivorous grin reappeared. 'You can do it, Colin. I have…some faith in you.'

Half a second later, his finger having no doubt hovered over the button, Leo terminated the call. Colin tried to resist the urge to sink his face into his hands.

He failed.

Possibly because he was tired from staying up so late and so often (last night had been an exception, because he'd been too exhausted from all those 2am expeditions). But his spare wardrobe was now a tad closer to empty, which unfortunately meant that it was still mostly full. Angela clearly hadn't looked inside or she'd have made her displeasure known by now. It was going to be a lot harder to get at the contraband with her in there…

Colin abruptly jerked upright when he remembered that he was supposed to be running a radio show. There was barely any time left on the current song. He'd forgotten the name of the artist, never mind the name of their supposed magnum opus.

Why did so many singers have to use autotune? Didn't they know it made their songs all sound the same?

'Hey there, it's DJ Coop and you're listening to Radio SPLATZAPP!,' his mouth started saying, several seconds ahead of his brain. 'So I didn't get fired, which is always a plus. But we *will* have to say goodbye to the Daily Inspo segment. Sad, I know. Not to worry, folks. You'll be getting a daily update on how things are going with Number Twelve instead…'

The official hashtag instantly became crowded with excited Tweets.

His listeners were already keen to know more.

Colin wondered if he could steal someone's TARDIS and go back to Tuesday, when he'd made the stupid decision to invite Angela into his home and into his workplace.

8

Angela stalked down the road with her hand wrapped around the wallet inside her handbag, disgusted with herself for even considering the sugary cereal that Colin favoured. It had been the only thing left in the cupboard (why on Earth did flats never come with actual pantries?) and she'd nearly *gone there*. Nearly fallen into a bowl of regret.

A complete absence of dairy products had saved her from that mistake.

Colin's closed door had also saved her from any exhausting social interaction. He claimed to have a virtual meeting of some kind at six every morning and so needed to run the kettle beforehand. She couldn't be mad about the noise he made in the kitchen, because someone needed to keep their job and pay the bills—and anyway, thanks to Ben dragging her out on morning jogs, her body clock already had a nasty habit of waking her up way too early.

Can't shift yourself off that weight plateau if you make too many excuses, Ben always reminded her.

Angela was fairly certain her plateau had lasted so long because A) her body had decided that this was her weight, no take backsies and B) she couldn't quit sugar. No thanks. Life wasn't worth living without chocolate croissants. And if she had to wear clothes a whole size bigger in return for that small privilege?

Well, it wasn't the end of the world, no matter what Emily said about it.

'Hey, I'm heading to The Bean and Gone,' Angela said into her phone, her sock-mask being sucked into her mouth at the end of each word. The call had gone straight to voicemail, but it had been nice to hear Ben's voice. 'Catch me if you can!'

Pleased with herself, Angela slid her phone into the generous pocket of her flowy brown skirt (she was in a boho-chic kind of mood today) and increased her pace. The cold air immediately bit harder at her cheeks. The sea breeze from Dover could be relentless, even on days when the skies were blazingly blue (*especially* on those days, come to think of it). She'd probably regret having complained about it when summer hit. But for now, she allowed herself a few choice words on the subject.

This was the one 'done thing' that she was comfortable with—practically everyone who grew up in Newfield could discuss the weather until the sun fell out of the sky.

She wasn't good at many things so she'd take it, however minor.

Angela stopped short. The café was open as usual, but it was deserted. She looked around, worried that a pandemic hotspot had blown into Newfield and taken out every Millennial who owned a Macbook Pro. She found herself wondering if the '5G spreads the virus!!' rumour was untrue simply because free WiFi was the culprit instead, then nearly laughed out loud at her own stupidity. Staying indoors was clearly eroding her brain cells.

Maybe there was an upside to exercise after all.

Still, Angela was wary as she approached the circular wooden frame that served as the café's takeaway service point (it had once been a porthole into a busy kitchen instead).

'Good Friday,' the barista explained when Angela hesitated, her fingers clutching her credit card instead of the fiver that no one had accepted from her in weeks. Totally fair, because the virus could survive on polymer bank notes for a while, but Angela hated carrying around smaller denominations. She really wanted to be rid of it.

This morning's barista was wearing a mask decorated with vibrant roses and thorns that matched the tattoos running the length of her sepia-toned arms. The simple silver studs in her ears provided the perfect punctuation for the larger studs adorning her black top, a sleeveless piece that somehow didn't result in goosebumps. The wind certainly hadn't let up yet.

'Are you new?' Angela asked.

'No. I'm the owner who decided to get her hands dirty for once. Or maybe getting out of bed before dawn is my idea of a good time…nah.' An exaggerated wink. 'Figured it was my turn to cover for everyone else and give them all a lie-in.'

'That's nice of you,' Angela said, taken aback. 'I thought for sure it was because you didn't want to pay them any extra for the public holiday and couldn't convince them to come in for their usual wage. Oh! Sorry, I didn't mean to make an assumption. But yes, very nice of you.'

'Shhh,' the café's owner cautioned, leaning out of the window to rake the street with narrowed eyes. 'Don't tell anyone. I'm not a nice person. Not at all. I'd never let Jon stay home to do a virtual church service and I definitely wouldn't let Lilly deliver emergency hot cross buns to her elderly grandmother. No. Not me.'

Angela choked back a laugh, unsure if it was appropriate or not.

The owner of The Bean and Gone winked again and held out a

hand. 'I'm Ishani.' She followed Angela's dubious gaze down to her latex-covered fingers and quickly withdrew them. 'Sorry. Force of habit. Let's not and say we did.'

Angela smiled behind her mask. 'So we did. How's business anyway?'

'Still selling a lot of coffee, but a lot less of the food,' Ishani said, tapping the wooden frame. Her nails were covered with delicate diamantes that still managed to twinkle beneath the gloves. 'Breaking even for now. I kind of like that the freelancers aren't taking up all the chairs anymore. But I'm seriously bored. Even had to start watching Korean dramas on my phone to pass the time. It's that dead.'

Ishani started humming a theme song. Angela couldn't help but join in. She knew exactly which K-drama it was from.

'You too, huh?' Ishani asked.

Angela shrugged. 'Lost my job and had nothing better to do than deep-dive Netflix. What would you be doing right now if you'd lost yours?'

Ishani waved a hand up at the café's sign hanging above them. 'I'm doing it. I took out a loan and created my dream job. Really didn't want to be forced back onto benefits. But I take it you mean what I'd be doing if I had nothing else to fill my time with?'

'Yes, that,' Angela said. 'By the way, I'm jealous. That takes a lot of gumption.'

Clearly Ishani had never let a single moment pass her by. A hustle success story. Angela conceded that she might hate hustle simply because she wasn't any good at it.

Instead of making full use of her unemployed freedom, she'd ended up staring out the window a lot. The pandemic had just made things worse. Idle hands might be the Devil's workshop to Ben's parents, but to Angela they were a quick path to a dark place. And that dark place often involved doomscrolling.

'If I had nothing else to do, I'd do something fun,' Ishani finally said. 'But it would have to make me feel like I'd accomplished something.' She snapped her fingers. 'I know! I'd watch every episode of every K-drama on Netflix and rate them all on Twitter. Good way to make friends with other fans, plus I'd have a log of what I've watched. Is there something that you could post about?'

Angela darted a quick look around. Ben hadn't appeared yet.

The coast was clear.

'I read romance novels,' she said quietly.

'There you go! You can review those. I think there's a website for that...' Ishani whipped out her phone and started scrolling. 'Yeah. You could even join a book club and discuss themes and shit like that.'

'But I don't want to review and discuss books. I...' Angela hesitated. It was hard enough to admit this to herself, let alone a complete stranger.

'Go on,' Ishani said encouragingly.

'I want to write my own romance book,' Angela rushed out.

To her surprise, Ishani didn't laugh. 'Not a bad idea. And when will you ever have this much time on your hands again? May as well take advantage of it.'

'But what if I suck at writing? Everyone will think I'm stupid.'

'How will they think that if you never tell them that you tried?' Ishani asked.

'*You'll* know,' Angela pointed out. 'You'll know I tried.'

Ishani pinched her thumb and forefinger together, then drew an invisible line with them in front her mask, right where her lips would be. She made mumbling noises and widened her eyes, as though panicked about a sudden inability to speak.

Angela snorted. 'Okay, fine, I trust you. Weirdly enough. Huh. This is the longest conversation I've had in months with someone who isn't my boyfriend, my roommate, or on the other side of the world.'

Sympathy threaded through Ishani's words. 'All your friends moved away?'

'Yes. And I only kept one of them after school.'

'The rest were wankers?'

'Pretty much,' Angela replied. She was a lot happier these days, but the memories refused to be formatted from her brain. 'Thank you, by the way.'

'For what?' Ishani sounded bemused.

It was so pathetic, but Angela felt she had to explain. 'For being a stand-in friend.'

'Tell me your name and I won't be a stand-in anymore,' Ishani said. 'Fair warning, though—I don't give away free drinks. Even to friends.'

Angela felt like she owed Ishani a lot more than three pounds.

Most days she was annoyed about how much a cup of tea cost here, but today it seemed like such a pitiful amount, especially since Ishani had written her phone number on the side of the cup just in case Angela needed to chat. Ishani had even agreed to take that troublesome fiver off her hands (Ishani had replaced her gloves after handling the till, so that she wouldn't contaminate any drinks she made afterwards).

When Angela checked her phone, she saw a message from Ben telling her that he was sorry, but he was filming a new video and was too busy to meet her. Angela grinned. It was nice not to worry about what Ben would say if he saw the chocolate melting onto her fingers.

The croissant, unlike the tea, had been complimentary.

Ishani had even eaten one herself, both of them chatting away like they'd known each other for decades. The masks had been doffed at some point, but they'd maintained their distance and it was frankly a relief to exchange smiles instead of muffled words and exaggerated eye movements. Ishani had quickly put on another stylish cloth mask when a new customer appeared. All Angela had was a wet sock and no replacement for it.

Completely unmasked, she dawdled along the footpath, sipping at her tepid tea and now suddenly unable to muster a glower whenever a passer-by walked a little too close to her. She really had to stop expecting the worst of everyone. People could surprise you.

And that included Colin Cooper. Shockingly.

9

'Colin has stepped up and agreed to transform his Daily Inspo segment into a romance serial,' Leo declared. 'And no wonder. Take note of his numbers from yesterday. Adaptation and innovation are the core tenets of growing an audience. I will speak to you all again on Monday, when I expect to hear ideas for new and challenging segments. Don't be late.'

As soon as his face disappeared from various screens across the country, his so-called 'stable' of DJs began the sacred ritual of piss-take (usually about some Draconian measure or yet another wholly unachievable goal thrown at their feet). The weekend DJs weren't inducted into this ritual, since they were high school students doing work experience. Leo ran a separate Zoom meeting for them.

It was probably for the best that the students didn't hear what the older and more mature DJs got up to when Leo wasn't listening. They'd probably develop bad habits, such as inventing increasingly vulgar titles for their future bosses.

Today, however, Colin knew he needed help from the collective instead of indulging in his favourite pastime.

'I'm in deep crap,' he said. 'I should never have agreed to this. I can't produce an ongoing romance serial, especially if it's supposed to make sense. You know I don't write my segments in advance and I definitely don't do fiction.'

Danger Jones, the DJ responsible for the afternoon drive programme, snapped his fingers and jerked forward in his seat so violently that his Ray Bans (Colin had never seen him without them) slid down to the tip of his nose. 'Get someone else to write it! There you go, Coop. Problem solved.'

Colin refrained from getting into it with Danger. Everything was easily solved in Danger's world. Even pandemics. Colin's fellow DJ was a very vocal supporter of the 'herd immunity' theory and didn't seem at all fazed that such a plan would result in even more deaths than they were already seeing.

It wasn't much of a surprise. He went by the moniker of 'Danger', after all.

'Great,' Colin said dully. 'I just need to get a ghostwriter by Monday.'

'Easy!' Danger insisted. 'So many birds are desperate for a gig right now. Can't visit their sugardaddies, can they? They're the ones who can write decent smut.'

Do NOT go there, Colin reminded himself. *He'll argue you into circles until you rage-quit and then he'll think he's won.*

He could tell that Graveyard Danika was also tempted to have a swing at Danger.

She looked sideways at her camera, kohl-lined eyes narrowed. Danika was no poser: she was a Gen X-er and had lived through the height of Goth popularity. With a Dutch father and a mother from Nigeria, she'd said it was inevitable for her to find some way to fit in that still allowed her to make 'a statement'.

Her phone was set up in her art studio (which also doubled as her radio studio) and today she was painting a self-portrait which depicted her surrounded by death and despair, all represented in shades of grey. According to Danika, it was meant to be as if Frida Kahlo had painted *The Scream*. It looked amazing, like all of her artwork did. Leo had even bought a few pieces and never had issues with Danika working on them during their Zoom meetings. No one else in the 'stable' was allowed to multitask.

'Men are more than capable of writing romance,' Danika said. 'Your thoughts, Peter?'

Peter stroked his chin thoughtfully, which meant that his opinion was imminent. Grey-haired, well-spoken, and an incurable romantic, he was known as 'The Love Doctor' to his surprisingly large legion of fans. He handed off to Graveyard Danika when it was time for her overnight shift—her first or second show of the day, depending on how you looked at it.

Peter's screen always featured a cat draped across the back of his armchair and Colin had yet to see it move. He and Danger had a bet going over whether or not it was actually alive.

'Danger. Colin.' Peter sighed deeply, then adopted the smooth-as-chocolate voice that a so-called 'Love Doctor' was probably required to possess by law. 'It might do your dating prospects some good if you read a handful of romance novels. The heroes therein provide a highly desirable blueprint. These books are also quite enjoyable with a glass of wine. And of course it goes without saying that men can both read and write in this genre.'

'Sure,' Colin agreed. 'But not *this* man.'

'Why don't you ask the girl staying in your flat if she can do it for you?' Danger asked, shoving his sunglasses back up his nose.

Colin tapped his desk, mulling it over. Not the worst idea Danger had ever come up with, not by a long shot. 'Huh. You know, I've actually seen Number Twelve reading romance novels when she doesn't think I'm looking. She might be able to give me a few pointers, maybe even draft up a cliché-ridden outline. I'll ask her.'

'Will you be telling her it's for your radio show?' DJ Sunshine asked, her image shaking as she mounted her camera on her desk.

Her screen had been black until now, a supposed 'technical difficulty'. She was the queen of avoiding eye contact with Leo, who could tell just by looking at her if she was lying about how she'd come up with her daily discussion topics (she was no longer allowed to let her grandchildren write down ideas on slips of paper to then be pulled out of a hat).

Danger laughed so hard the Ray Bans actually fell off this time. 'You think Colin should tell her about the show?'

Sunshine frowned. 'Why is that so amusing?'

'Because then he'd have to tell her how this all started,' Danika said. 'That she was only a good deed he needed to do, not someone he wanted to help.'

'Could he just not mention it?' Sunshine asked, distractedly glancing off screen. Her grandchildren had been screaming for several minutes but they'd abruptly fallen silent. Colin could hear actual sirens in the distance. 'Oh dear. I need to shut the door before I go on air again. Don't mind me.'

Her chair squealed as she vanished.

Colin rubbed his temples. 'Sure, I could keep mum. But Number Twelve might give me an idea that works great in a book, but is terrible for a radio show. She needs to know what it's for. But what if she googles my name, even listens to my show's archives? She's bound to hear my older segment if she does that. And she's finally stopped glaring at me all the time, which is a nice change, and she has a really lovely smile...' Yikes. Did he just say that out loud? 'Fudge!

I used her to fill a segment on my radio show. She's going to be horribly unpleasant to live with when she finds out.'

'Nice to see you're more worried about how it affects *you* than it does her,' Danika remarked, setting the stem of her paintbrush between her teeth and leaning in close to inspect her painting.

'You should have told her to start with, Colin,' DJ Sunshine said, reappearing. She shoved her long silver fringe up off her thick purple glasses. 'She still might have agreed to live with you. Who wants to hang out with Dear Old Mum, even in a pandemic? Oh well, this time my kids have got a good reason not to drop by. At least I have the grandchildren to keep me company. You really missed an opportunity to get things out in the open early, luv. Oh dear! I need to put you all into my headphones. I'm on in fifteen seconds…stupid song. I forgot it was the shorter radio edit.'

Sunshine was the only person Colin knew who didn't need to hear her voice through her headphones. Her pitch and volume were always perfect.

Danger chortled. 'No way, if he'd been upfront with her, she'd have buggered off. Coop, you needed to fill the segment. You did it. And you're gonna keep doing it. Doesn't matter how. Leo's the boss.'

'Leo's not listening, Danger, no need to brown-nose,' Danika said flatly.

The Love Doctor pursed his lips. 'Perhaps it is for the best that Colin was not upfront with Number Twelve, since he would not have otherwise been able to get close to her…'

Danika tsked. 'No, Peter. Do not encourage this behaviour.'

'My dear girl, it is practically impossible to meet a partner in the current climate. Colin has happened upon a rare opportunity.'

'I'm not a girl. I'm a woman. We went over this, Peter.'

He immediately made his apologies.

Danika nodded once, her forgiveness just as prompt.

'Whoa, hang on, back up a second!' Colin interjected, annoyed. 'I didn't invite Angela to live with me so that we could hook up. Come on. I really need some help here.'

'Your best bet…' Danika paused as she added the finishing touches to the frizzy hair in her self-portrait, using a cotton bud to do so. '…is to come clean. You might not want to date her, but you do want to be a decent human being, don't you?'

DJ Sunshine muted her mic for a few seconds, abandoning her show and leaving her listeners hanging so that she could rejoin the conversation. 'Oh no, luv, don't come clean now. It's too late. You'll hurt her feelings.' She hastily jumped back into the dead air she'd created. 'And coming up, a word from our sponsors. An online university thought we were highbrow enough to pay us for an advertising slot. Oh dear, what were they thinking?'

Danger Jones began to rant about how unprofessional she was being and how unhappy Leo would be with her on Monday. Rolling her eyes, Danika scratched her signature into the bottom-left corner of her canvas with her glossy black fingernails. Peter reached up to pat the cat behind him. Its whiskers didn't even flicker.

Colin facepalmed. 'Please. *Please.* Help me.'

'Can't blame us for your lack of morals, mate!' Danger told him. 'Do you want to keep your job?'

Colin sighed. 'Yes.'

'Then get Number Twelve to write your new segment for you. Easy-peasy.'

Panic began to swirl inside Colin's gut, like a potent vindaloo. 'Forgetting the ethics of it all, and the fact that I'm seriously feeling bad about this, how do I ask her to do this? What the heck do I even say?'

'At least you *feel* bad,' Danika said, her tone bland.

Colin scowled at her.

Danika was completely unperturbed. 'If you refuse to do this and lose a job you don't technically need, she'll never find out. You'll get a roommate who doesn't want to kill you. If you bring her on board but don't explain how you got yourself into this mess, there's a chance—a very high chance—that she will find out and stop helping you. Boom, you lose your job anyway. Let's not forget that she'll be deeply hurt by the fact that you only helped her so you could boast about it to a bunch of strangers. And if you hurt Number Twelve, I will get your address from Leo and hunt you down. I'm tempted to do it now, come to think of it.'

'Sistahs look out for each other,' Peter added helpfully.

'No, Peter,' Danika said. 'Just no.'

'I think that's enough fuss for now,' DJ Sunshine said, moving her purple headphones down to her shoulders and redirecting the meeting back to her phone's speaker. A BTS song was playing in the background. She'd declared them to be musical geniuses and Colin would have disagreed, except that they made a lot of money. 'Relax, Colin. Breathe. It'll work out, luv, you'll see.'

Colin sighed again. These people were like family to him, so naturally their advice was very contradictory and not at all what he wanted to hear. But he wouldn't trade them for his blood relatives in a thousand years.

'Okay,' he muttered. 'I'll ask her to help me. I think she will say yes. She'll want to pay me back for the free room. But I have to make sure she doesn't know what the segment used to be about or what I've said about her on air. I need her cooperation. But I also need to be prepared. This could go very, very wrong very, very fast.'

Danger visibly perked up. 'Create a Zoom meeting when the fireworks start!'

'I'll even microwave some popcorn,' Danika added.

The meeting broke up after that, to Colin's immense relief. It was a good thing they'd never met each other in real life. He probably wouldn't be able to choose between staging a group hug or murdering them all. But they weren't to blame for his current predicament.

Nope, that was entirely the fault of Colin Cooper, World's Worst Human Being.

There was only one solution.

He needed booze. A lot of it.

'Hey, I need a favour,' Colin said the moment his phone showed his best friend's lean face. Rob Chance was as scrawny as a *Doctor Who*-era David Tennant. The 'ladies' of their generation certainly appreciated it, according to Rob.

'Keen to exorcise another demon already?' Rob laughed. 'That was fast. A lot faster than last year's eviction.'

Colin ran a hand through his hair. 'Don't call my ex a demon, thanks. It was an amicable split. And it's not her fault she didn't realise that I wouldn't be as exciting as DJ Coop in real life. It's also my fault for dating a fan.'

'Yeah, let's not get into that again, mate. What can I do you for?'

'I need a delivery,' Colin replied, eyes drifting to the Talk Talk poster Blu-Tacked to the back of his bedroom door. 'Something to help me talk talk—er, talk.'

'Never thought that would be a problem for you, Mr DJ. Does your boss know you need a bit of a tipple to get going?'

'Haha. Lol. Seriously, though.'

Rob peered somewhere off camera, most likely at the collection of bottles behind the bar. Usually at this time of day there would be music and voices burring in the background, too loud for Rob to take a call anywhere but in his back office. But the restrictions had shut his doors (bars weren't deemed essential enough to stay open) and had thrown him into a new situation.

Not a dire one, because this was Rob. He always knew how to make a quid.

'It's the Easter weekend, Col,' Rob said cautiously. 'I'm expecting a lot of orders, so you'd better get yours in fast. Everyone's busy drowning their woes. Seems Newfield's got nothing better to do. So what'll you have?'

Colin explained his situation, then reluctantly hung up after Rob's insistence that he could be trusted with such an important mission.

A long, low breath escaped Colin.

He was supposed to be laughing at those memes inferring that introverts had been preparing for a pandemic their entire lives. He was supposed to *love* isolation. Except he hadn't realised how much he'd enjoyed being in the same room as someone else. His Zoom family was great, but he really missed knocking back a few with Rob. That good old vis-à-vis.

This lockdown couldn't end soon enough.

But for now, Colin did have company. And he was starting to appreciate it more than he ever thought he would. Maybe he'd go to the kitchen and make some more tea, use that excuse to talk…

It was a something of a rude shock to discover that Angela was missing.

10

Angela had meant to return to Colin's flat immediately, but her feet took her past the McDonald's instead, its carpark full and its queues six people deep. Everyone was lined up two metres apart, which Angela suspected was less to do with politeness and more to do with the fact that there were crosses taped to the floor, denoting where the customers should stand. Most places had such crosses now. Ishani had used spray paint on the concrete strip outside The Bean and Gone.

Crowds were Angela's biggest 'nope nope nope'. She had a perfectly nice chocolate croissant to finish anyway—and she had a different destination in mind.

Her body knew this route. Her mind knew it was forbidden.

But her heart just wouldn't listen.

Ten minutes later, Angela found herself standing outside Ben's front door. A charming two-storey affair, his parents' house blended into the row of identical buildings surrounding it. There was something soothing about every home on the street being constructed out of the same dark brown bricks, containing the same identical nuclear families, and having the same cropped lawns that were 'the done thing' on Newside Street.

No overgrown yards for us, thank you very much.

Everything had to look like it belonged.

The rather large non-Millennial population of Newfield might deride those who used Instagram, but they didn't need to take photos of their efforts in order to be vain.

Angela glanced down at her outfit. Her skirt probably should have been washed last week and the cuffs of her white blouse were coming unhemmed, too long to be hidden beneath the truncated sleeves of the brown velvet jacket that ended above her waist. Angela's mother would have said that a piece of the jacket missing, since it was so short—and how impractical, Angela might as well not be wearing it at all. And who was she trying to impress? The boyfriend who only ever wore sweat and spandex?

Angela was a frumpy blight in a neat and orderly neighbourhood. Someone would surely notice her standing there. Someone would realise that this street wasn't hers, that she was flouting the lockdown rules just by taking up space on the footpath.

Why was she here anyway?

Her phone buzzed: a message from Emily. *I am so tired delirious stop me b4 I go to bed with surfer dude*

The Emily Benson of last year would never have been available to chat at this time. Too busy, too much hustle. Working from home had its drawbacks, roommates among them. Emily constantly complained that staying inside the same four walls every day was actually more tiring than going *out*. Fortunately, Emily was still able to run her yoga instructor business online, though she often complained about how slow the Internet was in Sydney.

Distract me plzzzz, Emily begged.

The timing couldn't have been better.

Angela scuttled up to the front door, positioned her face so that the brass street number was right beside her ear, and then took a selfie of herself flashing the peace sign. The resulting photo went straight to Emily, along with the caption 'new address who dis'.

That done, Angela returned to the footpath and hunched over, feeling foolish.

Emily's response was blazingly fast. *U call that a distraction? No THIS is a distraction*

Her message contained an attachment, a photo of the roommate who featured in many of their conversations these days. The surfer dude was shirtless and doing the Shoulderstand yoga pose, his bare feet worryingly close to the low-hanging light fixtures. His tracksuit pants were also worryingly loose. There was a chance of a far more titillating view when his feet touched back down.

Angela nodded, acknowledging Emily's point. That *was* distracting.

Okay, but why was she picturing Colin Cooper doing the same thing?

A quick shake of her head did wonders for clearing her mind. She could hear a shower running, which meant that Ben had finished whatever workout he'd been recording for his YouTube channel. Angela rested a hand on top of the low brick fence running alongside the driveway and inhaled deeply, pretending that the wind smelled of Ben's aftershave instead of sea salt and whatever his neighbour was cooking.

Would it be so wrong to ring the doorbell? To go in? To join him in the shower for a long and steamy 'sesh'?

Not that she'd been able to do that before restrictions had forced them apart. On the rare occasion that Ben did invite her over—always when his parents were out, which made her feel like such a teenager—their showers had to be as quick as their lovemaking. They would then spend a good deal of time making sure that there was no trace of Angela's presence left behind. It had always been much easier to take him back to her cramped studio.

'That's it,' Angela muttered. 'As soon as this pandemic is over, I'm going to move in with you. No more sneaky showers.'

She spun on her heel and marched off, head held high. She didn't even duck when she saw the chunky VW belonging to Ben's parents peel down the road. Let them see her. Let them assume the worst, though they probably wouldn't. They could barely remember her name, let alone what she looked like.

Her phone vibrated several times in a row. Emily was the unsurprising culprit.

Crisis averted

Didn't end up shagging him

Say hi to Ben for me

Lucky bitch

Angela grinned. She *was* lucky. She wasn't sure what was so wrong about the surfer dude, even if his craft beer subscription habitually blocked the stairwell in Emily's apartment complex. And that manbun really suited him.

But Emily would probably prefer a caveman to a hipster.

Humming, Angela returned to Grace Park and accidentally tried to open Number Twelve's letterbox. She snorted in amusement and used a nearly identical key to open a nearly identical box, though this one bore the number twenty-two. Nothing for her, not yet. If all went well, she wouldn't get *any* letters until she moved in with Ben. It shouldn't take long. Lockdown permitting, of course.

Colin's mail in hand, Angela turned towards the stairs and stopped. She could hear his voice, his laugh—distinctive, genuine, and deep. Curious, and totally not checking to see if he'd illegally invited someone over and was keeping them on the ground floor so she wouldn't dob him in, Angela crept down the corridor, straining her ears. The corner she needed to peer around provided sufficient cover for her eavesdropping mission.

'I forgot it was Good Friday today as well, even though there I was reminding you about it on Tuesday,' Colin was saying. 'But not to worry. I'll pop to the shops in the morning and get a few things that will see you through 'til Tuesday. And I'll get something special delivered for Bernard. Something from my mate, Rob.'

Two full metres away from him, an elderly woman stood in her doorway, hands clasped in front of her, expression aghast. 'Oh, Colin. Please don't encourage his drinking. It makes him fancy himself a comedian. With the cricket matches suspended, he doesn't really have much else to do...'

'Are you letting a draught in, Loraine?' a man's voice demanded from out of sight. 'Don't be daft about the draught. Ha!'

Colin made a choking sound that might have been a laugh.

'Don't call your wife daft, Bernard,' he said. 'She cooks all of your dinners and I'd wager she makes your breakfasts and lunches as well. I'd watch your words if I was you.'

'I would never tamper with his food,' Loraine sniffed.

'That's what I'll tell the DCIs when they come by,' Colin assured her.

'Don't encourage *her*, Colin,' Bernard scolded. 'Now, what's this about something special for me?'

A grin coloured Colin's words; Angela could picture it perfectly, even though his back was facing her. 'You'll just have to wait until tomorrow night.'

'Why not tonight?' Bernard asked.

'I rather thought Loraine would take issue with you drinking on one of the Lord's days,' Colin said, suddenly solemn.

'Too right!' Loraine exclaimed. 'It's nice to see at least one person from the younger generations taking their faith seriously. I will allow Bernard a tipple tomorrow. He'll be insufferable all of Sunday if I don't. And that's when I'm supposed to watch my church's service on the Whiffy. Logging on is already too complicated for me as it is without Bernard complaining in my ear.'

'I can help with that,' Colin offered.

'Oh no, I couldn't ask you to do that. It was enough that you set up my Apple on the Whiffy in the first place.'

'*WiFi*, Loraine!' Bernard corrected. 'He's going to help us anyway. You don't need to pretend to be incompetent to guilt him into it.'

Loraine's face went ashen.

Obviously, she followed the same school of thought as Janet Tweedie—you couldn't ask for help, of course not, because you didn't want to offend your neighbour (translation: you were too proud to ask). But acting in such a manner that your neighbour would feel they had no other choice but to offer you their help? That was perfectly allowed.

Angela wasn't sure she ought to have rolled her eyes, given Loraine's age.

Colin adopted a measured tone, one that didn't acknowledge his feelings on the matter. 'Let me know if you see Number Twelve—Angela, that is. She hasn't come back yet.'

'Will do,' Loraine promised. 'So nice of you to take the poor girl in.'

'She's a woman, not a girl,' Colin said.

Loraine sighed. 'I can't keep up with the feminists and the words they're using these days. And I'm much too old to learn new tricks. Goodbye, Colin.'

The door clicked shut. Colin's smile froze when he turned around and caught sight of Angela, who was so preoccupied with the conversation that she had forgotten to duck back around the corner. They stared at each other for what felt like an age—or roughly the length of a too-loud ad on YouTube.

'Looking for me?' she finally managed.

Colin's cheeks tightened. 'I wasn't being a stalker or anything. Sorry if this seems creepy. But you know me, the neighbourhood creep. Lol. What I meant is, usually you're on the sofa when I finish my morning meeting.'

'Were you *worried* about me?' she teased.

After a short silence that made her very, very nervous, his green eyes gleamed. 'No, I was just stuck. I couldn't leave because there was no one around to hold the front door open for me.'

'You managed to open the door to your flat to come down here.'

'Oh, would you look at the time?' Colin inspected his naked wrist. 'I've got to start work soon. Better go!'

He shot past her and sprinted up the stairs. Angela studied the Colin-shaped hole he'd left behind, wondering if he hadn't wanted to admit to being worried about her—or if he'd been desperate for some form of companionship.

Well, she could sympathise with him there.

'Wait!' Angela called after him. 'Don't you dare touch that kettle. I'll be the one making the tea from now on—I refuse to let you brew any more of that fetid dishwater you're always scoffing down!'

11

Colin leaned back in his chair and rested his elbow on a raised knee, frowning at the Talk Talk poster on the back of his door. White suits, black ties, and a whole lot of suaveness.

They were definitely mocking him.

Beside Colin, the panel he used to run his show remained untouched, the volume meter dark and lifeless. On a weekday, he was in control. Dials and switches moved beneath his fingers and the smooth, confident voice that escaped the mouth belonging to DJ Coop caressed ears all across the world.

Today was Saturday. And Colin Cooper had no idea what he was doing.

Or why he'd gone looking for Angela yesterday.

The cynical side of him wondered if he'd done it to make sure Angela hadn't flown the coop. He needed her help. Colin had even checked the wardrobe in the spare room and made sure that his stash was intact, the minute hair still resting between the sliding door and its frame, right where he'd left it. So that embarrassing secret hadn't sent her storming off in disgust, at least.

'Oh for cripes' sake,' he muttered. 'You're not her keeper. Or her boyfriend.'

She did have one of those, apparently. Colin hadn't managed to get a name out of Angela, but she had told him over a pot of her excellent tea (he had to admit that his brews *did* taste like dishwater) that said boyfriend didn't have room for her at his place. Something about a home gym and religious parents. Colin wasn't sure whether to choke or thank the nameless boyfriend for sending Angela his way. On the one hand, he now had to live with her and her terrifying scowls. On the other hand, she might be able to help him keep his job…

What was he still doing in here anyway? Avoiding the pretty girl in the schoolyard?

Colin didn't need liquid courage. He just needed his mouth.

He stomped out into the living room. Angela was there as usual, reading yet another romance novel, though this one looked like it had a more modern setting, given that the shirtless Highlanders had been replaced by cartoonified people holding phones. Angela glanced up at him, sighed, and slipped her faux leather bookmark into a section about halfway along. She took a moment to jot something down in the lined journal resting on the arm of the sofa. Was she taking notes? Were romance novels required reading in some sort of university course? That wasn't impossible, actually.

'Save it,' Angela said.

Colin blinked. 'What?'

Angela lifted the book, resignation stealing across her face. 'I know it's silly. Reading romance novels. Sighing over fictional characters. Reading the same ending over and over again. Variations on a theme. A tale as old as time. Tropes galore!'

The opening she'd given him was perfect. Too perfect.

She was the reason he'd exploded out of his room in the first place—her showing off what she knew about the romance genre was a bonus. All he had to do was ask. She'd be so grateful to him for letting her stay rent-free that she'd immediately agree to plot out (maybe even write!) this ridiculous serial and never, *ever* listen to his previous shows.

But the moment passed. Or maybe he let it.

Colin wasn't sure.

'Do whatever makes you happy,' he said. 'There's no reason we should spend the entire lockdown depressed and miserable. And frankly, we don't want to come out of this thing with "pretending to shop for essentials to get out of the house" and "moping by the window" as our new favourite hobbies. I don't think our descendants would be terribly impressed with us.'

Angela didn't smile. Her fingers worried the edges of the book's pages and her eyes were bright behind her white-rimmed glasses. Colin cast about for something else to say, something that might cheer her up. Something that wasn't annoyingly optimistic.

His mouth ran away from him before he could stop it. 'Then again, our descendants are already going to think that the people of this time were selfish buttholes who liked to put others at risk when all the government was asking us to do was stay home. Look, reading romance novels is probably the best thing you'll ever do for your country.'

Finally, a laugh. *Yes!*

Angela slid off her glasses, cleaned them, and then popped them back on. Her magnetic smile remained firmly in place. 'Okay. Bless me, Father, for I have sinned. I love romance novels! And I wish I'd been able to read more of them before all this happened.'

'Not enough time?' Colin asked. 'I thought the train to London took ninety minutes?'

'I had plenty of time. I just…didn't want to be seen reading them.'

'Because you don't want people to judge you?'

Her silence spoke volumes.

Colin sighed and dropped onto the sofa beside her. 'I get it. My family's not exactly supportive of how I spend my time. Instead of making my millions, I decided to run a radio show. An obscure one at that, so they can't even brag to their friends about me or my salary. Nope, I'm still the black sheep of the family. Even in my parents' day, video was doing a good job of killing the radio star. But if I listened to them, I'd be just as miserable as they are. Maybe I'd be wealthier—my father's family owns half of Manchester, so the rumour goes—but I definitely wouldn't be happy.'

'Is that supposed to be the big rousing speech that absolves me of my obsession with romance novels?' Angela wondered.

'Yes,' Colin said solemnly. 'I so absolve you. Even after the pandemic ends.'

Angela shook her head and shoved the novel underneath her notebook. 'I'll have to go back to the real world when this is all over. Move in with the boyfriend. Start using my time to find a job and get trim instead of indulging in plots that have been done to death.'

'But you've got now, right?'

'Right,' she echoed. Dully.

Colin thought of a hundred different ways to continue the conversation, none of them helpful to Angela or himself. He considered coughing awkwardly. No, too obvious. She'd know something was up.

Fudge. Now what?

'Special delivery for Colin Cooper!' someone belted from outside. 'Enough grog to get pissed up in no time! All paid in advance! Unless I've got the wrong address?'

'Hold that thought,' Colin said to Angela and jogged over to the open window.

Sure enough, Rob Chance was standing on the grass in front of the building and waving a large brown paper bag, which completely and utterly failed to disguise its alcoholic contents. Bottles really did have a distinctive shape.

Rob performed a bow worthy of Shakespeare's Globe. 'At your service, Col. Where do you want me to dump these?'

'I'll be right there!' Colin replied.

'You want me to get it for you, mate?' someone shouted from a nearby window.

Colin scowled. That voice belonged to Number Twenty-Five, a bricklayer who wore only singlets and boxer shorts when he picked up his mail—yet another reason for Colin to avoid checking his letterbox during daylight hours.

'This is for Colin Cooper only,' Rob said, loyal to the last.

Bernard then tried to make a claim from downstairs. 'I'm Colin and so is my wife!'

Colin heard Angela burst out laughing and fought hard to keep his face straight. Monty Python never went out of fashion.

'You are not Colin, Bernard!' Loraine scolded. 'Lying is a sin. And I won't allow you to watch that terrible movie tomorrow until you ask for the Lord's forgiveness—just see if I don't!'

An elaborate shrug lifted Rob's narrow shoulders, along with the dodgy-looking trench coat he was wearing. 'Good enough for me, I guess. I could use a new mate called Colin. The current one's a complete wet blanket at parties. Always banging on about the house playlist having too many covers of his oh-so-precious 1980s songs. I think I'll get some local bands in to play covers every night when I reopen the bar, just to piss him off. I'll start with A Flock of Seagulls.'

95

'Don't you dare!' Colin bellowed. 'And Bernard? Don't expect me to share my stash with you, like I said I was going to! You thief!'

'Attempted thief only!' Bernard hurled in response.

Angela cleared her throat. Colin swung a look back at her.

'I could go down, if you like,' she offered.

'No! I am Colin Cooper and I have two good legs!' he cried, tearing out of the room and leaping down both flights of stairs. He couldn't afford to dawdle—Rob would 'donate' the alcohol if Colin made him wait long enough. He was the sort who went too far with a joke because he deemed a moment of humour worth more than the potential fallout.

And even though he'd been sworn to secrecy, Rob would love to give the game away. *I can see why Colin gave up his spare room, you're a fine thing. And here I thought he did it just so he could use you in his radio show.*

Rob would definitely say that. Because Angela *was* fine.

A leering grin (worthy of the cat that got the cream) greeted Colin when he stopped two metres away from his friend.

Rob held the paper bag aloft, as though he was Rafiki presenting Simba to the world in *The Lion King*. 'Your order, m'lord. Perfect for making the ladies pliable.'

'I thought you said that was the main purpose of alcopops,' Colin said, eyeing the bag suspiciously. 'Please don't tell me you got me alcopops.'

'Puh-leaze, Col. Those got left behind in the first decade of this century. Probably where Vin and his pals should have left those fast cars and faster plots, if I'm honest. Alright. You got me. I *do* have a stockpile of alcopops for the girls who come down from Essex on their way over to a hen do in Amsterdam. But you're classier than that, mate, aren't you? Then again, you're hoping to get your roommate to work for food and board and that's just rotten. You're not even planning on giving her any credit!'

'Just give me the fudging booze, Rob!'

Rob set his precious cargo on the ground and backed away, allowing Colin to scoop it up without getting too close. The bottles inside clinked promisingly.

'I probably shouldn't talk about the weather,' Rob said. 'Since that'd make this a social visit, which is illegal and all that.'

'Probably shouldn't make fun of your few friends either,' Colin replied.

'I'm not your friend. I'm just a purveyor of goods and hilarity.'

'Fudge off.'

'Gladly. Same time next week?'

'That's optimistic of you,' Colin said, turning his back on Rob to hide his grin.

He dropped by The Bennets', leaving a bottle of port (the good stuff from Portugal, aka the only stuff Bernard would ever touch) outside their door. Colin knocked and cleared his throat loudly. 'You really don't deserve it, but I've left you a little something. Go easy, Bernard.'

'I'll go as hard as I like, Millennial!' Bernard told him from the other side of the door.

Smiling, Colin ascended the stairs and re-entered his flat, finding Angela waiting on the sofa. She gestured at the coffee table. 'I found some cheese in your fridge and a whole packet of unopened crackers in the cupboard—sneaky grocery run this morning, I guess? You better have some wine on you.'

Colin held his breath as he reached once more into the paper bag.

He pulled out a bottle of Moscato. *Pink* Moscato. The kind you give a high school student on her eighteenth birthday, when she's wearing a tiara and buried inside a pack of her giggling friends.

'Thanks for nothing, Rob,' Colin grumbled.

'Oh, I love that stuff,' Angela assured him. 'Low alcohol content.'

Bother, Colin thought. How could he grease the wheels with this?

Angela snatched the bottle off him when he got too close and inspected the label. 'Five percent? That's more than enough to get me messy. I mean it. I'm going to be a handful. Are you sure about this?'

I meant my *wheels, Universe!* Colin thought.

He tried to smirk but it came out as a grimace. 'I guess we'll find out.'

12

Angela released a long, low moan, knowing it probably sounded pornographic but not particularly caring. 'So. Much. Cheese.'

'Too much,' Colin echoed, slumping down on the sofa.

'No such thing,' Angela said.

A wheezy laugh escaped him, as if he was buried underneath the combined weight of the smoked brie they'd just eaten. 'Liar.'

Angela held her hands protectively over the food baby that was growing inside her knitted tangerine jumper. She'd never admit this out loud to anyone, especially Ben who would think it juvenile, but she referred to her jumpers as fruit instead of by colour. Strawberry, peach, melon, blueberry, and guava—she owned more jumpers than she did pairs of underwear. Speaking of which, a trip to the communal laundry room downstairs was probably in order.

But those jumpers didn't survive quite so well as 50p knickers did when thrown into a dryer. Angela laughed out loud.

'What?' Colin asked.

'*Knickers*,' she gasped. 'It's the height of hilarity. Such a funny word.'

Colin stared at her. 'You weren't kidding about getting messy on five percent.'

She'd never thought of someone's eyes as 'delicious' before. But this was the first word that popped into Angela's head when she locked gazes with him.

Dark, mysterious green. A jumper in that colour would soon earn the name 'avocado'. Wait, was avocado even a fruit? It was, wasn't it? She was sure she'd googled it one time. Anyway. Avocados were probably more edible than human eyes.

Another laugh peeled out of her. '*Eyes*. Omnomnom.'

'Oookay,' Colin said. 'I think I overdid this.'

'Overdid what?' Angela asked, bemused.

Colin slid further down the sofa. 'I wanted to get myself tipsy, but now you're the one who's hammered and this feels all wrong. I shouldn't have done it.'

'You were trying to take advantage of *yourself*?' Angela snickered.

She probably would have reacted with a higher level of snarkiness if she'd been sober. But there were other things that annoyed her more than Colin Cooper just now: her bladder was a little fuller than was comfortable and the disgusting sofa was actively swallowing her.

'I wanted to ask you a question,' Colin muttered.

'So?' Angela said. 'Just ask. It's not that hard.'

He waved his hands in the direction of the empty wine bottle that had rolled halfway across the floor towards the kitchen. 'I'm no good at talking to people. I was hoping the alcohol would help. It was *supposed* to help.'

'Didn't you say you ran a radio show?'

'This is different,' Colin told her. 'When I'm on the air, I'm in control. I have a microphone, a panel, and headphones—and I have all the confidence in the world. I'm Colin Cooper, DJ. Not Colin Cooper, IRL.'

An excellent idea struck Angela. She leaned forward, clenched her hand into a fist, and tilted it towards Colin. 'Here you go! An invisible microphone. Ask your question, Colin Cooper, DJ.'

He gave her a stony look.

'Come on, Colin. What have you got to lose? I'm not going to judge you any more than I already do. Ha!'

He opened his mouth, then closed it again.

'You're a DJ!' Angela reminded him. 'So DJ!'

'Fine,' Colin said and abruptly sat up. It was as if a wave had rolled over him from head to toe; he stopped fidgeting, his posture (which had grown rigid over the past couple of minutes) softened, a rakish grin twisted his lips, and then he unleashed a voice that could only be described as 'dulcet with a side order of charm'. 'I'm Colin Cooper and this is Angela Tweedie Radio, known for savage commentary, strangely compelling beats, and better fashion sense than about ninety percent of Newfield.'

Colin paused, obviously gauging her reaction. Angela tried to hide her amusement behind a solemn expression, but knew she'd failed when he grinned and ploughed on. 'That wasn't a joke. I'm deadly serious—Angela Tweedie has the best selection of jumpers I've ever seen.'

Angela held up her other hand, as though she was back in class at Dover College.

'Our guest here in the studio has a question,' Colin said. 'She's the owner of Angela Tweedie Radio and she can read three romance novels in a single day, all while creating new ways to passive-aggressive me to death. Possessing that much talent must be exhausting.'

She rolled her eyes. 'Just get to the point, Colin. I thought radio was supposed to be punchy. This is *not* punchy. It's downright verbose.'

'Very well. I've been called out. Here's the problem: my boss is demanding that I create a brand-new segment for my show, one that runs over several weeks. Basically, he wants me to come up with a romantic serial involving two roommates. My boss is adamant about me using this trope. Worse still? I have to pretend that it's between me and my actual roommate. And it has to sound *real*.'

'Oh.' Angela sucked up the rest of her wine. 'Is that all?'

'I can't write fiction!' Colin exclaimed, sounding on the verge of panic. 'But you can.'

'What!?' She sprayed those precious drops of Moscato all over his carpet.

'You read romance novels, don't you? So you can help me write it.'

Angela set her glass down on the coffee table, right beside the chipped ceramic plate she'd used for their cheese board. Her buzz was quickly fading. '*No*. No, I can't. There's no way I can. Writing for an actual *audience*? God no.'

'Better you than me, I'm hopeless at this romance thing,' Colin said. 'So how about it? Would you like to help me out of this mess I've landed myself in?'

'Hold please,' Angela croaked out, distantly aware of her feet propelling her across the carpet and towards her door. She could feel his desperate gaze heating her back. Did he realise how ridiculous he sounded? How ridiculous this whole thing was?

Angela kicked the door shut behind her and slid her phone out of the back pocket of her jeans (blue denim really worked wonders with dressing down those jumpers).

Hey it's Angela

The woman who got tea yesterday

One of them anyway. I was the romance novel person

Shit I've buggered this up and spammed you

She didn't expect a response, nor one so soon. But Ishani didn't leave her hanging.

No worse than my ex after we broke up

And I've got no customers atm so all the time in the world

What's up?

This is rude, Angela texted back, biting her lip. *Asking for help when I should be using our first phone convo to get to know you better*

Convo? Ishani inserted a laughing emoji. *Is this 2002 and r we on MSN?*

Angela grimaced. It had been years since those days in high school, when her life had been full of drama and bullying—all played out on MSN Messenger, because social media hadn't become A Thing yet.

Many a 'convo' on MSN had reduced Angela to tears. Her own mother had said she needed to ignore the taunts (Janet Tweedie had never been bullied, so she'd parroted the advice expected of a Newfield parent), but when Emily's mother had heard about it, she'd immediately swooped by and picked Angela up in her car. They'd gone to McDonald's, grabbed a sundae each, and then they'd both read and discussed a battered old book that Mrs Benson had plucked out of her rather large collection of Mills & Boon medical romances.

Angela really missed her. Emily's conversations never featured her mother, who had been stolen from them years ago by cancer. Angela wished they could at least reminiscence together. But just having Emily on the other side of the phone was enough sometimes.

Sometimes.

Angela tapped her phone with both thumbs as she typed up her response, outlining what Colin had asked of her. She glanced nervously at the door. He hadn't followed her in, but he had to be wondering about her mental state. Most people didn't head for an exit when someone asked for their help. It just wasn't *done*. But springing something like this on your roommate probably wasn't 'done' either, so...

Wait, was that the mysterious thumping noise?

Ishani hadn't replied yet. Had Angela been left on read? There was no way to tell with her generic phone. It didn't have any of the fancy trimmings.

Thump. Thump. Thump.

Nope, she hadn't imagined the noise. Colin was at it again.

Angela's grip tightened on her phone. She could run out there right now, catch him in the act—and be forced to give him an answer. Or she could keep running until she hit the street, leaving all of her possessions behind (except Wills the stuffed bat, of course, who she would cram into her pocket) and hoping that there was some other friendly soul out there who didn't mind taking on a broke roommate during a global pandemic.

Thump. Thump. Thump.

What on Earth was he doing out there!?

Angela had just touched the doorknob when her phone buzzed repeatedly. Within half a second, she was staring down at a collection of text messages.

Sounds like he'll be passing ur work off as his own?

R u ok with that?

Ok I guess it'll be less pressure if it's his career on the line not urs

Do it. But make sure u get something out of it. ASK. Worst case scenario he kicks you out and u get to crash at mine. Dooooo tits

Shite autocorrect dooooo ittttttt

gtg soz a customer heading my way

104

MSN slang for nostalgia ONLY don't start using it back at me

Angela's cheeks ached fiercely and she was startled to realise that she was grinning from ear to ear.

Wish I could send you an MSN nudge, Ishani continued.

NUDGE NUDGE dooooo tits

No autocorrect this time lol really gotta go now

Angela stared at her phone. She wasn't sure if Ishani had really meant that bit about Angela crashing at her place. They'd only just met. Even Emily had never made that offer when she'd still been on this side of the world, though Angela suspected they'd kill each other if they had to share the same space.

Strange, once upon a time no one had wanted to live with her.

Angela's mother would say that it was only polite to give Colin something in return. No one likes a houseguest who demands too many liberties of their host without making it worth their while, of course not (Janet Tweedie thought that anyone asking her not to snoop through their things was one such liberty, even if that request came from her own daughter). Angela bit her lip. This was not how she'd have chosen to try her hand at writing, but if not now—then when? After she'd moved in with Ben? She'd be too afraid of his laughter to give it a real go.

It wasn't like she had anything better to do at the moment.

She threw open the door and found Colin frozen in the middle of the living room, one foot hovering above the floor in front of him. He'd shed the ratty ankle-length slippers he wore everywhere except to the shops (a spotless pair of black-and-white Converse high tops replaced the slippers for those excursions) and was now barefoot.

Angela's own feet, encased inside thick socks and matching purple slippers (tidy and clean, unlike his which looked like they had been rescued from a dumpster), ached in jealousy. She had Raynaud's and always paid dearly for letting her toes get even slightly cold.

'I'll do it,' Angela said. 'But I want to keep our free rent arrangement going if I mess this up. And I want something in return. I want to know your secret.'

His eyes flew to the doorway behind her. 'I'm not opening the wardrobe.'

'Huh? Oh. Not that! What makes the mysterious thumping noise? It drove me nuts when I was living downstairs!'

'Mysterious thumping…?' He looked perplexed.

'What were you doing just then?' Angela demanded. 'Did you take your slippers off so you could stomp as loud as possible?'

Realisation dawned on his face and he straightened, lining his feet up on the floor beside his disgusting slippers. He lifted his arm and the long sleeve of his Cutting Crew shirt fell away, revealing the fitness tracker he was wearing. 'Walking in circles. It's how I get my exercise. Hard to get a good pace going when your feet are flopping around inside slippers.'

Well, he did have a point about the slippers.

But hang on a second. 'You walk…in *circles*?'

'Yes,' he said, sounding defensive. 'I hate going outside. This does it for me.'

'This *does it* for you, huh,' Angela echoed, painfully aware that her biting tone and the matching eye-roll were a concerted attempt to hide how terrified she felt. 'Takes all sorts. And here I thought you were doing it on purpose to drive me insane. Do you know how many days I spent glaring up at the ceiling, wanting to strangle you?'

Colin raised his eyebrows. 'Should I be worried?'

'Yes, you should be! I've never actually *written* a romance. Unless you count some slash fanfiction when I was a teenager.' Angela flushed. 'Alright, I know that fanfics get their own books and movies these days, but those are the good ones. I can't count my attempts as actual writing. I barely had any readers. And I was writing for a pretty popular pairing, by the way. So this could go horribly, horribly wrong. But I'll…I'll give it a go.'

He visibly sagged in relief.

Angela marched forward and knelt down, rescuing the notebook that she'd dropped on the floor earlier. That done, she settled herself on the sofa (which was actually less terrifying than those slippers of his) and waited for him to join her.

Colin stayed right where he was.

Angela patted the cushion beside her. 'Sit.' When he did so, she continued, 'I know how to write prose, I guess, even if I'm a bit rusty. But I don't think your listeners want to hear you sounding like you're reading a book, since they can just go onto Audible in their own time. And DJing's a bit different, isn't it? This is a show and you'll be…um…'

'Presenting a serial,' Colin supplied. 'Think of it as bite-sized bits. Singular scenes, always with a punchy ending, or a cliffhanger. No extended dialogue, since I'm more of a narrator than anything. And it can't be too long. The sponsors want their ads played on time.'

Angela dug a hand into the gap between their respective cushions and retrieved a pen she'd misplaced. There was never any point in looking elsewhere; sofas had a magical ability to magnetise any lost items. She pressed the nib to a fresh sheet of paper. 'It's always better to write something you'd read. Maybe it's better to present something you actually like as well. So what's your favourite romance? Surely you have one.'

'Not really, no.'

'No books, no movies, no TV shows?'

He pursed his lips. 'Does real life count?'

'Yes! It'd be nice to know that this stuff happens in real life, because I always wish…' Angela quickly cut herself off. 'Um. Go on. Just pretend I didn't say anything.'

Thankfully, he obliged her. Which said a lot about how much he needed her help.

'There's a story in my family,' Colin said slowly. 'No one's sure if it's real or not, but my grandfather certainly thought so.'

Angela peered at him over the top of her glasses, intrigued. 'Tell me.'

'One time, when I was about seven, Grandad sat me down with some whisky.' Colin smiled. 'His way of making sure my cousins and I didn't become alcoholics was to give us a dram when we were kids. Disgusting stuff. But it put us off alcohol until we were eighteen, so I guess he had a good reason for doing it. Anyway, while I was gulping down some water to get rid of the taste of the whisky, he asked me if I was looking forward to The Great Big Romance in my future. I did the usual thing any kid my age would. Laughed and said "ew".'

'Still ew?' Angela asked with a grin.

'Less ew, but relationships are a lot more work and a lot less romantic than I realised.' Colin cleared his throat. 'Grandad's skin was a lot more olive than mine and he had a slightly different look to him. So I guess I wasn't all that surprised when he said, "My father was a Gypsy! Yes, he was. He had his Great Big Romance, something everyone in this family's forgotten they need. This lot are always looking to make money instead of love, don't you be like that, Col."' Colin paused. 'Fudge. Am I allowed to use the G word? I've got this work friend, more like an aunt, who would yell until my ears went red if she heard me using that word.'

'You're quoting a story,' Angela pointed out. 'And I suppose if your grandfather's father really was a...you'd be allowed to...oh, I don't know. It's too confusing!'

'Yeah, you see my dilemma, don't you? Anyway, so the story goes like this. My great-grandfather stopped by Manchester in the early 1930s. Good place for transients of all kinds back then—there wasn't much work going. He was travelling with his family and intended to keep on doing that, because that's what was expected of him. He always followed their rules. But then he met my great-grandmother, who was working in a soup kitchen. He fell. He fell *hard*. Within a month, they were married.'

'Ohh,' Angela sighed. 'How romantic.'

Colin's grimace suggested that he didn't quite agree with her assessment. 'Their families didn't attend the wedding, since neither side approved. Grandad said all this like it was the best thing ever, like it was a typical happy ending, but it really must have been awful for my great-grandparents.'

'Your great-grandfather gave up everything he knew for love?' Angela whispered.

Colin shrugged. 'I've never thought about it that way before. He must have done.'

She scribbled away in her notebook for a couple of minutes, then leaned over and slapped his shoulder, Moscato-induced dizziness nearly tipping her sideways into his lap. 'You've been holding out on me.'

'I have?'

'You had this great forbidden romance stored away in your family tree and never mentioned it, not once!' she exclaimed.

Colin snorted. 'In my defence, you spent the better part of two years glaring at me and insisting that my sole purpose in life was to annoy you.'

'Yes, well, there is that,' Angela admitted. 'You can't believe how jealous I am right now. None of my relatives or ancestors have ever done anything really, truly romantic. I wish I could *live* something like that.'

'Looking for work in Manchester during the Great Depression?' Colin mused.

Angela laughed. 'Maybe not. But this is good. We can use this.'

'How? My boss wants me to use the roommate trope.'

'Yes, I know, I heard it the first time you mentioned it,' she said briskly. 'I *do* listen to what you say, Colin Cooper, contrary to popular belief and contrary to what you deserve.'

He managed to look contrite, even though the corners of his lips were twitching. 'Sorry. So how are we going to work this in, exactly…?'

13

'Sunshine, you should purchase a new phone if the camera keeps dropping out like this,' Leo said severely, making Colin feel like he was the one in the naughty corner. Monday mornings were already bad enough without Leo's judgemental stare.

'With what money?' DJ Sunshine's faceless voice challenged. 'Is this a business expense? Say the word and I will gladly expense you, luv. But I have a show to run right now—unless you want me to leave our listeners hanging?'

Leo's expression went briefly murderous, then smoothed out again. 'Of course not. Focus on your show.'

He might have challenged her further if he hadn't lost the battle over her on-air moniker two years ago. Leo had told her not to use a pseudonym, because morning listeners would only trust someone using their real name. Sunshine had promptly emailed him a scan of her driving licence. He'd allowed her to win many of their arguments since then.

Colin's snicker shrivelled up inside him the moment Leo's attention found a new target. 'Colin. I look forward to hearing your new segment. Do not disappoint me.'

The words 'or else' were left unspoken but hung around, as oppressive as dead air. Undeterred, Colin swung his leg up onto his desk and slid on the easy smile he used to polish his voice whenever he became DJ Coop. 'With this talent? How could I possibly fail?'

Leo gave Colin a long, lingering look. 'I'll be waiting with bated breath for 9am. Good luck, if you need it.'

He left the Zoom meeting without another word. Sunshine immediately appeared.

'Are you alright, dear?' she asked.

'Yep,' Colin said. 'I've never been this prepared before. It'll be great.'

Her eyes were squinted in suspicion as she left the conversation to resume her show. She repeated her cheerful intro, speaking over the top of a song that was just finishing—one of her favourites, 'Walking on Sunshine' by Katrina and the Waves. Leo never went off at her for playing tunes from previous decades.

Colin had once complained about this preferential treatment, but he'd quickly backed down after Leo had told him in a patronising tone that DJ Sunshine's generation were quite capable of finding Internet radio stations when they wanted to. And she was the one they listened to, not 'some young thing' like Colin.

Never mind that Leo was a decade younger than him.

'Careful, Col,' Danika said, turning away from today's painting. It was oddly sunny and bright for her, but she had threatened the artwork with a bucket of black paint since apparently it wasn't doing what it was told. 'You're a little overconfident. Pride goeth and all that.'

'There's no goeth and no fall,' Colin said breezily. 'Just you wait.'

Someone knocked on his bedroom door. Repeatedly. And at length.

Colin jolted upright in surprise and his leg fell off the desk. He was lucky his chair didn't slip too far or the rest of his body would have followed.

'Who is it?' he called out.

Danika snorted. 'Who do you think? Your roommate.'

'Let her in!' Danger Jones commanded. Along with the usual Ray Bans, he was also wearing a red cap that bore the letters 'MGBGA' in bold white font. 'I want to see this bit of fluff!'

'No! No way!' Colin said.

The Love Doctor cleared his throat. 'It would be nice to meet her and gain an idea of her suitability as a girlfriend. I've told you before, Colin, it's very hard for young people to meet prospective partners right now. We could help you with this.'

'Nope, not happening, Peter, not in this universe,' Colin said and exited the meeting.

He rearranged himself in his chair, elbow on the desk and fingers curled beneath his chin in what was supposed to be a sophisticated pose, then laughed at his own vanity. Who was he trying to impress? And never mind the slippers. Angela hadn't made a comment about them yet, but he just *knew* one was brewing behind those glasses of hers.

He was almost looking forward to hearing it.

'Come in!' Colin shouted.

'Took you long enough,' Angela said from the doorway. She was a much more welcome sight than the Talk Talk poster that should have been filling the gap. Her pink jumper was already brightening up his room and she hadn't even stepped inside yet. 'Your co-workers sound like…fun.'

'Wait, has that door been open the whole time?' he fretted.

She simply smiled.

Colin felt the blood drain out of his face as he frantically tried to remember if he'd said anything incriminating.

'Anyway,' Angela said, knotting her fingers together, 'I thought I'd say my goodbyes now, since once your show starts I'll be heading down to The Bean and Gone to meet up with my boyfriend. The thought of you presenting something I've written to thousands of strangers…ugh. Nope. I really, *really* can't be here when you do it.'

Colin laughed. 'Shouldn't you have another reason to go see your boyfriend?'

'Do you really want to get into this with me, Colin?'

Yes, a traitorous voice said somewhere between his ears.

And then his mind decided to conjure up images involving her glistening lips—images that involved a lot less talking and a lot more of something else.

'No, I really don't want to get into it,' Colin said quickly, more than a little perturbed. Where had *that* come from? 'Since you'd resort to personal attacks and I'm too fragile to hear your opinion on my slippers today. Even though I'm sure you're dying to tell me. Crap. Is that an insensitive thing to say right now? I'm sorry if it is. I think I understand Peter's generation a bit better now. It's exhausting to make sure you're always saying the right thing.'

Angela rubbed her temples. 'Great, now I'm going to be rethinking every word *I* say today. Ugh. Not that Ben would notice or take offence, but anyway. I'm off now. Have fun.'

'Have fun,' he repeated distastefully. '*Fun*. I have to work. And my boss is a whisker away from attempting world domination.'

She rolled her eyes. 'Well, at least try to have fun. Bye, Colin.'

'Goodbye, Angela.'

He definitely wouldn't miss her, Colin vowed.

'Thanks for your concern, DJ Sunshine, but I'm still alive and kicking, as you can hear,' Colin said, grinning. She'd just finished telling her listeners to take pity on him because of his roommate problem. The handover between their two shows was now complete. 'I was going to make you all wait for an update on Number Twelve—or the former resident of Number Twelve, I should say. But since Sunshine has pumped you all up and you're going bonkers in the hashtag—and at-ing me so often I can't keep up—I'll get straight to it.'

Leo's insistence that he keep to the usual running order was not a request. There was no way Colin could have delayed the segment, but he was supposed to bait the listeners, reel them in, have them eating out of his hand before he offered them anything of real substance. You had to train them to stick around for the reward.

'So last night I tried to build a bridge instead of burning one,' Colin said, restraining a laugh as he remembered Angela's dismay that he hadn't stocked up on more than one type of cheese. 'I bought wine. I figured that Number Twelve might be more pleasant with a buzz going. And you know what? She was. I didn't hear a single sarcastic comment out of her for ten whole minutes. She was downright social, actually. I've definitely had worse roommates.'

Get on with it!!! #splatzapp demanded more than one listener.

But he wasn't done reeling them in just yet.

'No, romancegurl007, there was no kissing or romance of any kind,' Colin said, raising the pitch of his voice as he performed the indignation. He then jumped back into the words Angela had given him, beginning with a truncated retelling of his grandad's story, one that was punctuated by observations of his roommate's reactions and how much she enjoyed hearing it. He finally conceded, 'Okay, there was a bit romance. But we were only discussing it! I guess it was more fun than rewatching the same old rom-com on the telly? Mind you, I can't stop myself when that same channel replays *Pretty Woman*, just like they do every year around Mother's Day...'

His listeners had a lot of opinions about *Pretty Woman*, apparently.

Colin had never actually seen it, but Angela had insisted that he pretend he had. Something about making him sound more appealing to his female listeners.

He was a romantic hero now, after all.

'Hey!' Colin said. 'No one disses the Gere to me. Or Cinderella retellings. Older movies are always going to be problematic in some way, so let's enjoy the ones that aren't completely awful. Anyway, I'm not here to discuss whether or not Grandad's story was in any way true. Definitely don't have the time for that. But I will say this: it was nice for Number Twelve and I to find something to do that didn't involve sniping at each other.'

He knew he needed to end the segment. And soon.

The sponsors had to be appeased—but so did his listeners, who were demanding more, more, *more*. Angela had written him a good script, for a first-timer, but the segment lacked punch. It needed a killer ending.

Colin took the plunge and went off-script. 'One last thing before we hear from our sponsors...do you ever get those random thoughts that make no sense? Or you picture yourself doing something completely bizarre? Like kissing someone, for example. Someone you would never consider kissing, someone you absolutely will *never* kiss. Maybe the boredom of this lockdown is getting to me. I don't know.'

His Twitter feed exploded.

'Well, that's today's Number Twelve update over and done with,'

Colin said, cheerfully ignoring his listeners. 'Stick around, though. I'll be playing some Roy Orbison after the ads. Because I can. No guesses as to which song it'll be. And then maybe I'll play you some Depeche Mode, though you clearly don't deserve their awesomeness. You should see some of the song requests I get from you lot! DJ Coop out—for about ten minutes. Enjoy my absence.'

He leaned back in his chair, grinning at his phone when it began to vibrate, Leo's number clearly displayed on the screen.

He already knew what his boss was going to say.

'Hey, Leo,' Colin greeted, finally answering.

'You,' Leo said, 'are a genius.'

Colin's grin only got wider.

14

Angela stood awkwardly off to the side, certain that the other caffeine-starved Millennials were giving her an even wider berth than usual. Definitely more than two metres. They didn't say anything about her lack of mask (she'd run out of socks she was willing to deface), or accuse her of lingering for too long, but this was Newfield. They were obviously thinking it.

She was going to die of a judgemental stare the instant someone weaponised their eyeballs.

The line outside The Bean and Gone slowly dwindled until Angela was the only customer. It wasn't like Ben to be more than twenty minutes late, but then again it wasn't like him to want to meet at this time in the morning either. She'd been so relieved when Ben had suggested 9am instead of his usual 'crack of dawn'.

'Boyfriend stood you up, huh?' Ishani asked.

Easter Monday had also proven difficult for her to find staff to cover the morning shift. Ishani had finally admitted, after some complaining, that it might have had something to do with the alcoholic Easter eggs she'd given everyone as a treat.

Angela sent off another text to Ben, frowning. 'Seems that way. He might have forgotten about me and started recording another video for his "Workout in Lockdown" series. I guess I can't really blame him. He's got about fifty thousand subscribers on YouTube and at least ten percent of them pay him for shirtless videos. He needs to keep uploading things. Whatever. I'm just happy to be out of the flat.'

'Yeah, I'm glad we're allowed to stay open for takeaway,' Ishani said. 'I'd go mad if I could only go out for a jog, or a wander through the barren toilet paper aisle at Sainsbury's.'

Horrible and hot-as-boiling-water realisation flooded through Angela. 'Shit! I'm not exercising and I've already finished my "takeaway" tea, which I should have actually *taken away*. I need an excuse to wait here.'

Ishani leaned out of the circular window she served from, peering around dramatically with a hand flattened over her eyes, as if she was a sailor in some old movie. The white cloth mask she was wearing certainly helped to enhance this image. It was covered in blue embroidery that seemed to emulate waves.

Ishani laughed and retreated back inside. 'The coast is clear for now. And I think you'll make it back to your flat before the rozzers show up.'

'I can't go back yet,' Angela all but wailed. 'My roommate's doing that radio thing. What if I accidentally set him up to fail? I can't witness that. I mean, before now my only writing experience was unpopular fanfic. Seriously unpopular. I've no idea what I was thinking. I might have just cost him his job!'

'He'd have lost his job anyway, by the sounds of things,' Ishani said with a shrug.

Angela opened her mouth to say something, but she was interrupted when her phone buzzed. She glanced down. The message wasn't from Ben. It was from Emily. *See what happens when ur not here to stop me!*

Attached was a photo of Emily's bed. Facedown on one of the white satin pillows, a matching sheet twisting up towards his torso, was a shirtless (and presumably naked) man with shoulder-length blond hair and wings tattooed onto his shoulder blades. Surfer dude. Even with the manbun missing in action, there was no mistaking his identity.

'Oh my God,' Angela said.

'What? What's happened?' Ishani asked.

'My best friend slept with her roommate.' Angela shook her head, dazed. 'Oh my God. You *never* sleep with the roommate.'

Ishani raised a single eyebrow. 'I thought you wanted to move in with your boyfriend? You'd be sleeping with your roommate all the time then, wouldn't you?'

'That's different!'

'Sure it is.' That sounded a lot like sarcasm.

Angela was saved from further argument when Emily sent her a barrage of texts.

U can call now

CALL ME NOW

NOWWWWWW

'Em, are you okay?' Angela asked as soon as the call connected. She power-walked away from the café and began a loop around the block towards the McDonald's, hoping it looked like legitimate exercise and not an excuse to keep busy until her boyfriend showed up.

'*Nooooo!*' Emily cried. 'You should have stopped me!'

Angela threw her eyes up to the clouds. She didn't trust herself to speak.

'I couldn't call you during Ben's live video,' Em continued, her whine carrying a vague echo that suggested she was currently hiding in a bathroom. 'I know he gets you to hold the camera for him when he's running about, but I needed you more. You knew there was a risk of this happening!'

Several thoughts flew through Angela's mind just then. She tossed the least relevant ones away. 'Why did you do it, Em?'

'You didn't stop me!'

Angela fought the urge to growl; even Colin Cooper didn't inspire this kind of aggravation. And the sense of dread she felt whenever Emily sent her a text? Completely absent around him.

She actually didn't mind his presence, maybe even enjoyed it. When had *that* happened?

They'd been roommates for less than a week!

Momentarily flummoxed, Angela called to mind various things Emily had said over the years and combined them with the dialogue she'd read in various chick lit novels. 'I'm sorry. It must be very upsetting. But you've scratched that itch, right? Now you can focus on something else, like work. Or a productive hobby. Or something.'

'Ange! I'm stuck with this guy! We're in the middle of a pandemic!'

Angela grimaced. Yes, Emily was stuck. Short of enlisting the help of potentially contagious movers, anyway. Australia might be doing better with the pandemic, but it was still floating around, unseen. Emily's life was about to become very awkward.

Unless…

'Do you like him, Em?' she asked.

'What kind of question is that?' Emily demanded.

'Um, a good one? If you do like him, then maybe this isn't so bad. You could actually date him. Where else are you going to find a guy at the moment?'

'Ange! This is serious. You're the one who got me into this mess and now you need to get me out of it.'

'Yes, I know, it's my fault you shagged your hot roommate,' Angela said, her patience wearing thin. 'But if you're not going to listen to me, like always, then what's the point of me even talking to you? What's the point of our friendship if we can't be honest with each other? If we only ever pick up the phone when we want something from the other person? And let's be real. The main reason you didn't ditch me like the other girls at school did was because your mother wouldn't have let you. And you're only talking to me now because you'd feel guilty about upsetting her memory. You know what? I'm done. I'm so done.'

She hung up and switched her phone to silent.

Reality slammed into Angela with the force of an out-of-control lorry. 'Oh my God. What did I just *do*?'

Angela's eyes stung. No amount of words could fix the damage she'd just done. But she had other things to worry about right now.

She circled back to Ishani's café with her phone still out, watching the video that Ben had been streaming a few minutes earlier. He was sprinting through the hallway on the first floor of his parents' place, darting from side to side, making his way past the master bedroom where an oval mirror in the corner stood facing him—

—and she saw a flash of pink.

Frowning, Angela clicked back a few seconds and zoomed in.

A blurry figure in bright Lycra. Holding up Ben's phone to record his antics.

This was of course the moment that Ben chose to text Angela, telling her he was 'so sorry, babe' and he'd be on his way after a quick shower. Would she mind ordering him some tea? Hot and herbal, with a squeeze of lemon and maybe a drizzle of honey? His voice was on the way out. Too much talking during his most recent Q&A, apparently.

Angela's stomach dropped down into her woven ballet flats.

The Bean and Gone had just come back into view when a series of waspish messages arrived from Emily.

Btw pink really isn't ur colour

Might b a reason Ben never shows ur face in his videos

Just saying

Honest enough for u???

That would have hurt—on a normal day. But Emily was on the other side of the world. Unreachable even at the best of times.

Ben was only up on Newside Street. And he was headed her way.

Angela increased her pace and frantically clicked through the last few videos, jumping forward in thirty-second increments. She'd only watched a couple of them in the last few days and not all that closely. Minute, insignificant details suddenly became astoundingly obvious. Every video contained a hint of someone else, someone holding Ben's phone, someone inadvertently knocking over a water bottle emblazoned with the logo belonging to Ben's major sponsor.

Someone who was too good at keeping up with Ben to be one of his elderly parents.

'Oh my God,' Angela chanted. 'Oh my *God*.'

She was breathless by the time she reached The Bean and Gone. Ishani took one look at her, swiftly sent her current customer away without any of her usual friendly banter, and asked, 'What's wrong? Are you okay? Angela?'

The story tumbled out of Angela before she could stop it, before she could edit it, before she could make herself sound less insane. She could already picture the red twine criss-crossing over the four walls of her room, connecting dots that didn't exist.

She was obviously imagining things. She had to be. The alternative wasn't bearable.

'Right,' Ishani said briskly, rolling up imaginary sleeves. 'I know just what to do. I'll make his usual cup of tea—why anyone would claim to love chamomile brewed that strong I'll never know, I'd break up with the bastard over that—and you'll stand off to the side when he comes to collect it. Let's see if I can't get him to mention something about his mysterious houseguest. I'll keep it casual, keep it shallow, indulge in some wink-wink-nudge-nudge. You know what I mean. I'm bisexual, so I'll use our mutual appreciation of a fine feminine form to get him to open up.'

Angela wavered on the spot, paralysed by indecision.

'Shoo!' Ishani said, waving her hands towards the footpath.

'You…you believe me?' Angela managed to croak out. 'You're not going to tell me I'm imagining things and spiralling into a dark pit of sitcom-grade jealousy?'

Ishani pitched her an impatient look. 'Well, *someone* is hanging out with your boyfriend. If he hasn't bothered to mention it by now, then he's clearly up to something shady, right? Now get over there and look innocent!'

Meekly, Angela obeyed, her heart thumping faster than a Lexus on the M20 belonging to a man saddled with three children, an ex-wife, and a mid-life crisis.

Ben came down the hill a few minutes later. It felt like only seconds had passed.

Angela lifted a hand and gave him a half-hearted wave, which he didn't return. But he did flip her the smirk that had managed to turn her knees to jelly and custard when they'd first met. He wasn't wearing his exercise gear this time, having swapped it for the button-up shirt and black trousers that his mother always insisted on him wearing if she was planning to 'do brunch' (aka sequester herself in the kitchen and cook for everyone else, then spend hours cleaning up while complaining about a woman's lot in life).

Angela had been invited to every other brunch before now.

'I've ordered for you,' she said distantly. 'It should be ready.'

He sauntered over to the window and almost immediately chuckled, responding to some sly comment that Ishani had made. More murmured words passed between them.

Angela bounced on the balls of her feet, fighting the urge to march over and listen in. Their heads were bent too close together in a total disregard for social distancing, all in the name of—what? Uncovering a cheat? Was risking Ishani's health worth it? Her mask wasn't even surgical grade, because of the shortages.

Ben turned around and made his way towards Angela, that smirk still smacked across his face.

'French Earl Grey, whole milk!' Ishani bellowed.

'Black tea, babe?' Ben said, looking horrified. '*Whole milk?*'

Angela scurried forwards to avoid having to defend herself—and also because Ishani was tossing her head to the side repeatedly, a painfully obvious 'come here' gesture that even Ben wouldn't fail to notice once he stopped checking his subscriber count on his phone.

Angela's fingers closed around the insulated cup and jerked it towards her. Hot liquid sloshed onto her skin, reminding her that she hadn't grabbed a lid from the nearby self-serve table (which also featured a bottle of hand sanitiser that had been duct-taped down, to discourage thieves looking to make a quick buck on a suddenly scarce item).

But the brief scalding was nothing compared to the pain spearing her chest.

'Well, I don't know who that bint from the videos is,' Ishani said in a low voice, 'but he definitely gave her one this morning. And the past few mornings, the way I hear it. The sleaze even joked about moving her in, just so he'd have easy access for when the police really do start taking the PM's rules seriously out here. Whatcha going to do?'

Angela looked down at the clouds in her tea, which were as miserable as the ones filling the sky above her. She sighed. 'The only thing I can do. Toss the whole man out and mine the experience for material. For Colin's show.'

Ishani laughed. 'That's the spirit!

'I was joking,' Angela muttered. 'I'm really not that brave.'

'Well, you can't stay with him, can you?'

Ishani had a very good point.

Angela just wished she didn't have to implode yet another relationship fifteen minutes after the last one.

15

She left her room after midday, her expression so pinched he wasn't sure if she could see out of the gaps between her eyelids.

Colin swallowed. She *knew*.

Somehow, she knew that he'd let himself into her room to access the wardrobe. But he hadn't touched any of her stuff (or even looked in the direction of her suitcase) and there were so few times that he could do this without arousing her suspicion. Colin steeled himself. Rob had already had a lot to say on the subject. But Rob was nowhere near as blunt as Angela. This was going to hurt.

'Oh my God,' she breathed, pressing her back flat against the door.

Colin waited. He wasn't going to apologise prematurely. He'd seen enough movies, most of them comedic in nature, to know better. There was still a chance that he had managed to get away with it.

'You look wrecked,' he observed.

Angela threw him a blistering look.

Colin held up his hands, a gesture of surrender. 'Sorry. But you do. And I'm sure you wouldn't waste any time pointing it out to me if our positions were reversed. I suppose I should ask if you're alright, let you say something cutting in response, and then wait for the canned laughter to erupt from the audience.'

There, a small smile pricking her lips. 'No canned laughter today, please. There's some good news, at least. I managed to get an idea for tomorrow's show.'

'Do tell,' Colin invited.

Angela levered her body away from the door and slouched towards him, her hand targeting the mug she'd left on the coffee table earlier. She slung back a mouthful of whatever was inside it and retched. 'Nothing's worse than cold black tea. At least green tea is forgiving. Herbal's even better, actually, because you can pretend it's iced. But whatever. Cold black tea is a *mood* today.'

'Right,' Colin said, though he had no idea what she was going on about.

Angela dropped heavily onto the sofa beside him. 'So here's what's going to happen in your segment. You'll tell everyone that your roommate broke up with her boyfriend, because he had a peroxide-blond bint visiting him on the sly. During a lockdown, of all things. Bint's too offensive, isn't it? It's also incredibly misogynistic and she's not the only one at fault here. Better not use that word then.'

Colin mutely shook his head.

'He was even planning to introduce this hot new thing to his parents,' Angela went on, a potent scowl ripping across her face. 'What about his girlfriend? Shouldn't he be taking her to brunch instead? And who is she anyway? Someone who should have known better than to withhold sex during these uncertain times, apparently. He can't have really loved her. He didn't jump at the chance to move in with her when this all started.

'Maybe he knew they were never going to last.'

Angela seemed to have finally run out of steam. She went for the mug of tea again and shuddered before she even swallowed the next mouthful.

'I'm so sorry,' Colin said.

'Why?' She laughed bitterly. 'It's too cliché. It can't possibly have happened in real life. This stuff only happens in fiction. And it's just an idea for your show tomorrow. That's all.'

Colin wasn't game enough to object. 'Just an idea, got it. Should I ask Rob for more Moscato?'

She eyed him.

'For inspiration, of course,' he clarified.

'I haven't given you enough already?' She snorted. 'Sure. Why not. But I should probably drink alone. I'm *this* close to losing it. Better if I do that in my room.'

'You can cry on my shoulder, if you'd like,' Colin said.

'You did not just say that.'

Colin chuckled uneasily. 'It's an idea. For my show. Your dashing roommate gallantly offers you his shoulder and tries not to sniff your hair as he pulls you in close and whispers assurances that everything will be okay. Well, maybe not everything—there's still a pandemic doing its best to completely upend billions of lives. But apart from that.'

Angela pulled a face.

'Too creepy?' he asked.

'Yes. Let's not use the hair-sniffing thing.'

'Duly noted.' Colin slid his phone out of his pocket and shot off a message to Rob. 'I've made an order for more wine. Shall we get started on tomorrow's segment?'

She hesitated. 'Will we have to wait long for your mate to show up?'

'Could be an hour or more, depending on how busy he is.'

'Oh God,' she moaned. 'I'm going to need something to tide me over.'

'I have just the thing,' Colin said cheerfully. 'A spicy chai tea I picked up in Borough Market one time. Might have been a few years ago, mind…I don't *think* tea goes off. The flavour loses some of its potency, that's all.'

Angela held out her mug and shook it at him. 'It'll have to be better than your usual dishwater or you'll be writing this segment yourself.'

'I'll do my best!' Colin promised as he darted past the kitchen's saloon doors.

***

The cold night air was unrepentant as it clawed through his cheap disguise, causing Colin to upgrade his wonky shuffle to an even wonkier run. The fresh oxygen in his lungs was like a drug. He had to have more. Maybe he'd jog all the way down to Dover when the sun came up, get some proper exercise in. Pre-pandemic, he'd always hired a taxi to take him there, and only so he could grab a pint at Rob's bar.

Circling the sofa wasn't enough to tame his restlessness. Not anymore.

A car blew past on the road.

Colin slowed to an inconspicuous walk and adjusted the scratchy beard fastened to his face, thankful that there were no streetlights up this way. He couldn't be caught out here, not in this get-up. He looked downright shady. The police would have a thing or two to say about his appearance, he was sure, and the local paper would have a field day with it.

Something this bizarre might even surface on the Internet. He could always shrug off yet another long-winded email from his parents, who seemed to take turns in berating Colin for once again proving himself to be the black sheep of two families. But if their good friends and neighbours saw just how much of a disappointment he was, courtesy of a viral news article? They might actually come down to Newfield and express their displeasure *in person*.

There were already enough scary things going on in the world right now.

At least they didn't listen to his show and complain about every little thing he said—but of course they would never do that. They'd never taken a close interest in him. He wasn't a person with hopes and hobbies. He was an asset.

Colin made it back to Grace Park without incident, though he wasn't sure how long he'd be able to get away with this. There was still too much of the stuff left in Angela's wardrobe. By his calculations, he needed to do four more weeks of night-time excursions before he was in the clear.

Colin slunk his way into the foyer, pausing to check his mail. Despite himself, he looked up the stairs, as if that alone could have summoned the usual visit from Angela, the usual haughty expression, the usual waspish comment. But not tonight. She was sprawled across the sofa in his flat and kept warm by a blanket he'd thrown on top of her before heading out.

She hadn't even touched the Moscato. As it turned out, a good pot of tea was all she needed to fuel her writing and her rants.

Angela's ex-boyfriend had earned quite a few interesting names over the afternoon and evening, growing notably less sweary and more ridiculous. 'Narcissistic Pec-Obsessed Organic-Loving Keto Slag' was still his favourite.

Since Colin's experience with romantic disasters was rather limited (his relationships tended to amicably fizzle out, not self-destruct), mostly he'd nodded and hmmed whenever appropriate. Colin had asked Angela if she had some friends she could talk to, since apparently Dear Old Mum was out (he could totally understand that). Angela had confessed that her only friend was someone she'd only just met at The Bean and Gone, because she'd ditched her oldest friendship minutes before dumping Ben. Angela was reluctant to lean too heavily on Ishani this early on in the game.

Colin closed his letterbox and shook his head. 'No letters. Great risk you took there, Colin. You need to get out of sight ASAP. Maybe you should have done this when you weren't dressed like…'

'Why on Earth are you dressed like Father Christmas?' a very familiar voice demanded from the stairs.

His heart rattled against his ribcage.

'What are you doing down here?' Colin wheezed out.

Angela raised her eyebrows, as if it was obvious. 'You know this is the best time to check the mail. And tea doesn't send me into a drunken coma, shockingly enough.'

'Oh,' Colin said.

'"Oh"? Is that it? Where's your silver tongue, Mr DJ?'

Colin wished he hadn't immediately imagined doing certain things with his tongue. Wait, *no*. Not again. Not with Angela. And even if she wasn't still reeling from a breakup with the 'Complete and Utter Chav-Wannabe Wanker' (Colin's second favourite insult for the ex-boyfriend he'd never met), he definitely wouldn't do that.

It had to be an intrusive thought. It had to be.

Bother. It wasn't. He really did want to kiss her. This realisation pulled the blood right out of his face. He had no idea what he was supposed to do or say. Was she expecting a coherent response?

Happily, she was focused on another topic, even if it was similarly unwelcome. 'You look like the world's sorriest Santa. What's that about?'

'I was…exercising,' Colin improvised. 'Yes, that's legal. I was out exercising.'

'In a red and white suit, complete with hat and beard,' Angela said flatly.

'Yes. Why? This isn't how *you* exercise?' he shot back.

She crossed her arms. 'Colin. You'd have a hard time convincing any policeman that's what you're doing out past midnight, dressed like that. And besides which…you're wearing your Converse.'

'So I am,' Colin said, bemused.

'You always go barefoot when you're walking in circles. Oh, I'm sorry, when you're—' She grinned mercilessly and held up two fingers on each hand to perform air quotes. '—"exercising" in the living room.'

Colin had the alarming feeling that he was about to lose control of this encounter. 'I wear my Converse for *outdoor* exercise.'

'And if I ask your mate, Rob, about your history of outdoor exercise?'

'I only exercise barefoot inside because I'm trying to make these last longer than my previous pair,' Colin said, trying a new line of defence.

Angela paused, studying his shoes. He knew they were still in good condition—the white soles were spotless, largely because he never went anywhere except to the shops (or to Rob's bar, but that was before the restrictions came along). After a few tense seconds of silence, Angela shook her head, clearly unconvinced. 'If the state of your shoes was so important to you, you'd replace those awful slippers. The ones you wear all day, every day. I swear I can smell them from my room sometimes.'

'No you can't!'

'Can too,' Angela countered. 'And I can smell your attempt to change the subject.'

'Is it a successful attempt?'

'No.'

'I suppose I'd better go in and change,' Colin said and headed up the stairs, yanking off the scratchy synthetic beard as he went. He wasn't running away, he told himself. This was a tactical retreat. And he was going to be sensible and get some sleep and definitely not think about what her lips might feel like against his.

'You are *infuriating*!' Angela called after him.

'And you'll wake up our neighbours if you keep insulting me out here!' he said, a much safer option than the 'and you look ridiculously sexy when you wear one of those long jumpers over the top of your nightie!' his mouth threatened to spill.

Once he'd shut his bedroom door and was safely hidden away, Colin tumbled into his desk chair and clapped his hands over his face. What was wrong with him? How was he supposed to look Angela in the eye from now on?

Wait. Was it really such a bad thing to fancy her?

Well, aside from the fact that he'd only invited her to live with him so that he could make himself look good in that Daily Inspo segment. Was he allowed to strike up something with her, given how all this had started? Would he have to tell her at some point?

Did it even matter? *Nothing* was going to happen. Even if he wanted it to.

Colin groaned and prepared himself for a sleepless night.

16

He was avoiding her. He had to be.

Angela could excuse his absences in the living room at 6am. It was perfectly acceptable for him to attend that Zoom meeting every day—well, perfectly acceptable for people whose bosses had decided that their employees didn't need a lie-in. Colin's boss seemed the type to never relax the rules, never mind that it was getting harder and harder to roll out of bed after seeing the updated national death toll on Twitter each morning. It felt like a couple of centuries had passed since the year had begun.

Surely a lie-in would be acceptable at this point.

Aside from the meeting, Colin was also making himself scarce at other times. It was now Wednesday and, outside of their brainstorming sessions where he sat as far away as possible, Angela hadn't seen him for more than a handful of minutes since she'd caught him sneaking about in that red-and-white suit. If he wasn't collecting groceries or visiting the elderly couple downstairs, he was suddenly and inexplicably fond of exercising on the grass out the front instead of following his usual route around the sofa.

It just wasn't *normal*. For him, anyway.

And it wasn't normal for Colin to be doing his laundry in the morning—and on a weekday, no less. If her previous observations were correct, he usually left it until some ridiculous hour on a Sunday night. That was something they'd never managed to sync up, unlike the mail run; Angela preferred to do her laundry on Tuesday mornings. She'd never do it on a weekend.

Because that's when the laundry room downstairs became an all-too-polite version of the Hunger Games. Abandon your clothes for two seconds and they'd somehow be shunted into the one washer/dryer that took hours to finish a load. As a result, people tended to congregate in the basement, keeping an eye on their chosen machines.

It could get downright crowded. Not a terribly safe thing during a pandemic.

Anyway, Angela had been sitting patiently on the sofa ever since Colin's Zoom meeting had started. She only had to wait until 6:30am for his attempted escape.

'Is that why you had to wear the Santa suit?' Angela asked idly as Colin crept out of his room. His back was bowed, his laundry bag was clutched to his chest, and his foot was hovering in mid-air as if he wasn't sure what to do with it. He seemed to be trying to audition for the role of a cartoon miscreant in *Hugo & Victor: Bunglers in Crime*.

'Is what why?' Colin echoed, still frozen in place.

'You ran out of clothes, obviously,' Angela said, giving him a convenient out.

He bit his lip, clearly seeing the trap for what it was.

Angela grinned.

'I'll be back later,' he grumbled and shuffled his way across the carpet. She noticed that he was wearing new slippers. 'When my show starts.'

She raised her eyebrows. 'You're going to stay down in the basement until nine?'

'Why not?' he challenged, now most of the way to the front door.

'It's kind of boring down there, isn't it? There's nothing to do. Except look at that supposedly motivational poster with the picture of a kitten falling off a cliff. You know the one I mean. It has the words "hang in there!" written along the bottom.'

Colin kept his back to her.

Angela dearly wanted to strangle him just then.

'At least take a book with you,' she said instead.

Colin spun around, his eyes bright as inspiration struck. 'I have my phone on me! Some of us read books on tiny screens these days. Our own personal guides to the galaxy. Douglas Adams had the right of it there. The man was a genius. So ahead of his time.'

'Did you get those new slippers because of me?' Angela said, interrupting his attempt to distract her. She indicated his feet.

'Contrary to what you believe, Angela, I don't structure my entire wardrobe around you,' Colin said airily, his usual confidence oozing back into place. He clearly wasn't going to give her an honest answer. That hurt, actually, and she wasn't sure why.

Angela sighed. 'Have fun, then.'

'You know, I think I will, since there'll be no one down there to judge my footwear,' he shot back and then practically ran out the door. It didn't even close properly behind him.

The silence he left in his wake was deafening.

Angela's phone lay unlocked in her hand, open to the message thread she'd had running with Emily for years, imported from at least three other smartphones. Before that, on their ancient Nokia bricks, they'd racked up even more messages, lost to time and format changes. But she could still picture the best conversations in her head. Their own personal 'greatest hits'.

Jeremy Clarkson = hawt, Emily had sent one time.

R u fucking serious? Angela had demanded.

Emily's reply had been lightning-fast. *'Yes, that too,' Remus said.*

They'd both laughed about it for days, sometimes in the middle of class. That was the one thing they could agree on back then—Sirius/Remus 4eva. They'd spent hours each day reading Harry Potter fanfiction together.

Their English teacher had caught them at it and had told them that no real writer indulged in fanfiction. But what was *Wide Sargasso Sea* then? And what about *Paradise Lost?* Angela had never received satisfactory answers to those questions. That teacher had also been very vocal about her dislike of romance novels, so Angela had made sure that she'd never taken any to school in her backpack.

She and Emily had shared some good times, hadn't they? She shouldn't have exploded like that. An apology should be easy enough to write.

But Angela's fingers remained poised above the screen instead of typing.

Did half a lifetime of memories, some of them fantastic and some of them wince-worthy, make it worth hanging onto a friendship that had been frayed even before distance entered the picture?

She was rescued from making a mistake when a text message arrived from someone else. Someone no less cancelled.

Babe we should talk, Ben implored.

I'm not your babe BABE, Angela wrote, furious.

Don't get ur panties in a twist babe. Just want to talk

Oooh, she would gladly disobey social distancing laws to wring his neck (and then she'd have a good go at Colin Cooper, of course). But at least she'd already thought up a good response before this situation had arisen. Ishani had impressed upon her how important it was to plan ahead and arm herself with a few choice phrases. Just in case.

Ishani had more than a little experience with ex-boyfriends and their wheedling ways. Angela was a most willing student.

Don't get your balls into a twist, she replied. *I don't owe you the time of day.*

This is so silly, Ben complained.

Angela consulted her mental list of comebacks and used another. *If infidelity is silly to you then we've got nothing to talk about. Don't ever text me again.*

Then she miiight have gone off-script. *TWAT*

Grinning, Angela blocked his number. She couldn't wait to tell Colin about this. And she couldn't wait for him to stop being so childish and stop avoiding her. Maybe she'd been too judgemental. Maybe dressing up as Father Christmas was some sort of weird fetish of his and she'd offended him. Whatever. At least he wasn't hanging out with someone who thought pink Lyrca was a good look.

Colin Cooper was a much better roommate than Ben could ever be. He had let Angela crash with him at the drop of a hat and he didn't care about the romance novels. None of them were hidden away in her suitcase anymore. And he had given her the opportunity to try her hand at writing. He didn't even laugh at what she came up with.

He was also kind of hot.

Are you fucking serious? a little voice asked inside her.

Oh my God. She was not going to have this conversation, even with herself.

Angela shook her head vigorously. Time for a distraction.

Somehow she ended up browsing a clunky fanfiction site, just as she had done as a teenager. Her old account was still there, along with all those old stories she'd spent countless hours reading when she should have been studying for her GCSE. Nothing really died on the Internet.

Excellent. She knew exactly how she was going to pass the time until Colin returned from his exciting adventure downstairs. And she might even get some ideas for his show in the process.

Fanfic writers were brilliant at remixing tropes, after all.

**

Colin returned five minutes before 9am. No time to chat when he was starting work so soon.

It was such an obviously deliberate attempt to continue avoiding her. Twitter was currently full of links to articles about the nationwide lockdown being extended for several more weeks, so he was going to have to give her a real conversation at some point. He bloody better. She'd go mad otherwise.

God, he could be as stubborn as her sometimes.

Not exactly the best attribute split between two people sharing a flat, but Angela consoled herself with the knowledge that they hadn't killed each other yet. Oh well. She could always pick up the phone and chat to Ishani—once the café owner was finally out bed. According to yesterday's text, Ishani was far too old to be covering as many morning shifts as she had over the weekend and needed to sleep like the dead for a bit.

Colin made it from the front door to his bedroom in under four seconds.

Notably, he'd lacked a bag of laundry.

Angela killed a few minutes by reading a book, but soon found herself trying too hard to listen in to Colin performing their latest effort. She couldn't bear to hear it. Even if he'd assured her that his listeners were enjoying the serial.

Nope, she had to get out of there. Angela left the sofa and padded her way downstairs to rescue Colin's clothes. He had indeed left them in one of the machines. He didn't appear to be the only person to have forgotten their laundry, but there was no mistaking his load. She recognised those band shirts: Devo, Duran Duran, Adam and the Ants, Pet Shop Boys, New Order. He really had an obsession with New Wave. Admittedly, it was one of her favourite music genres, but Angela had always been careful about who she revealed that to (Emily had thought it downright daggy). She had a feeling she didn't need to be careful around Colin Cooper, Retro Addict.

When Angela returned to the flat (making sure to wait at least fifteen minutes before doing so, to avoid catching even a second of the serial), she found Colin looping around the sofa. He didn't notice her at first. He was too busy arguing with his boss.

'I don't care!' Colin exclaimed. 'I've already changed the format twice this year for you *and* I've started giving my listeners the romance serial you demanded of me. There's no way I'll stop playing the music I like.'

The phone exuded a stern, paternalistic voice, one that didn't match the young face on the screen. 'Colin. While I will allow the occasional indulgence on your part, your music tastes are not as important as what your listeners want. And the sponsors want what *they* want. Have you seen the complaints on your Twitter feed? Play some music from this century, please. Before I decide that you are not suited for this job.'

Colin stared at his phone, mouth wobbling soundlessly.

His boss sighed. 'You don't need to start doing it right this second. Tomorrow is soon enough.'

Angela cleared her throat loudly as soon as the call finished. Colin's stunned expression was almost too perfect and she wished she had her phone ready to take a photo of it. He was adorable right now, especially with his hair mussed up like that; it made him look like he'd just rolled out of bed.

His laundry was still in her hands. Right, this could help break the awkward silence.

'I got your stuff,' she said, offering the bag. 'Folded it too.'

'I have to get back to my show,' he said distantly. The music wafting out of his bedroom revealed that he was barely halfway into the epic intro of 'I Ran (So Far Away)' by A Flock of Seagulls. It was up there with 'Twilight Zone' by Golden Earring as one of the greatest driving songs ever made, in Angela's opinion. Some people might claim that 'Radar Love' was better, but they could all sod off.

God, she missed her car. She missed getting in and going for a long, aimless drive with the music blasting. But it hadn't been worth spending the money to keep it when she'd been taking the train to London five mornings out of seven.

It was a good thing that Colin didn't own a car. She was willing to bet that he'd have driven to France by now, pandemic be damned. All to avoid her.

'Can you stop being such a mysterious prick?' Angela demanded.

Colin blinked at her. 'I wasn't aware…?'

'I did you a solid,' Angela told him, waving the bag so vigorously she was sure her careful folding had gone to waste. 'Just like I did you a solid by writing this romance serial, something you clearly couldn't manage on your own. And I can do you one more, if you'll let me.'

Colin was already backing away towards his door.

'Stubborn git,' she said. 'I'm not going to ask about the Santa suit. Or the wardrobe. Or your insulting efforts to avoid me—which, by the way, you're going to stop doing or I'll stop helping you. Got it?'

He swallowed. 'I'm sorry.'

'Apology accepted. Don't do it again. Now do you want to keep your job or not?'

'Yes, but...'

'You *are* allowed to ask for help, you know.'

'That's...that's not the issue here,' Colin managed, his voice strained. At least he was now doing her the courtesy of meeting her eyes.

'Tell me or don't tell me "the issue", I don't care,' Angela said. 'I don't want you to lose your job. And not just because I'm worried you'll need to bring in a roommate who actually pays rent.' She dropped his laundry bag onto the floor and crossed her arms, jerking her chin towards his bedroom. 'If that's the extended version of "I Ran" I can hear, you've got time to hear this. So. Colin. Do you have a thing against cover songs?'

'Who doesn't?' Colin asked, grimacing. 'No one makes original songs anymore.'

'Just as I suspected. So you're aware that "Talk Talk" by Talk Talk is a cover, right?'

She'd chosen that band because she'd seen the poster on the back of his door. And since he was a radio DJ, Angela was fairly certain she knew which of their songs appealed to him the most.

'Wh—what!?' Colin exclaimed.

Angela grinned, sensing victory. 'Yeah. The frontman first recorded it in the 1970s with his other band. I'm partial to the pop remake myself. But there you go. That's your way forward.' When Colin said nothing, presumably still processing the bombshell she'd dropped on him, Angela went on, 'Do you know how many covers of New Wave songs are out there? Let me introduce you to my Spotify playlist after your show. "I Ran" alone has over a hundred remakes, ranging from smooth jazz to heavy metal. *And* they're all from this century. Even Darude's given it a go.'

Colin bit his lip. A Flock of Seagulls were now long past walking along the avenue.

He'd have to go back into his room soon.

'It's a bit cheeky, I'll admit,' Angela said. 'Playing new versions of your favourite songs, but…'

'But it might just get Leo off my back,' Colin finished, exhaling deeply.

Angela laughed. 'Maybe. No promises. Now get back to your show before the song runs out.'

'FAB, Jeff,' Colin said with a sloppy salute, then dashed back out of sight.

Angela watched him go.

No, there was no reason to admire about that view, none whatsoever.

He was wearing those skinny black jeans again (folding his laundry had revealed that he owned more than one pair, thank God) and though they probably felt comfortable to him, they were tight enough to show off his assets.

Had she just been ogling Colin Cooper? Of all people?

Why, yes. Yes she had.

I'm single, I can look now, Angela silently justified it to herself as she stared at his bedroom door, which was now firmly closed.

Angela's fingers flew across her phone's screen before she could stop them. Ishani might not be awake yet, but this was definitely the sort of thing that would amuse her. Once the laws were relaxed, hopefully before summer, Angela was sure a bit of space (aka a few hours at The Bean and Gone each day) would provide her with some perspective and eradicate this sudden and bizarre attraction to Colin Cooper.

Except it was probably a lot less sudden and bizarre than she'd like to admit.

17

'No way, not a chance,' Colin said.

He was well aware that they already had him cornered. This was inevitable—and he'd known it ever since he'd agreed to this conversation. He didn't like it. Not one bit. And to make matters worse, his face was now itching something chronic because of that stupid synthetic beard he'd been wearing for his night-time excursions.

Colin sighed, but he wasn't about to cave just yet. 'Why can't I go with the you-folding-me-laundry thing? The segment's already written. We finished it last night.'

Angela set her hands on her hips, looking frighteningly like his Maths teacher from fifth grade, although Ms Jones' stern expressions had never had the same puzzling effect on him that Angela's did. She was also far too awake for someone who had rolled out of bed at 5:30am, determined to convince him they needed to rewrite his entire segment.

'Leo, back me up here,' Angela said.

Colin's boss stroked his beardless chin. The gesture was annoyingly dignified, despite it being performed on the small screen of a phone that was propped up against a mug on the coffee table. Leo had agreed to a pre-meeting meeting, but only because Angela had requested it. He was very curious about 'the roommate'.

Colin wished Leo had at least pretended he was surprised that Angela had been helping him write the serial all along. Introducing them had definitely been a mistake. Leo and Angela had banded together against him within seconds of meeting each other.

Colin's fingers scratched their way over his face, trying to dispel the itchiness. He was willing to bet he looked deranged instead of dignified.

Finally, Leo gave a sharp nod. 'I like Angela's idea. You need to accelerate the pace of the serial, Colin. Your listeners will lose patience if we drag this out too long.'

'Drag this out?' Colin repeated. 'Leo, we only just started doing it!'

'Colin, you are forgetting our competition.' Leo frowned heavily at him. 'They don't remain static. They've started cobbling together romantic serials of their own, though theirs are noticeably paced slower, to keep the segment going for as long as possible. We do not want to lose our listeners to boredom or to choice. We'll offer them a serial that isn't open-ended, that *will* have a satisfying conclusion. And they can replay it to their hearts' content afterwards, safe in the knowledge that there is no cliffhanger. You need to be the first to finish. Speed up the romance. Change today's segment.'

'But you like me to have my stuff prepared well in advance,' Colin argued.

'No,' Leo corrected. 'I like all your *stuff* to be prepared before 9am. A rewrite of one segment in three hours is hardly going to do you in, Colin.'

'But...'

Leo waved an impatient hand. 'Listen. Angela folding your

laundry is a cute gesture, I'll admit, but there's only so much "slow" that our listeners can take in their slow burn. Your target audience isn't used to waiting, Colin. They're *Millennials.* They've been fast-forwarding through the boring bits since the times of VHS.'

Angela nodded along with Leo's words. No argument from her. For once.

Colin slid his stare from his boss to his roommate. How the heck had this happened? Why had he agreed to let Angela talk to Leo? It can't have been because she'd ambushed him while looking adorably rumpled in a grey nightie that featured two pairs of sunglasses set above a certain quote about the distance to Chicago and a full tank of gas.

'Leo, you're a Millennial too,' was all he managed to say.

Leo went dangerously silent. Colin felt the sweat gather between his shoulder blades.

'Fine.' Colin deflated. 'Fine, fine, fine. We'll frantically rewrite this segment in the limited time we have left. But you know, Leo, I won't be able to attend the usual Zoom meeting if I'm too busy doing this.'

He might have crossed his fingers behind his back.

'Colin. You are not the one writing it. As I have just discovered.'

Fudge. Leo wasn't going to let him get away with ditching the meeting.

'Not that I have a problem with you outsourcing,' Leo went on. 'I'm actually quite impressed with your problem-solving methods.'

Angela patted Colin's shoulder, her grin downright feral. 'You go get ready for your meeting. Say hello to Sunshine, Peter, and Danika for me. But not Danger. I don't know how he manages to imply offence without actually saying anything remotely offensive, but it definitely doesn't make me like him any.'

Uh oh. He really shouldn't have told her so much about his

colleagues. But what else were they supposed to discuss over a pot of tea in the late afternoon? He was fairly certain he hadn't mentioned Danger's presentation style, however.

Had she downloaded the Radio SPLATZAPP! streaming app?

Was she now *listening* to the shows?

The only things she could have heard lately from DJ Coop were fairly innocent. But if she started trawling through the archives…just how long did those go back anyway? Surely Leo eventually retired the old show files. Or maybe he never did, because the ads in them were constantly replaced to reflect the current paying sponsors.

Radio never used to be this permanent, nor the past this difficult to bury.

The Internet was forever.

'It's a shame you have no experience in radio or podcasting,' Leo told Angela. 'I could definitely utilise your wit. Maybe pair you with DJ Sunshine. Her show has been lacking some bite of late. You'd be the perfect whip crack there.'

'You know what else is a shame?' Colin groused. 'Sunshine's camera not working.'

Leo sighed deeply. 'I may have to consider allowing her to expense a new phone.'

'Oh no, don't do that!' Angela said, eyes wide and accusing as she flung them at Colin. She'd somehow guessed what he was up to. 'You can't set a precedent, Leo. If just one person expenses their phone…it'll snowball.'

'Right you are, Angela,' Leo agreed gravely. 'I'll see you in a few minutes, Colin.'

Leo's face vanished from the phone and the call disconnected.

'You did not just do that to DJ Sunshine,' Angela snapped.

Hot waves of guilt immediately swamped Colin. He identified his motive as pure jealousy. He didn't want Angela to go to another show.

Yikes, he was going to turn into Danger if he wasn't careful.

He bowed his head. 'It was petty and wrong and I totally deserve to get pummelled for it. I'm going to do better in future. This is character growth, you know. To prove myself as the romantic lead.'

'Romantic lead,' Angela repeated. 'This is *real life*, Colin.'

Colin's stomach hollowed out. She was right. And he was going to have to stop avoiding her, saying snippy things, and being generally unpleasant. It wasn't her fault that he'd somehow, irrationally, formed a crush on her.

If he wanted to ask her out at some point, he had to do a *lot* better.

'Yes, you're right, I really need to adjust my attitude,' Colin said distantly, wondering if he should be worried by the thought process that had just occurred inside his head. 'Have fun writing this awkward encounter that never occurred between us.'

'Would you rather it did?' Angela asked, a pen twirling through her fingers. She always used a notebook first before going for her laptop. Colin rarely wrote or typed anything, because it was always printed across his mind's eye. And frankly, he couldn't be bothered. Probably why he wasn't a novelist.

'Because we can set the encounter up, if you'd prefer,' Angela continued. 'For authenticity.'

'No!' Colin exclaimed.

She affected a gruff, Wolverine-esque voice. 'Come on. Afraid you might like it?'

Colin was seriously wondering why he'd bothered to get out of bed. His day had already gone downhill at an alarming rate and he hadn't even had breakfast yet. But he was going to grapple his way to a win against Angela, even if it killed him.

She was waiting for a response, smirking slightly, and he wanted nothing more than to wipe that smirk right off her face.

So he went for honesty.

'Not afraid,' Colin said flippantly. 'Because I'd definitely like it.'

Her mouth dropped open.

He spun on his heel and marched triumphantly back into his room. Colin thought he'd made it away unscathed, but then she shouted after him, 'Not as much as I would! The scene is meant to feature you in your birthday suit, so I'd definitely be getting the better view.'

For goodness' sake. Was she ever going to let him win?

Well…if he was honest, he kind of liked the challenge.

18

An A4 sheet of paper slid across his desk at 8:55am.

Colin inspected it closely. 'You typed this up pretty fast.'

'Bullet points,' Angela told him as she retreated, hands flat against her thighs. 'Size sixteen. Arial. I didn't have time to put the new segment into prose, not that I'll bother doing that anymore. Because you'll probably go off-script anyway—I managed to make myself listen to the archived serial last night, Colin, don't look so surprised—and I figured this would make it easier for you to keep *mostly* on track.'

Colin pulled a face.

But that was a pretty good idea and he might have to steal it. Because he did forget things. Like giving a shout-out to a sponsor who preferred to be mentioned organically in segments, as opposed to having blaring, intrusive ads played on their behalf.

He was willing to bet that if Angela ever decided to become a radio DJ (and he suspected Leo would definitely give her a shot), she'd nail it with ruthless efficiency. Colin could already hear her upbraiding her listeners, but of course they'd keep coming back for more. Just like he did.

She was almost out of the room, incidentally, her fingers glancing across the faces of Talk Talk as she passed the door.

'Do you want to stay?' Colin asked.

Angela looked over her shoulder at him. 'I never picked you for someone who liked being watched while they work. Where did that come from?'

Colin shrugged. 'No idea. Probably the same place my next question will come from.'

'Oh?'

His confidence abruptly deserted him.

'Stay for my segment and I just might ask it,' Colin said into his keyboard instead of doing something stupid, like actually asking her out. A near miss, that.

'Am I going to need to call your mate and get some Moscato?' Angela teased. 'So we can loosen you up a bit?'

'I can't get drunk on-air!'

'It's only five percent.'

'Look who's talking,' Colin fired back. 'If you're staying, please shut the door, sit down, and keep quiet. You can put your hand up if you want to say something, though. I'll point at you if I think it's a good idea for you to jump in. If I wind my hand in circles, that means you need to wrap it up and get to the point. Got it?'

Angela wet her lips. 'You want…me to *say* something?'

'Up to you, really. Plenty of people without experience get behind a mic to spruik their wares or give distasteful opinions. But I don't want to make you uncomfortable.' He hesitated. 'Hearing the segment on the app yesterday was probably bad enough for you, so I understand if you can't stay in here for it.'

She surprised him by shutting the door and taking his other chair, an orphan from a second-hand dining set that had barely survived

Rob's ownership. Trying not to grin too widely, Colin lobbed a spare pair of headphones across the table at her.

Angela dutifully slid them on. But she held a thumb over the tiny bead-like microphone that was attached to the AUX cable. Colin didn't trust Bluetooth.

'Thank you, Sunshine,' Colin began, finishing the handover between their shows. 'It might be a beautiful day up in Whitby, but down here near Dover we've got the typical sort of weather we're always complaining about to our neighbours. It's a tad dreary, is what I'm saying. The perfect day to be social distancing, working from home, and/or self-isolating. If you're bored of your four walls, maybe you should get a load of the Twitter account belonging to that famous actor who has a pig for a pet. You know the one I mean. Man, I'm getting really attached to that pig.'

Angela lifted her hand and started twirling it.

Colin stared at her, momentarily taken aback. Dead air filled the room and hovered, until he was sure he could hear Leo listing all the things he'd done wrong inside the first two minutes of his show.

'I can take a hint, folks, you want me get on with it this morning,' Colin rushed out, then forced himself to slow down. 'Whatever happened to delayed gratification, I ask you?'

ok Boomer #splatzapp said about a hundred different Twitter profiles.

'I'm not a Boomer, by the way,' Colin told his listeners, frowning. 'I'm Gen Y. And if you've never heard that label before, then you're too young for my target audience anyway. I was born in the 1980s.'

Yeah and you never left that decade #splatzapp someone observed and was retweeted fifty times in as many seconds. Colin felt a little indignant. But hopefully soon his listeners would stop ragging on his song choices. He had a whole list of Angela's suggested covers to play today and that *should* appease a good portion of them—and most importantly, Leo.

'I have absolutely no time to get into a generational argument right now,' Colin said, managing to force himself back on track after a quick glance at the piece of paper in front him. 'And I, DJ Coop, intend to deliver as promised: an update on the roommate situation. But it's kind of embarrassing. I'd rather you didn't hear this, no matter what my boss says about me needing to give you what you want. Because it concerns me, my junk, and my shapely backside.'

WHATTTTT was the resounding response on social media.

It suddenly occurred to Colin that Angela was missing half of the conversation. He swung his secondary monitor around so that she could see the Tweets appearing under the hashtag. A grin crept across her face. He could tell that she was already as addicted as he was to the instantaneous feedback.

She whipped out her phone and began flicking through the hundreds of new Tweets herself. Colin moved the monitor back into its previous position.

God help him if she posted something.

He held the piece of paper out further from his eyes in an attempt to stop the words blurring together. So maybe he avoided reading things up close because he was slightly long-sighted, but there was no way he was going to admit defeat and head down to an optometrist. And besides, he wasn't game enough to get checked out during a pandemic.

He didn't want to risk both his life *and* his pride.

'So who else is stuck in a flat right now?' Colin asked. His listeners immediately started posting about their woes; most of them were his age and a large chunk of them couldn't afford anything bigger. 'There's some communal grass outside, sure, but I'd have to use a stairwell that has bits and pieces of everyone else lingering in the air. And who wants to do that when all the disposable masks are sold out and that fancy cloth one is lost somewhere in transit? Sea post is making a comeback, folks, and it's not pretty.'

Angela twirled her hand at him again.

Colin restrained the sigh; he *was* taking too long. 'Anyway, my flat has its eccentricities. The saloon doors in the kitchen. The pee-coloured stain shaped like a heart underneath my bed. But how did I not notice that the bathroom door didn't have a lock? I'm not used to sharing my space, I guess. Can't believe I forgot that anyone could just walk in.'

The feed lit up with excitement.

'Yeah, you can see where this is going,' Colin said, grinning across at Angela.

'Pee-coloured stain?' she mouthed at him.

He nodded emphatically. He'd show her later.

'So there I am, about to take a shower.' Colin swallowed quickly, keeping his voice oiled up and smooth. 'Maybe if I'd been just a bit quicker with the taps, Number Twelve would have heard the water running and kept well away. But I wasn't expecting her to be up. Only we morning radio DJs roll out of bed at a ridiculous hour, right? Nope! The bladder wants what the bladder wants, no matter who you are.'

Angela clapped both hands over her mouth, shaking with suppressed laughter.

Colin tried not to look too closely at her, in case he caught a case of the giggles himself. 'Anyway, I've just dropped my boxer shorts and I'm about to get in when I feel a draught. Now, the window in there is tiny and hardly going to let in *that* much wind. So I look around and there's Number Twelve. Just standing there. Wanting to use the lavatory. Oh and she's also holding her toothbrush, since she doesn't deign to leave it next to mine.'

That much was true to life. Angela always kept her toothbrush in her own room. Did his bathroom really look that unsafe? When was the last time he'd cleaned the basin anyway?

Another hand wave from her side of the desk. *Get on with it, Colin.*

Ignoring both his monitors, Colin flicked his eyes over the bullet points in front of him. 'I'm in my birthday suit. She's in her cute *Blues Brothers* nightie. I'm kind of staring, because she's obviously got good taste in movies and I didn't expect that—and she's full-on staring because, oh yeah, I'm completely starkers.'

Angela was staring at him now, actually. Was it because of the unscripted bit about the nightie?

Well, it *was* cute. And it did show taste.

'So I tell her I'm sorry, we ought to sync our schedules better in future,' Colin continued, slowly building up to the climax. 'She agrees, says alright, but if I accidentally return the favour and get an eyeful myself, she won't be too mad. It'd only be fair. I quickly promise her this will never happen. To which she says, in her best Wolverine voice, "Afraid you might like it?" My God, I could not stop laughing. And then—only then—did I remember to grab a towel and cover myself.'

Angela had managed to put together an utterly hysterical scene for him. And it seemed his listeners agreed. The gifs of fictional characters laughing came thick and fast. But he was more interested in smiling at Angela, whose eyes were shining. He couldn't look away.

He wanted to ask her the question he was sure he shouldn't ask.

Angela, will you go out with me? Or go 'in', since there's not many places we can go...

Angela, I really like you and I know you just got out of a relationship, but I was wondering…

Would you…will you…can we…

It was on the tip of his tongue, poised and ready to go.

But then her phone lit up. Her gaze fell to the screen—and her expression fell much further than that when she read whatever was on it.

'Yep, that was my mortifying experience of the day, week, month, maybe even my year,' Colin said quickly. 'And the less said about it the better. Now here's a rock version of "Blue Monday". Okay, it's a cover of a 1980s song, but listen to that instrumental!'

He slapped the 'play' and 'mute' buttons simultaneously. 'What's wrong?'

Angela looked equal parts miserable and furious. 'I can't believe he did this. It's bad enough that he was shagging that woman, but now she's given him…oh God.'

'Angela. Take a breath. Tell me what's happened.'

'I've been exposed to the virus,' Angela said grimly. She stood, leaving her headphones on the desk. 'I'll get out of your hair. A contact tracer is probably going to ring me soon. They'll need to ask me who I've been in contact with, so they know who needs to go into self-isolation.'

The door snapped shut behind her.

Silence crowded in, relentless and heavy.

Suddenly his burning need to ask her out didn't seem quite so important.

19

***

Day One

Angela stared out the window at the recently-shorn grass in front of Grace Park. The gardener must have been by with his lawnmower, though she couldn't remember hearing him at it. Odds were she'd consigned it to background noise. The grass itself didn't get any attention from her most days; it was easy to forget what was bordering the footpath when you had somewhere to be, some place to escape to.

Angela had only stood on the grass a few times, mostly to avoid whoever was coming the other way. Notably, the last person she'd had to circle around had been Colin. But she didn't have to do that with him anymore—and now she wasn't even allowed on the grass. Not for fourteen whole days, according to the contact tracer who had rung her a few minutes ago.

Fourteen days of mandatory self-isolation, for the safety of the community. Fourteen days of wondering if the police would come knocking on her door to make sure she was home. Fourteen days of waiting for the symptoms to show.

She'd taken so much for granted. She'd taken *grass* for granted.

Speaking of which, there was someone she shouldn't be taking for granted just now. Friendship being a two-way street and all that.

'Hey,' Angela said, her phone pressed to her ear. 'Are you okay?'

Ishani's response was dry, with a side order of done-with-this-shit. 'I think you and me are gonna have to agree on a definition of "okay" before I answer that.'

Angela covered her face with her hand. 'I'm sorry. I'm so sorry. If I'd just gone home instead of waiting for Ben, he wouldn't have brought his plague-ridden body down to the café and landed us both on the contact tracers' hit list. He must have had a positive test if they made him tell them everywhere he's been lately. And your text earlier said you did a test as well? Why? You'd only need to do that if you actually had symp…oh God. But you were wearing a mask! Are you *okay*?'

'Slow down, Angela,' Ishani ordered. 'What did I just say?'

'Arrghh! Fine. I'll be more specific. Do you have a sore throat or something?'

'No, not that. I've got a fever and an occasional, reluctant cough.'

'*Noooo*,' Angela said, the phone slipping inside her sweaty grip. 'I'm going to kill him. I really am. Oh no. I shouldn't say that. He might actually die. *You* might die!'

'I'd rather not talk about that, if it's all the same to you,' Ishani said, just as one of her reluctant coughs made an appearance. 'Masks work better if you're both wearing them. You know that. And it might not be his fault. My symptoms did come on pretty fast for it to be him. Yuck. I haven't felt this bad since I caught con crud off a hot Cyberwoman when I went to see John Barrowman in London last year. I always tell myself I'll take some hand sanitiser to the next convention. I always forget. More fool me. Can't even buy tiny travel-sized bottles of the stuff right now because everyone's busy hoarding it. But hey, my test might come back negative, right?'

'Ben's didn't,' Angela muttered.

'Aren't you exhausted from being this down all the time?'

'Better that than getting my hopes up.'

Ishani's ensuing sigh was sharp and truncated. 'Angela. I'm not going to bail on you. I promise. I get the feeling a lot of people have disappointed you before. But maybe wait until I disappoint you before deciding that the world is over, okay? If the world isn't actually over because of this pandemic, that is. *Okay*, Angela?'

'Okay,' Angela echoed quietly.

Ishani wasn't going to let her off the hook just yet. 'I know you'd rather be alone than risk getting hurt, but I'm not going to let you wallow. It isn't healthy.'

'I'm…I'm glad I met you,' was all Angela managed to say, her eyes burning.

She took a few moments to watch a couple walk down the concrete path towards the road, one of them entombed by a baby carrier with more straps than Doc Ock had arms. She couldn't actually see the baby loaded inside, just a dark hood that was pulled down so low over its head she wasn't sure if it was in fact a tiny human.

The unshed tears threatened to spill over.

They were probably out for some fresh air. But was it even safe for them to *be* out? Had Angela touched the railing beside the stairs or the front door without washing her hands first? Had they forgotten to sanitise their own hands after touching those things themselves? Was the highly contagious virus now walking among them, like a fourth family member?

At least they could leave Grace Park. No contact tracer had rung them (unless they had been rung but were flouting the laws, as some were). It was a calculated risk, taking a baby anywhere near other people.

But you couldn't stay locked up forever, even if you were a dedicated introvert.

'I'm jealous of a baby,' Angela muttered.

'Well, that's an interesting non sequitur I don't particularly want to chase right now,' Ishani said, but at least she sounded amused.

Angela shook her head, annoyed at herself for being distracted when she needed to be there for her friend. 'Sorry. Just saw a baby going outside. God knows how long I'll be stuck in here with Colin Cooper, Distractingly Hot Roommate. I might do something stupid. Just like Em did with *her* roommate…oh.' Yay, she totally needed that reminder. She missed hearing Emily's voice. 'Wait, you've met John Barrowman? That's really cool.'

'Yeah. For about five seconds. He signed a photo for me, then signed thousands of others for everyone else waiting in the queue. He was pretty nice, though, considering how short our acquaintance was. You should come with me to the next convention.' Ishani paused, which made Angela worry that she'd regretted making the offer. 'You could dress up, go wild, buy a graphic novel or a Pop! Vinyl or something. They'll even have a TARDIS for you to pose with.'

Angela began to grin at the images Ishani's words were inspiring, but then her heart abruptly sank. 'If conventions are ever a thing again.'

'Oh, they will be,' Ishani said darkly. 'Probably a lot sooner than they ought to be, mind. And don't you dare say "if we live to see it", because we bloody well will, Angela. I can *sense* your anxiety from here. Hang on a minute.'

A coughing spiel followed.

Forget seconds. It felt like an actual age had passed before Ishani's coughs faded into ragged breathing.

'Can I...' Angela's voice faltered.

'Get me anything?' Ishani finished with a brittle laugh. 'Well, I'm out of Penguins and gin, but I can't really ask you to pop down to the shops. My brother can't head out either because he's stuck in quarantine with me.'

Angela tapped her fingers against the windowsill. The young family had vanished down the road. 'How desperate is your Penguin and gin situation?'

'I'll live. Can't say the same for my brother, since how dare there be tea and no biscuits to go on the side. Worst sister ever! But it'd nice to have some groceries. Sainsbury's is slammed for delivery slots until next week. Can't imagine why. You'd think everyone was stuck inside or something.'

Angela fought the smile. It didn't feel right. Not now.

'You can laugh, you know,' Ishani told her. 'I'd much rather you did.'

'Um. Haha. Ha.'

A snort from Ishani's side. 'I'll take it. Anyway, at the risk of sounding Millennial as fuck, the problem with owning a house is that your neighbours want to talk to you all the time. I'm definitely not into that, so I fobbed them all off. Maybe that was a mistake, since none of my neighbours would go to the shops for me if I asked. I should befriend them in case another pandemic hits, hey? And I could finally figure out why they keep giving me stink eye—is it the height of my hydrangeas or is it the topless sunbathing in the back garden?'

This time Angela did laugh.

It made her feel marginally better. Maybe things weren't so bad.

Maybe she hadn't caught the virus off Ben—she hadn't stood as close to him as Ishani had, after all. And maybe Ishani's test result would be negative. The common nasties were still floating around, after all.

'I'll see what I can do about your grocery problem,' Angela said. 'What's your address?'

***

'I'm going to need a favour,' Angela said.

Colin remained in that same hunched-over position on the sofa, where he had been ever since she'd made him sit down so she could explain the situation. His face was uncharacteristically pale.

Guilt crept in. She'd dropped that quarantine bomb on him mid-show. She might listen to the archives later to make sure the rest of it had gone okay. Ever since she'd Googled the names of Colin's colleagues and found the Radio SPLATZAPP! streaming app, those long quiet evenings after Colin had vanished into his room didn't feel so lonesome. The voices in her earphones did a good job of crowding out the pessimistic voices in her head.

Chances were that Leo had already delivered a stern lecture about what the show had been missing and Colin didn't need a reminder. His boss could probably even make a busload of enlisted men soil themselves.

Leo might have been charming to her, but Angela had seen sharks with less teeth.

'What kind of favour?' Colin asked finally.

'My friend, Ishani, needs a grocery drop. Penguins and gin are a top priority. And I was wondering if your mate...'

'Done,' Colin said. 'Anything else?'

Angela shook her head slowly, but her mouth didn't get the memo. 'Colin, I'm *terrified*. It was so much easier to believe this whole thing would blow over when I wasn't exposed. When no one I knew was in danger. It's not some news story on the telly anymore. It's too real. Make it stop! Er, not that I think you could actually stop it...'

His lips warred together for several moments before he spoke again. 'I don't want to sound presumptuous here, but do you need a hug?'

A watery laugh escaped Angela. 'Yes. Please. I never thought I would have to give up hugs, except those aren't safe anymore. And grass! I can't even touch *grass* with my hands for fourteen days. Not that I ever did it that much.'

Colin waved her over. 'Come on, then. We can infect each other.'

He gathered her into his arms as soon as her backside hit the sofa and Angela felt herself go boneless, the tension draining right out of her.

Thank God she didn't have to quarantine on her own.

Thank God he'd asked her to move in.

Colin's presence made everything seem that little bit more bearable, which was strange because she'd spent two years glaring at him when they could have been conducting adult conversations. Maybe they could have even been...who knows...*flirting*.

He abruptly stiffened and pulled away.

Too soon. Much too soon. But Angela supposed it would have to do. They were roommates, possibly even be friends (she hoped), but they weren't something else.

'Colin?' she asked, concerned. Maybe he had a reason for pulling away.

His distant gaze snapped back to her. 'Sorry. Just concocting a plan. I'll give Rob a call. Hang tight.'

'Hanging,' Angela promised with a small smile that quickly segued into a frown. 'I've also got a plan and I'm not sure I should concoct or enact it.'

'Do tell.'

'My friend, Em.' Angela ducked her head, feeling rather stupid. 'I know everyone on Reddit says to ditch toxic relationships, but I miss her. Maybe I shouldn't flush two decades of friendship down the toilet just yet. I never told her I had a problem with her only ringing me to complain about her life, or that it was frustrating that she was never interested in hearing about my own problems. But I can't call her. I'll end up apologising for everything and hating myself.'

Colin indicated the phone in her hand. 'You could just shoot her a text.'

'She might have blocked me,' Angela protested.

'Do it anyway—you should at least try,' Colin told her. 'Knowing you did all you could might stop you pouting and torturing yourself when you could be doing something productive. I'm the one who has to live with you, by the way. I'd rather we didn't go through the pouting and torturing. It wouldn't be fun for either of us.'

Angela slapped his shoulder. 'Colin!'

'Well?' he said, grinning.

'Fine, fine.' Angela dramatically waggled her thumbs above her phone, pretending to type. 'Hey, Em. I'm not sorry about what I said, but now I have The Killer Virus and my dying wish is to make amends.'

'Give me that!' Colin snatched her phone.

Angela made a half-hearted attempt to grab it back from him.

Colin was already swiping his fingers over the screen. 'Let's see...something short and simple, something that doesn't demand a response from her, something that makes her *want* to get back in contact. You need to bait her.'

'Colin!' Angela cried. 'This isn't the time for DJ Coop! She's not a listener. She's my friend. Or was. Or could be. I don't know.'

He pursed his lips. 'Okay, how about…*Hey Em. I've had to go into quarantine. Just thought you'd like to know.* There. Easy. Do you want to add anything about breaking up with the boyfriend? Him cheating and giving you a potentially fatal virus is definitely grounds for some sympathy.'

'No! That will definitely make me sound desperate. And I don't want to burden her with *all* of my problems.'

'Nope, that's what you've got me for,' he said cheerfully.

Angela nudged him with her elbow and felt a girlish smile bloom across her face, as if she was sitting next to her teenage crush. Okay, she was sitting next to Colin Cooper. And maybe she did have a crush on him.

Oh. She really did, didn't she?

'I suppose I do,' Angela said with a laugh, one that was more aimed at herself. 'Have you, I mean. Fourteen days stuck in here together. What on Earth are we going to do with ourselves?'

'Well, first I'm going to send this text.' Colin targeted and hit the send button. 'And then I'm going to call Rob. After that? Maybe I'll find something that can entertain us for a while. We have two weeks to kill, possibly more if we start to show signs of The Plague. You into board games?'

Angela shuddered.

'That's a no then. Leave it with me—I'll think of something that's not complete rubbish!' He flipped her that irritating, irresistible smirk. 'It'll be alright. You'll see.'

Damn it. Why was it so easy to believe every word that came out of his mouth?

20

Day Two

Angela decided the very next day that she really shouldn't have been so trusting.

The smoke alarm was wailing unhappily and Colin was jumping around underneath it, waving a tea towel in an attempt to clear the haze settling against the ceiling. He didn't own a ladder, so they couldn't reach up and turn the damn thing off.

All this for chocolate and marshmallows, melted into an indistinct and scorched lump on a tray in the oven—the decadent, sugary lunch had apparently been part of 'The Plan' Colin had concocted yesterday. She'd definitely heard capitals when he'd given it that name. Well, she had to give Colin this. So far The Plan hadn't been boring.

'It'll be fine! It'll be fine!' Colin shouted, much like a broken record. Or a CD that kept skipping. Or a digital file that hadn't been copied across correctly. Angela was tempted to come up with an updated simile involving streaming services just so she could use it on him.

Someone knocked at the door. 'Colin! Are you alright? Loraine and I heard you screaming.'

Angela dropped her head into her hands and tried not to laugh.

Colin hurled the tea towel aimlessly over his shoulder and raced towards the front door, checking that it was still locked. 'Sorry! We'll get the smoke to clear soon. I can't let you in and you should wash the hand you used to knock *immediately*. Just in case. We're in quarantine. I honestly can't remember the last time I touched that side of the door.'

'Right,' Bernard's voice said. 'Is this place going to burn down in the next fortnight? We'd like some advance warning, Colin. It's going to take time to arrange a move in these current conditions. I'm sure you understand.'

'It is *not* going to burn down,' Colin insisted.

'But Colin might burn up all of our groceries,' Angela added.

A pause, then—'Do you need me to get you some bits and bobs from the Sainsbury's? I'm taking Loraine out later with her walker.'

Colin's face paled. 'Bernard...'

'It won't be much, mind,' Bernard went on, either not hearing Colin or ignoring him completely. 'We're not as spry as we used to be, but I'll get you the staples. Bread and milk. Maybe some meat and veg. We should be able to carry that back. Hang the bags on the walker's handles. Yes, that ought to work.'

'Bernard...' Colin tried again.

'Colin. We are neighbours. We're supposed to help each other out. And if not during a bloody pandemic, then when?'

'But...'

'Go on, let him,' Angela interrupted. 'He's got to get his jollies somehow.'

'Loraine and I are perfectly capable of getting our jollies while staying in,' Bernard said. She could have sworn she'd heard a wink accompany those words. 'Let us help you, dear boy. You've done a lot for us. And you've kept me sane with your visits. Lord knows I wasn't created to have only Loraine for company, much as I love her. Telephoning the grandkids doesn't really help things. It's not the same.'

'But I don't deserve this,' Colin said quietly.

'What did he say?' Bernard asked.

'He said yes!' Angela called. 'He definitely agreed. He's even nodding.'

Colin's scowl deepened. But he didn't correct her.

'Of course he is,' was the droll response from the other side of the door. 'Make yourselves comfortable. I'll be heading out in an hour or two, so it may be some time before you have groceries that aren't burnt to a crisp.'

His footsteps padded away down the corridor.

The smoke alarm had switched off at some point, Angela realised.

Colin turned away, stubbornly evading her questioning look. 'You shouldn't have accepted his help.'

'Why not? You've done the same for him in the past.'

'That's not...it's not the same,' Colin muttered and stormed into his bedroom, slamming the door behind him.

Angela could only stand there, utterly confused.

And a little pissed off.

***

Day Two of The Plan had so far not gone to plan at all.

Colin stewed in his chair, folded into a position that was probably going to give him shooting pains in his back later, and listened to Graveyard Danika make wry commentary about teenagers using 'Danse macabre' as the soundtrack to their pandemic-related TikToks. She was impressed with their musical education and pleased to see them dealing with death in manageable ways, but she was wondering if they shouldn't be funnelling their creative energies into a longer-lasting medium.

The world was just one more disaster away from losing the bulk of its history, Danika decided. Especially if the next global shakeup wasn't a pandemic but an EMP. Humans needed to return to using pen and paper, perhaps even chisel events of import into stone. How else were visitors from Alpha Centauri supposed to know how Earth had met its end?

This gave Colin a few moments of existential panic when he realised that his radio files could vanish in the blink of an eye. Maybe the Internet wasn't so forever after all.

Danika finished her segment. Then the ad break hit.

Colin immediately created a Zoom meeting and held his breath. Everyone joined in, much to his (and his lungs') relief. They probably didn't have anything else to do with their time—with the exception of Sunshine, who had to look after her young charges all day. Something audibly smashed the moment her face appeared on his screen.

'Don't make me come out there and get the wooden spoon!' Sunshine barked over her shoulder towards the door.

Everyone looked as stunned as Colin felt. Sunshine never raised her voice.

'Homeschooling in lockdown: week four,' she said grimly, by way of explanation. 'If my eldest daughter wasn't a nurse and their father wasn't a doctor...well, it is what it is. We must all do our bit for society right now. Even if it means living with those terrors full-time. This is a lot safer for them than staying with their parents.'

Mute nods of understanding all round. Colin fought the grimace.

His 'bit for society' involved staying home for fourteen days, which paled in comparison to what other people were doing. He didn't have a mask to wear, but he also hadn't gone out of his way to make one like Angela had. A part of him had lived in happy denial. Newfield had felt safe, insulated against a virus that only affected other towns.

'Col, do I have time for your Freak-Out of the Day?' Danika asked.

'It's not a freak-out,' Colin insisted. 'I just need some help with a romantic complication. That's all.'

'Oh no,' Danger Jones said, horror causing his Ray Bans to slide down his nose. 'You banged the roommate! Should have made sure she wasn't going to get all clingy before you did that, Coop. Boundaries, you've gotta set them *beforehand*. Trust me on this one.'

'I haven't banged anyone!' Colin said.

'Why not then?' Danger demanded, changing his tune. 'What are you waiting for?'

Peter pressed his hands together, looking thoughtful. Either that or he was making prayers on Colin's behalf to some deity of love. 'It's possible that Colin wishes to hear serious advice on how to woo his roommate. It was inevitable, really.'

'I have a plan,' Colin said confidently.

Danger burst out laughing.

'You can't plan these sorts of things, dear,' Sunshine told Colin, smiling gently and making him feel about six years old. 'Just let it happen naturally.'

Danika crossed her arms and leaned back in her brand-new chair, which for whatever reason was shaped like the grim reaper. For a moment, all Colin could see was the hooded skull affixed to the top of the chair, leering at him as if it knew he was doomed to fail.

After a few tense moments had passed, Danika gave a short, sharp nod. 'Let's hear what he's got to say. I'm curious. He's not one for planning, our Colin. The most stubborn, ad-libbing DJ in Leo's "stable" is finally growing up. Or at least, we all hope that's what's happening here. His plan could be entirely workable or utter rubbish.'

She glanced at the monitor on her desk, her dark lips curling in satisfaction. 'Go on, Col. Tell us everything. I've got seventeen minutes since I just put on the album version of "In-A-Gadda-Da-Vida". It's only the second time this week—I'm sure my listeners can't get enough of it. And I'll be able to schedule in another set of ads directly afterwards.'

'Leo lets you get away with murder,' Danger accused.

'He might but the cops won't, so you'll live to see another day,' Danika said flatly.

'Love should be ad-libbed, not planned,' Peter murmured, seemingly to himself. 'Or where is the surprise? The spontaneity? The spice of life? What is the point of life without that spice?' He began to spiral into more rhetorical questions, expression grave and fingers curled up underneath his chin like he was The Thinker, or some forgotten philosopher.

'You can write your next "Love and Mid-Life Crises" segment on your own time, Peter,' Sunshine interrupted. 'I want to hear what Colin has to say.'

Now they were all waiting on him. Colin had no choice but to feed the beast.

'So Angela and I have to be quarantined for fourteen days, thanks to her infectious ex-boyfriend,' he told his eager audience. 'We could actually have this crappy virus. The whole immediacy of it all, life and death and ventilators, has me questioning why I'm dancing around the issue. What's stopping me? Aside from the recent breakup she just went through.'

'High-risk situations tend to hasten connections, as do close quarters,' The Love Doctor noted. 'But be careful, Colin. These sorts of relationships are fast-burning and potentially explosive.'

'The good ones always are,' Sunshine sighed dreamily. 'Best time of my life.'

Danika's kohl-lined eyes lit up with fascination. 'Okay, now that's a story I definitely want to hear at some point. I had no idea your past was so interesting, Sunshine.'

'You might need a few pots of tea for the whole story,' Sunshine told her.

'*Anyway*,' Colin interrupted and his hodgepodge family fell silent. 'I came up with a fourteen-day plan to court Angela. Technically Day One was planning the plan, but I digress. Day Two was supposed to involve chocolate and marshmallows for lunch, except that one fell apart in about five minutes. Smoke alarms are not my friend. Moving on. So, by the fourteenth day of us doing activities together and growing ever closer, I'll be ready to ask her out. And then we'll be able to actually go out the next day.'

Sunshine sighed again, her eyes glazing over. 'That's beautiful, Colin. Poetic even.'

'And completely unnecessary,' Danger added.

'Colin can use this time to forge a meaningful connection instead of just a physical one,' Peter said with a disdainful flicker of his eyes at the camera. He resumed stroking the seemingly frozen cat stretched out behind him. 'There is no need to look down on something simply because you do not understand it.'

Danger adjusted his Ray Bans and huffed. 'Yes, I know, *Love Doctor*. Even I like to forge meaningful connections sometimes.'

'Is this a sign of the apocalypse?' Danika wondered.

Danger pulled a face. 'No need to sound so surprised. What I'm saying is, why doesn't he ask her out now? Just cut to the chase, man. But you don't get to whinge about it after she rejects you, okay? There's only room for one Nice Guy™ in this group and it's me.'

'Just acknowledging that makes you even worse,' Danika told him.

'It's progress, isn't it?' Sunshine asked wearily.

Colin shifted in his chair. Something clunked beneath him and he dropped about an inch. Not a good sign. If it broke completely, he'd have to order another one to be delivered, not that it would actually make it up the stairs. Most couriers were allergic to going past letterboxes, even when people needed door-to-door deliveries. And this was one item that Bernard couldn't risk his back on.

'I need time to build up my confidence,' Colin said.

'You don't need confidence to ask someone out,' Danger muttered. 'I should know.'

Colin cleared his throat. 'I'm going to tell her everything, including why I invited her to stay with me. I'll do that on Day Fourteen. And then I'll ask her out. She needs to know all the facts before she can make an informed decision.'

'So you're going to butter her up, then *butter her up*,' Danger said, nodding.

'No, Danger, do not encourage him,' Peter said severely. 'I will admit that I was supportive of Colin's deception to start with, but my conscience will no longer allow me to support such trickery.'

Sunshine looked torn. 'Colin, luv…'

'This is way above our pay grade,' Danika said. 'But personally? I think you're in for a world of well-deserved hurt.'

Colin looked away from his phone, his stomach twisting into knots. 'What choice do I have? I made this mistake right at the start and I can't go back now. Let me try to fix this. Please.'

'It's not us you need to convince,' Danika pointed out.

Fudge and bother. She was right.

No one said anything for a while, allowing Doug Ingle to fill the silence with the epic organ solo that Iron Butterfly's 'In-A-Gadda-Da-Vida' was famous for. But the solo, instead of making him drum his fingers on his desk like it always did, just made Colin feel like he was attending a funeral. Possibly even his own.

And with that morbid thought, he said goodbye to the other DJs and stewed some more, not quite ready to face Angela again.

But he had a plan. It had to work.

It had to.

21

'What's up with you?' Angela asked when Colin finally emerged two hours later.

He went stock-still, his eyes wide, like a proverbial deer caught in the headlights. 'I have no idea what you mean.'

Angela was briefly tempted to throw her notebook at his head, but managed to stop herself—mostly because it contained scraps of scenes from a romance novel that might actually make her money someday (ha). Denting Colin wasn't worth the risk of him holding her words hostage.

She sighed and reached for her mug of chai tea.

Yes, a much safer object to fill her hands with.

'Colin.' She pushed the mug across the coffee table, putting it out of harm's way. 'You're acting a lot stranger than usual, and that's saying something. You promised—well, not so much promised as heavily implied—that you had a plan for killing time while we're in self-isolation. Right now I'm working on my first ever novel. It's very exciting and new for me, but I'll go mad if I've got nothing else to do. So if The Plan is actually a thing and you're not just pulling my leg, *please* tell me.'

'I'll need to eat something first,' Colin muttered.

'Not a problem. I made you a ham-and-cheese sandwich. It's on the counter.'

Colin's bemused stare moved between her and the kitchen's saloon doors. 'But we don't have any ham or cheese. Or bread.'

'Bernard came by again.' Angela crossed her arms, mentally daring Colin to find some way of disagreeing with the existence of the sandwich. 'He seemed very pleased with himself, though I can't be sure if that's because he was successful in his mission in obtaining groceries or because he had an excuse to leave Loraine downstairs for a bit. Apparently he complained about the lack of Bible verses that are relevant to daily life, she tried to educate him, and then he retaliated by quoting several passages from "The Song of Songs" back at her. That conversation didn't end well.'

Concern creased Colin's expression.

'No, no,' Angela quickly assured him. 'I didn't open the door until after Bernard left. I guess he thought that sandwiches were a safe, fireproof lunch. Any other excuses or misdirects you want to try?'

Game. Set. *Match.*

Colin rubbed a hand over his jaw. 'Fine. I will eat the sandwich. And I will not burn the place down in the process. Thank you, by the way.'

Angela felt her cheeks grow warm and jerked her eyes back down to her notebook, annoyed with herself. All he'd done was thank her for a sandwich, not proposition her for sex on the sofa. Oh God. She was in the midst of writing a sex scene and...definitely not picturing Colin in a tartan kilt.

Colin returned from the kitchen and perched on the edge of the sofa, as far away from her as he could get without sitting on the arm—and seemingly entranced by the sandwich on the plate balanced across his knees.

Nope, definitely no sex on the cards today. Wait, why was she even thinking about this? He was her roommate. Her very distracting roommate. And Angela was now *'single single single get it girl'*, according to Ishani. But her breakup was still new, though somehow not as raw as it should have been. Ben had been convenient, not the love of her life.

Right. Yes. She needed to think of reasons *not* to hook up with Colin Cooper.

Number one. If things went sour, she'd have to move back in with her mother. Not ideal.

Number two. She was going to be stuck inside with Colin for an entire fortnight. There would be no escaping him or the remnants of an imploded relationship before the end of their law-enforced quarantine. Definitely not ideal either.

And lastly, she'd never know if they'd only got together because they had no one else to ogle.

That was the least desirable outcome, actually.

'Don't make this awkward, don't make this awkward,' she muttered.

'What was that?'

'Oh, nothing,' Angela rushed out. 'Nothing at all.'

'Well, if you did say something, I'd say it was too late for that,' Colin said, then took a giant bite of his sandwich, deftly removing himself from the conversation. Again.

'Arrghhh.' Angela threw her hands up. 'Why are you so...*you?*'

Colin grinned at her. Another large corner of the sandwich disappeared into his mouth.

He was enjoying her frustration, damn him.

Angela shook her head, exasperated. 'Tall, dark, and mysterious might work in novels, but personally? I'm sick of secrets and hidden motives. It's not an admirable quality, certainly enough to make the entire package less attractive. Um. Shit. I mean...'

'So the entire package is attractive, huh?' He preened.

'Colin! What I'm trying to say is, I need you to be more forthcoming if you want me to trust you. If you want me to go along with whatever devious plan you've got up your sleeve.'

His expression grew solemn. 'I understand. Right. Forthcoming. I can do that.'

Angela gave him her best sceptical look, bunched eyebrows and all. Forthcoming wasn't exactly one of his traits.

There was so much uncertainty and confusion surrounding him and his odd habits, though she wondered if this was by design rather than by accident. It definitely ensured that someone lay awake late at night, mulling over every single thing he'd ever said to them—and maybe this also led to someone wishing they really had walked in on him mid-shower. He was ridiculously good-looking, even in those loose band shirts, but she just wasn't comfortable enough to take the plunge and ask him something really stupid. Like if he wanted to go on a date. There was still so much she didn't know about him.

Throwing questions at the men in her life hadn't really worked out for her, anyway.

'Good,' she finally said. 'You being forthcoming, that is. It would make a nice change.'

Colin nodded vaguely. 'Well, I'd better get on with it then. Yes. I should.'

Angela waited, tapping out a tattoo on the arm of the sofa. He scraped the underside of his plate along the coffee table and brushed the crumbs off his jeans.

'I feel like a teenager again,' Colin grumbled.

'Why? Because you're trying to ask me out?'

There was no other rational explanation for how nervous he seemed. But she really wished she'd been able to keep those words locked up inside her instead of blurting them out like a teenager herself. Had she lost all common sense since moving in with Colin? Or had it all started before then, when she'd been unable to resist locking horns with him every time they'd run into each other?

'No!' Colin exclaimed. 'That's not…no!'

'Oh,' was all Angela managed to say.

Colin combed his fingers over his scalp, looking far more distressed than she currently felt. 'I mean, yes. Yes, I do want to ask you out.'

Angela closed her eyes in relief. 'Thank God. For a second there, I thought I was going to be stuck in here with you for twelve and a half more days after making the enormous error of thinking you fancied me. Talk about embarrassing. No, wait. This is *still* embarrassing. I should probably give you an answer of some sort.'

'No, no,' Colin said, rearranging his hair with his hands again. 'That's alright. I won't be officially asking you out until we're allowed to leave. The Plan is supposed to involve two weeks of wooing. Courting instead of actually dating.'

'Did you trip and fall through a henge into the Medieval Period?' Angela asked with a grin, trying not to listen to the enthusiastic thumping of her heart. How wonderfully old-fashioned.

Colin blinked. 'No?'

Oh well, he had his flaws, not knowing about *Outlander* being one them. Then there was the mysterious wardrobe that may or may not lead to Narnia.

And how could she forget the Santa suit thing?

'Anyway,' Colin said, sitting up straight and suddenly looking a good deal more animated. 'I figured that if we start going out now, then we might never know if it happened because we had nothing better to do.'

Angela nodded emphatically.

But he wasn't done. 'And I'd rather be careful. I don't want this to blow up in my face. My past breakups were boring. Adding you into the equation…'

'Are you saying I'm a volatile part of this so-called equation?' Angela demanded.

Colin winced. 'That didn't come out right.'

'You bet your arse it didn't.'

'Sorry.' He did seem suitably contrite.

Angela tried to temper the smile that he hadn't quite earned yet. 'Well, I suppose I'm willing to see where this goes. But I'm not going to walk in circles around the sofa with you, okay? I'm going to sit *on* the sofa and eat copious amounts of packet cupcakes. Bernard seemed to think we needed three boxes of those. He made me promise that I'd be the one making them.'

Colin scowled. He was too easy to rile up sometimes. And touchy. Very, very touchy.

Especially when he was hiding something.

'You're not doing this for your show, are you?' Angela asked, suddenly suspicious.

'What? No!' Colin laughed. 'You're still the resident expert at contriving ridiculous situations for us to theoretically find ourselves in.'

Angela slid off her glasses and pressed a cool palm against her flushed face. 'It's not that, Colin. I just…I just need this to be real, okay? Not something that someone made up with pen and paper. So I'll go along with The Plan, but on the condition that none of this gets put into the show. This is real life, *my life*, not some entertaining story. Okay?'

'Okay,' Colin agreed, a smile warming his words. 'I understand. And I've never planned any of my segments anyway—I tend to just wing it and see what happens. This is totally different. You deserve more forethought than that and I really don't want to screw this up. Planning is my new hobby.'

'So what are we doing this afternoon, Mr Planner?' Angela teased. 'Arts and crafts? Movie marathons? I hope you've pencilled in an *Outlander* binge session, because you are seriously behind in your pop culture knowledge.' She held up a hand. 'I'm not going to make you watch *Game of Thrones*. That's something you have to come to in your own time. I can probably trade you *Outlander* for *Knight Rider,* though. It's a sacrifice I'm willing to make.'

He stuck his tongue out at her.

'Very mature,' Angela told him—right before she returned the gesture.

Colin stood and grabbed his plate on his way to the kitchen. 'You'll see. This day will turn out perfectly, burnt chocolate and marshmallows aside. I just need you to make yourself scarce for a bit. You can come back out in fifteen minutes. It's all a part of The Plan.'

'Why doesn't that make me feel reassured in the slightest?' Angela wondered.

'I have no idea why,' Colin said, completely straight-faced. 'As we've just discussed, I have a *lot* of experience with planning things.'

Shaking her head in amusement, Angela headed for the bathroom.

***

Angela found herself staring into the mirror that hung on an angle above the sink. She'd run her hands under the tap for a few seconds and patted every stray hair back down with her damp fingers, but she still managed to look dishevelled and slightly panicked at the thought of 'courting' her roommate.

What if this *did* blow up spectacularly?

'At least he doesn't own any pink Lycra,' she muttered, transcribing those same words into a text meant for Ishani.

There's that, Ishani agreed. *And it's not like he can leave and go cheat on some sidepiece for the next fortnight hey*

Angela clapped a hand over her mouth, catching the laugh, and typed out a response. 'He's still not telling me everything though.'

R u ok with that?

'I think so. I feel like I've known him forever and I can't help but trust him. Oh God. What is *wrong* with me? No one falls in love this fast in real life. It only happens in romance novels. Right?' Her phone trilled loudly, as if it was mocking her, but Angela didn't hesitate to answer the call. 'Ishani! You shouldn't be talking. Your test came back positive and—'

'You stopped texting, so I figured you were muttering to yourself again,' Ishani's hoarse voice replied. 'Also, virus or no virus, I'm still bored out of my mind over here. Angela. You're not in love yet so there's no need to stress. Sit back. Relax. Enjoy yourself, no matter the outcome. And let me wait for my Penguins and gin in peace.'

'Colin's friend still hasn't dropped your groceries off yet?'

A string of ragged coughs answered her.

'Ishani?' Angela asked, worried. 'You should be sleeping or something.'

'Or something. I've got a Netflix account and I'm not afraid to use it.'

Angela smiled. 'Maybe humour your brother and turn down the volume for once. Wasn't he going spare from overhearing all those K-dramas of yours? You did say you're always promising him "just one more episode" until suddenly it's midnight.'

'It's not my fault those shows have forty or more episodes. And I'm the one who's sick! Ungrateful blighter. I never make him pay rent and this is how I get treated.'

'Have fun,' Angela said. 'And maybe hide the remote! You've got to fall asleep sometime and he'll definitely risk catching the virus to pinch it off you. I would.'

'It's a good thing he didn't hear you say that,' Ishani remarked. 'Bye for now.'

Well, Colin's fifteen minutes were now up.

Angela wondered what awaited her on the other side of the door. It better not be strip poker. She drew a breath, steeled herself—and left the bathroom.

Angela wasn't sure what she expected, but it certainly wasn't the sight of Colin holding a purple wizard's hat upside down and pouring tiny shredded pieces of paper into it. She opened her mouth to say something. Not a single word made it out. All because Colin had looked at her, that slow grin creeping across his face.

Her stomach did a funny dance and so did her heart. Oh God. They were supposed to be taking things slow.

Enjoy yourself, Ishani's voice reminded her.

Angela suddenly found herself unable to stop smiling back at him.

22

'What?' Colin asked. 'Never seen a lucky dip before?'

Angela gave him that patented look of scorn, just as he'd expected (maybe even *hoped* for), but he definitely hadn't imagined the smile she'd quickly stowed beforehand.

Colin waved at the coffee table, where two steaming mugs of chai tea waited—on coasters this time, because he was starting to see her point about cups leaving marks all over the wood. He could tell she'd noticed the coasters. The usual waspish comments she would have made swiftly fell by the wayside.

Angela sat down on the sofa and linked her hands over her crossed knees. Her jumper today was mauve and hung off one shoulder, revealing a tempting stretch of pale skin. She raised an eyebrow at him.

He just winked at her in response.

'Alright then,' Angela said. 'I can wait for you to explain, if it'll kill more time.'

Colin had no intention of making her wait.

'Part of the courting process,' he began, offering her the hat with a flourish and a bow, 'is getting to know each other. To find out if we're a suitable match. And to make sure we don't have any incompatible deal-breakers.'

'I thought the sexy banter was already a massive plus in our favour,' Angela said dryly.

Colin blinked at her. 'It is?'

'Never mind. Please continue this courting ritual of yours.'

Angela reached for her mug, sipping at her tea and meeting his gaze without flinching.

He wouldn't break the silence first. He wouldn't.

'So this is what we'll do every afternoon,' Colin declared, unable to stop himself. He jiggled the hat at Angela. 'If you put your hand in here, you'll be able to pick out a subject we have to discuss, or a question that we both need to answer. I read about this on the Internet. It's supposed to be quite the icebreaker.'

'You, a DJ, needing an icebreaker,' Angela mused.

'Don't really need to approach people if they're the ones tuning in to *me*,' Colin said.

Shrugging and apparently conceding the point, Angela reached into the hat and rummaged around with a thoughtful expression on her face. Colin tapped the floor impatiently with the heel of his new slipper (it was nice not to be able to feel the carpet through a hole in the bottom, but of course he'd never tell Angela that).

Finally, she held her hand aloft, a piece of notepaper curled up on her palm.

'Will you do the honours?' Angela asked, offering him the scrap.

Colin accepted the paper and unrolled it, then cleared his throat in an exaggerated fashion. 'Exchange anecdotes about the cars you drove during your high school years.'

Angela grimaced. 'Now that's a walk down memory lane I didn't need.'

'I can pull out another one…' Colin suggested, inwardly berating himself for trying to plan something for once. It clearly wasn't working out for him. And he'd only been at it since yesterday.

'No, no, no,' Angela assured him. 'It'll be fine.'

A small shudder passed through her. One hand went to the collar of her jumper and reefed it up to her neck, the fabric bunching there and then expanding back out like an accordion once she'd let go of it.

'Maybe I should go first,' Colin said.

Angela smiled gratefully. 'That'd be wonderful.'

He plonked himself down on the sofa beside Angela, knee pressed against hers, and grabbed his mug of tea, gulping down the too-hot water. He had an awful feeling that his anecdote was going to be silly compared to hers, but it might just evoke another smile. And he really wanted to see her smile again.

'When I was fifteen,' he said, the mug now safely consigned to the coffee table, 'I stole one of my father's Porsches and took it for a joyride.'

'*One* of his Porsches?' Angela repeated, eyeing him. 'Wait, I think I know where this is going. You were pulled over, some policeman took pity on you because you just wanted attention—*any* attention—and then they let you walk. Rich parents who ignore you all the time? No problem, we'll let you off, but not the next young thing we catch speeding in a stolen Nissan. Here, have a tissue.'

Colin snatched the box of tissues from the coffee table before she could beat him to it. She ducked pre-emptively. Poorly aimed and hastily thrown, the box hit the wall and bounced onto the floor. Angela gave him A Look. Then she burst out laughing.

Colin grinned, enjoying the way her glasses slid down to the end of her nose. Once she'd pushed them back up, he said, 'They probably would have let me off, if I'd been caught. But I wasn't. Something of a letdown, actually. I was trying to be rebellious.'

'Were you drunk? Tipsy, at least?'

'Nope. Completely sober.'

'Surely you must have broken some rule, the initial theft aside,' Angela said. 'Were you using your phone? Recording your little jaunt?'

'*Noooo*,' Colin replied. 'Too rich for my blood.'

'Too rich! That's funny coming from someone whose father owns multiple Porsches.'

Colin performed a deep sigh, but he couldn't quite mask the laugh underneath it. 'Alas, I had a flip phone at the time. The cameras on those back then were terribly poxy and I insisted on having the cheapest model possible. Because I was a rebel. Obviously.'

'So what happened when you got home, Colin Cooper, Master Rebel?' Angela asked, watching him with a mixture of disbelief and supressed amusement. 'Were your parents waiting for you, like they always are in the movies?'

'Nope. That would only have happened if Father had known I was gone. He had no idea. I even refuelled the car.'

'*Oh my God*,' Angela gasped, tears leaking out of her eyes as her laughter returned in full force. 'Did the people at the service station say anything?'

'No! I kept waiting for them to ask for my ID.'

'Did you steal a packet of crisps?'

Colin shook his head. 'I was the perfect customer.'

'You don't have a single rebellious bone in your body, do you?' Angela teased.

'I have other attractive qualities, obviously,' he said with a wink.

Angela mimed retching into her lap.

Colin quickly smoothed out his burgeoning grin. 'Well, that's my anecdote. You don't have to tell me one of yours if you don't want to. Not all of us have parents with more money than emotional capacity. I think my going into a low-paying career bothered them a lot more than my decision to use my trust fund to move away without telling them where I was going. They do make the occasional token effort to reach out, but only because their friends expect them to. Got to make sure they look like model parents, you see. Yeah, I could probably still get a policeman to feel sorry for me with that story.'

Angela didn't respond, but her mouth curved as she took a draw from her mug. Colin watched her drink, unable to look away. He would listen to every word that passed those lips if he could and he was sure his listeners would too, if he could just get her to feel comfortable enough with a microphone. Leo would love that, he thought. Especially since they were actually 'courting' now. His numbers would go through the roof.

But Angela didn't want any of this to make it into the show. Real life and fiction had to remain separate. For now, that is...he had plenty of time to convince her otherwise, since they were going to be stuck inside for a while.

'Alright, stop that,' she said.

'Stop what?' Colin was half-convinced that she'd been listening in to his thoughts and immediately felt guilt-induced bile crawl up his throat.

Angela rolled her eyes. 'I'm not *that* distracting, am I? Your attention's wandering.'

'*Noooo*, you definitely are that distracting,' Colin blurted out.

Angela snorted but she didn't comment on that, apparently mollified. 'Okay. I didn't steal any Porsches. I actually had a job at the Sainsbury's when I was in high school, so I was able to save up for a second-hand car. It was awesome: twin cam, spoiler, white tyre rims. It did lack airbags and ABS, but anyway. It was the best deal I could get at the time. And it made me look like a real speed demon.'

'You, a speed demon?' Colin scanned her from head to toe, maybe lingering a little too long on where the jumper was hanging low on her shoulder again. 'Somehow I doubt it.'

'Maybe I just wasn't caught!' Angela said.

'Or it could be that the local police are just as terrified of you as I am.'

Angela picked up her mug of tea, her grip uneven, the water level continuing to wobble. 'I sometimes wish I hadn't bought it. I was the first one in my grade with a car and a provisional licence. This made me everyone's best friend.'

'Of course it did,' Colin agreed. 'You could give them independence. Even as an adult I hate relying on the infrequent buses around here.'

'I assumed they actually liked me.' Angela laughed harshly and peered down into her chai tea. Colin realised he'd forgotten to add a dash of milk, but the dark depths seemed to suit her mood. 'Mum said I should have realised something was up when they never bothered to thank me for the rides I gave them. I didn't care about that. I was doing what anyone would do for their friends. Because they *were* my friends. At least, I thought they were.'

'They took you for granted,' Colin said quietly.

'Yeah. My use to them was more important than me as a person.'

'What happened in the end?' Colin asked.

'Nothing dramatic. Someone else got a car and the licence to go with it. Suddenly everyone forgot my number. I'd ask to hang out and all I'd get was silence. I tried talking to them on MSN, because I was desperate, but I wouldn't even get the "so-and-so is typing" message. I felt really stupid. I was no one, just a way to get around. Just someone to use when it benefited them.'

Colin wondered if that sandwich she'd made him had contained an eel, because he didn't feel terribly good just then.

Angela's shoulders sagged. 'Em—she's the friend I yelled at recently—was the only one who stuck around. Her mum took me out for ice cream and made me realise that things would get better one day. Sure, my situation still sucked, but high school isn't forever. You don't want it to be your peak anyway.'

'Wise woman,' Colin noted.

Angela nodded. 'She died five years ago. I miss her. More a mum than mine ever was.'

'I'm sorry.'

'Anyway,' Angela charged on, 'I was afraid that Em only agreed to hang out all those times because her mum told her she had to be friends with me.'

'I guess she had another reason then?'

Angela reached for her mug, her frown hitting the rim. 'I asked her about it later. She said that was part of it, but she also stuck around because all the others kept going to McDonald's or driving in circles. I did more exciting things, like late-night runs over to Hastings. We didn't do much, just roamed the beach while giggling like proverbial schoolgirls, but still.'

Colin stared at her. Words had completely escaped him.

'She eventually decided that I was decent friend material, even without the car or her mother's prompting,' Angela said. 'Apparently this honest answer of hers was supposed to make me feel flattered.'

'Ouch,' Colin managed.

'She was my only friend, so what I could say to that? "Piss off"? I still don't know if I should have gone off at her like I did the other day. But I did. And I've probably lost her.'

Colin hesitated. 'I've no idea what I'd do in your shoes. I was a bit of a loner as a teenager and was quite happy to avoid people. But then I moved here, met Rob, became friendly with the other DJs when I started my show…I'm spoilt for choice, if I'm honest. It's been kind of easy for me.'

'Lucky,' Angela said with a sigh.

Colin glanced away, ashamed. He'd often thought that his life was difficult, but he'd really just coasted through everything, hadn't he?

'I'm not sure Em and I can move on from this,' Angela said quietly, more to herself. 'Things can't go back to how they were. We'd have to treat each other completely differently.'

'Like equals,' Colin agreed.

'Yes, that. If it's possible. I'm no longer so desperate for a friend that I'll do anything for her, or take her shit without complaining.' Angela paused. 'I'm not really sure what she likes about me. She's always telling me how I should be living my life and what I should be doing if I want to avoid dying alone. And it'd be nice if she didn't go on and on about both of us getting old and losing our looks.'

'Validation,' Colin said. 'If she can get you to worry about the same thing, then it means she's not anxious about something irrelevant.'

Angela raised her eyebrows. 'Very deep.'

'Hey, I'm more than just a pretty face and epic band shirts,' Colin defended.

'Epic,' she repeated. 'Try "so worn and ripped even punks would drop them in the dustbin". Don't you have something nicer to wear? Something with…*buttons?*'

Colin looked down at himself and immediately noticed the mysterious stain right in the centre of his shirt. He was sure it hadn't been there a second ago. 'Okay. When The Plan calls for a fancy dinner—and there'll be one on Monday night, I've just decided—we will both put in some effort and dress up.'

'We? Hmm.'

How could she put so much meaning into so few syllables? Colin stared at her for a moment, impressed, then shook himself out of his stupor. 'Fine. *I* will dress up. You always look good. Especially when you wear the long black skirt. I still remember the day you first wore it, because the price tag was hanging out the back.'

'Just how long have you been checking me out, Colin Cooper?'

'Oh, would you look at the time?' Colin said, dramatically holding his bare wrist up in front of his face. 'Let's move on.'

'No, let's *not*.'

The acerbic bite to her words was back, but her dark brown eyes held stars in their depths. There was also a tantalising flush spreading across her cheeks. He had the distinct feeling that he was standing too close to a precarious ledge.

Uh oh, Colin thought.

He was saved from falling off that ledge when his phone buzzed. He snatched it out of his pocket so quickly he actually tore the lining with a jagged nail.

'Rob?' Colin answered. 'You have impeccable timing.'

'Coward,' Angela mouthed.

Rob's terse voice battered his eardrum. 'Colin. Mate. Did you have to do this to me?'

'Uhh,' Colin said. He would never have let that syllable escape him during a show (he would be dead to Leo if he did), but he needed to stall while he tried to remember what he'd done to Rob lately. A year ago, he'd hidden Trolls throughout Rob's Hyundai and some were so tiny that it was possible they hadn't yet breeched the rubbish that formed a crusty layer on the bottom of the car. But Rob had never sounded this annoyed about the Trolls before.

'What did I do, exactly?' Colin asked.

'You. Made me. Deliver. Groceries. To my *ex*.' Rob swore under his breath. 'Damn it, Col. Really?'

'I had no idea,' Colin protested. 'I swear.'

'Yeah, that doesn't help me any. My head's a mess. I'm going back to the pub.'

Rob abruptly hung up.

Colin stared at the phone in his hand. 'That was…unexpected.'

'You're in luck,' Angela said, clearly having overheard their conversation. 'I'm far more interested in this sudden revelation about Rob and Ishani than I am in your sudden inability to answer a harmless question.'

Colin laughed. 'Thank God for that.'

23

Day Three

Angela sat up against the wall and bounced the balls of her feet off her mattress. Wills, currently cradled in her lap, gave her a lopsided stare that looked all the more judgemental because one of the buttons posing as an eye was missing—and it definitely didn't help that half his face had always bulged a little more than the other. None of this was her fault; she had rescued the stuffed bat from a discount bin.

Not that he'd ever shown how grateful he was.

'Ishani is *not* ignoring me,' Angela told Wills. 'And I'm not going to blow up her phone. It'll make me look clingy and it's totally inappropriate. You can't just bring up someone's juicy past without their consent. If I was the doddery old dowager aunt in a Regency novel, I'd say it was unseemly. Okay, maybe I should've picked something other than historical romance for my first book...I swear, for every full day of research I do, I might be able to write a single sentence. Ugh.'

The bat, now strung up by his wings in her hands, offered no wisdom.

Angela sighed. 'I can't afford to lose this friend, Wills. And besides which, Ishani is sick. Really, really sick. She's got a good reason for not replying yet. Unless…oh God. Unless she's so sick she can't reach the phone and she's dying and her brother is driving her to Buckland Hospital right now.'

Wills' one-eyed stare didn't alter in the slightest.

Angela flung him down onto the mattress and buried her fists into her eye sockets. 'I'll call her later to see how she's going and that's it. That's all. No asking her what the deal is with Rob.'

She looked to Wills for guidance again. He didn't seem particularly pleased about being upside down. Hastily apologising, Angela propped him up against her pillow and frowned. Wills was filthy. And it had been months since she'd dressed him in his little tuxedo. It felt wrong to keep hiding Wills in her suitcase, but she didn't want a certain roommate to see him.

Colin chose that rather inconvenient moment to knock on her door.

Angela shoved Wills safely behind her. She squashed the immediate urge to yell 'who is it?' and instead called, 'What? Did you forget that The Plan for today included solo leisure time until after lunch? You do realise that "solo leisure time" sounds dirty, right?'

Colin cleared his throat. 'If you'd prefer I came back later…'

'No! That is not what I'm doing. There is nothing dirty happening in here.'

'If you say so,' he said noncommittally.

'Open the bloody door, Colin!'

'Are you sure?'

'Arghhhh!'

'Well, it's not "open sesame" but it'll do,' Colin said cheerfully as he pushed the door open and flashed a diagonal smirk at her. He was wearing yet another band shirt (Men at Work today), but at least this one didn't have a stain on it. 'So you too, huh?'

Angela stared at him.

He gestured towards her lap, where her phone was resting. 'You're also waiting for a certain friend to get back to you, right?'

Angela immediately turned her screen off, paranoid that he had somehow seen the texts she and Ishani had exchanged about him. 'Yes! And the only thing I can distract myself with at the moment is panicking about how I'm supposed to dress up for our fancy dinner on Monday—assuming we'll have something a bit more exciting than baked beans on toast, like we did last night—because I don't have anything fancy *to wear*. The last fancy thing I owned was my formal dress from high school. I sold it two months ago so I could buy groceries. Not sure why I kept the dress that long. I haven't been that size in over a decade and the memories attached to it aren't especially fond.'

'You always look good to me,' Colin said. 'I'm the one who needs to put in the effort this time. I'll have a look in my wardrobe. I might even find something with buttons!'

Angela rolled her eyes. 'Your dressy look is not the same as *my* dressy look. I can't wear an everyday outfit. Mind you, I'm not sure why I'm so worried about impressing Mr Colin Cooper. I could probably get away with wearing your favourite black skirt five days in a row...I'm not sure you'd notice.'

Colin straightened against the doorjamb. 'I absolutely would.'

'Well then, I need something else to wear,' Angela said and whipped out Wills, sad state and all. 'He's even got formalwear. But I'm shit out of luck with my own wardrobe.'

'Who or what is that?' Colin asked.

Angela pursed her lips, deciding on the safest answer. She didn't want him to think she was weird—well, weirder than he already thought she was. It then occurred to her, in a voice that sounded suspiciously like Emily's, that if Colin had a problem with Wills, then that was a good reason not to go out with him. She could nip this thing in the bud right now.

'Wills,' Angela said slowly, 'has been one of my best friends since kindergarten.'

Colin nodded, his expression solemn. 'I see. Do I have to impress him in order to impress you? Because I can talk to Wills if necessary, but please don't record me doing it.'

Angela snorted. 'He's a stuffed bat. Named after someone who now has even less fuzz on the top of their head than he does. No, you do not need to ingratiate yourself with an inanimate object.'

'Thank God for that,' Colin said with feeling. 'So, did I pass your test?'

'Was I that obvious?'

'Just a little. Maybe we can avoid the tests for now. I think it's a bit early in our courtship for me to kiss your stretch marks.' Colin's left eyelid blurred; it might have been a wink. 'But that test is not off the table—when it's the right time for it, I mean. Anyway, I hope you're ready for this afternoon's activity. Let's see if we can survive it.'

'I'm pretty sure I can survive walking on carpet,' Angela said. 'Since it can't burn me.'

'But the whole point of "the floor is lava" is that we're supposed to pretend it can,' Colin told her. 'For...drama.'

Angela grimaced, the saliva souring in her mouth. 'Colin. I don't need any more drama in my life. I've recently gone through the cheating ex-boyfriend thing, even if it didn't happen in that excitingly catastrophic way it does in my books.'

She paused, wondering if she was disappointed by that. No, she wasn't. But it hadn't felt particularly good either. Oh well. A bit of silliness to break up her afternoon routine might be nice. Finally, she conceded, 'Oh, alright. The floor in the common area is lava after midday. But I'm not coming out to help you if I hear a thump.'

'You mean, a suctioning noise followed by my pained screams,' Colin corrected.

'Might be a good thing if a ratty old band shirt gets incinerated today,' Angela said. 'But I'd be sad if your Duran Duran shirt, the one with the *Rio* cover, got burnt to a crisp. I'm rather fond of it.'

Colin mimed writing something down on an invisible pad of paper, the corners of his lips twitching. 'I'll make sure it gets bequeathed to you. And I won't change into it, in case disaster strikes. I'll see you later, Angela.' He grinned. 'Bye, Wills.'

Angela lifted one of Wills' wings and waved it at Colin.

'Kissing my stretch marks?' she muttered as soon as the door shut. 'What's he on about?'

***

Angela caught sight of Colin nursing future bruises on the sofa as she made her way over to the kitchen for a tea refill. The laugh spilled out of her before she could stop it. She'd already copped his earlier accusations of cheating, which were to be expected from someone who had just injured themselves while attempting to jump from their door to an unattainable sofa.

Angela had to admit she'd deserved his ire; she had sticky-taped several A4 sheets of paper together and laid them out from her room to the saloon doors for her earlier cup of tea. She'd left the common area immediately after acquiring the much-needed caffeine.

But the proverbial paper trail had remained.

It had been a mistake, thinking that he wouldn't need to use the bathroom before she did, that her untoward methods would go unnoticed. Colin had a steel bladder—usually. But he'd made a rather large mug of tea without realising how close it was to 12pm, the starting time of their game. The desperate urge had apparently struck him an hour after the carpet had become deadly.

'You didn't stipulate that I couldn't create non-lava floor,' Angela pointed out, repeating her earlier argument.

Colin rubbed his temples. 'The paper would have disintegrated before it even had a chance to hit the lava.'

'The sofa *might* last a fraction longer,' Angela noted. 'But it would go up in flames almost instantly. I don't fancy your chances. You'd survive just long enough to laugh at my folly before yours got you in the end.'

'An observation worthy of Douglas Adams,' he said dryly.

'Are you saying I'm wrong?'

'No, no.' Colin gave a brisk shake of his head—but this didn't dislodge his small, creeping smile. 'I'm once again defeated by you and your logic.'

'Get used to it, Colin.'

Angela wandered into the kitchen, grinning, and was still filling up the kettle at the sink when she heard a knocking sound. She froze, momentarily panicked.

'The done thing' in this situation, at least before a pandemic had flown its way into the country, would be to answer the front door, no matter one's introverted status or how strained their relationship with their mother was. Admittedly, Angela would usually ignore whoever was there (this had once earned her a 'Millennials can't even talk to other people anymore' lecture from the righteous Janet Tweedie) or tell them to go away if they got pushy.

But she had a damn good excuse for not answering the door this time.

Angela tiptoed back into the living room just in time to see Colin nudging the door shut with his backside, a box clutched in front of him. He marched over to the coffee table, ignored her raised eyebrows, and set it down, a pair of scissors appearing out of the back pocket of his jeans. Angela had no idea how long those had been in there. It couldn't have been comfortable sitting on them.

Colin pressed the tip of one blade between the cardboard flaps of the box. He paused, eyes narrowed in concentration, then slowly began to saw his way down the tape.

'Hurry up!' Angela said. 'And don't be gentle about it. This is the most exciting thing that's happened since yesterday. Give us a look.'

'I don't want to rip the contents,' Colin said defensively.

Angela huffed. 'Okay, fine. I guess I can be patient, since you've given me privilege of witnessing your grand unboxing event. If I had any money left myself, I too would resort to online shopping just to make the days in quarantine a bit more bearable.'

'Bearable?' Colin laughed. The scissors didn't pick up any speed as he kept working on the box. He did, however, toss her an infuriating wink. 'You can be a bit of a bear sometimes, but I actually don't mind your company. Huh, I never thought I'd say that.'

'I know, right?' Angela said. 'We couldn't stand each other barely a fortnight ago.'

'Yes, I remember, you always had a problem with my presence coinciding with yours.'

'Oh, do not repeat what I then said,' Angela teased.

Colin stared at her, scissors slack in his grip.

'Never mind, you don't get the reference,' she said, then rushed on before he could say anything, 'Open the bloody box or so help me God—!'

After performing a ridiculous bow, Colin returned to liberating the contents of the box. Her exasperated sighs only made him move slower, so she did her best to remain silent. He ground to an actual halt once his hands were buried inside the box.

'What?' Angela demanded.

'I did get the reference, by the way,' Colin said, holding her eyes. 'Why else do you think I call Loraine and Bernard "The Bennets"? But I think you should refrain from quoting any more marriage proposal scenes. You might not be so grateful when you see what I've done. I think I've just horrendously overstepped.'

'Colin! For crying out loud!'

He laughed and pulled something out of the box with a flourish.

A dress. He'd bought a dress.

'For Monday night,' Colin said, as though it were obvious.

The dress was dark blue and twinkled in the afternoon light skimming in through the window, its fabric like a miniature galaxy that had been spun together and shipped straight to them. The dress was gorgeous. And A-line too, a flattering fit for just about anyone.

'Umm, okay,' Angela said to buy time, not wanting to blurt out the first thing that had popped into her head, which would have been rude and inappropriate and entirely not a 'done thing'. So what if he wore dresses? Newfield didn't exist in the Dark Ages (anymore…). He might look pretty good in it. In fact, she would probably enjoy him modelling it for her.

God, she really hated her head and the thoughts that popped into it sometimes.

'I bought several different sizes,' Colin nattered on, seemingly unaware of the mental pictures she was getting. 'I have no idea how sizing works outside of the men's department and I didn't want to insult you by getting something too big. Or something too small. Yikes.'

Angela looked at the dress, then at his embarrassed expression, then back at the dress. '*Oh.* Oh! Good thinking. It's actually really creepy in romance novels when the billionaire, kidnapper, and/or Mafioso springs a dress on the heroine in her exact size before they're anywhere *near* dating. Especially if a generous bust like mine is involved.'

Colin swallowed a couple of times.

Angela grinned at him, enjoying his discomfort.

'Er, well,' he said, waving vaguely at the box. 'There's a thirty-day return policy on them, so we'll be able to take back the ones that don't fit. I got the lot from Suzie's Magical Couture down the road. I paid Suzie (or someone I presume to be Suzie) extra to drive the contents here herself. Anyway, I'll leave you to it.'

Colin all but fled into his room, his feet tearing up her A4 sheets of paper as he went.

Somehow managing not to laugh, Angela dug into the box and began sorting through the sizes. He'd bought five of them! No price tags and no invoice. Probably a good thing—Angela wasn't sure she could bring herself to try them on otherwise.

There, a size 16. Only one way to find out if the sizing ran true.

Angela darted into her room and put the dress on in front of the mirrored wardrobe doors. Even before she'd pulled the capped sleeves up to her shoulders, Angela knew it was a winner. The fabric wasn't tight across her thighs and nor did the zipper force her to do yoga. Colin had either figured out exactly what she'd always wanted in a formal dress—or he'd managed it through sheer dumb luck.

'I guess I don't have any more excuses to avoid that fancy dinner,' Angela told Wills.

Her faithful friend's sole eye twinkled.

24

***

Day Four

Angela emerged from her room, irritably rubbed her eyes, and glared at Colin.

'It's Sunday,' she said. 'You should be having a lie-in.'

Colin glanced up from the paper he was busily scribbling away on and grinned. Sitting beside him on the sofa, as though he'd been there all night, was Wills. Vague memories of allowing Colin to spend 'man-to-man' time with the stuffed bat floated through her head. It had seemed funny at the time. Clearly that had been a mistake, since Wills and Colin were now suspiciously chummy with each other.

'Do you have any suggestions for The Plan today?' Colin asked. 'Wills has come up with a few ideas already.'

Wills looked oddly pleased to have earned Colin's favour.

'Traitor,' Angela told the stuffed bat—and went straight back to bed.

Some hours later, when Colin declared that they would be playing Twister (using a battered old copy that the previous owner of the flat had apparently left behind in the shower cubicle, which raised all sorts of disturbing questions), Angela was sure Wills had told him just how bad she was at the game. Clearly to torture her in return for her rough treatment of the bat.

Angela groaned from her mangled position on the floor. 'Can't even trust my own soft toys anymore.'

'I think Wills is an excellent judge of character,' Colin said.

'You would,' she grumbled.

***

Day Five

'Alright, folks,' Colin said, affecting a weary voice worthy of a veteran reliving some long-ago battle from World War Two. 'Enough already. There's definitely *two* separate beds in my flat, so no one is being forced to share.'

He grinned across at Angela who was in the chair on the other side of his desk, where she'd parked herself at 8:57am. Not to keep an eye on him and how he was handling her serial—he hoped so, anyway. He was sure he'd earned her trust by now. No, her presence probably had more to do with the fact that last night he'd Blu-Tacked a piece of paper to the wall in the living room (right between the framed *Red Carpet Massacre* and *Pop Trash* posters) with today's to-do list written on it permanent marker. One item in particular had very large letters: 'Angela to sit in on Colin's show—ALL THREE HOURS OF IT'.

Okay, maybe Colin had been seeking some revenge after yesterday's 'pull a question out of the hat' thing. The scrap that had emerged had told them to share their impressions of each other before they'd become roommates. It had somehow turned into a debate (with supporting arguments from three-second Google searches) about whether or not Angela should have held the door open for him back before Easter.

Back before. It really wasn't that long ago. Just one day shy of a fortnight, nearly the same amount of time required by self-isolation.

Wow. The pandemic had really done a number on his perception of time.

It hadn't taken more than ten minutes for Colin to be soundly beaten by Angela's social distancing argument. He really couldn't wrangle a win out of that one—and he knew she would never let him. At least she was more enthusiastic about sitting in on his show than she had been about playing Twister.

Colin was almost relieved that Angela had so far showed no signs of jumping into his show today. Almost.

'Sorry to disappoint, but there are no convenient leaks in the roof,' Colin said in response to an overly optimistic Tweet. 'Both our beds are dry. *Anyway*, I thought you'd all be more interested in what happened in one particular bed, not worrying about which bed may or may not be useable. Maybe I should put a song on and let you stew for a while.'

Angela performed a silent gasp of shock, as if she hadn't known about this plot development. She'd been the one to come up with it. Colin was glad she was now using bullet points instead of paragraphs; it was a lot easier to add in his usual comments, to make it seem natural when he deviated from her words. It was bad enough that someone else was writing for him. He didn't want to start *sounding* like someone else.

Colin waggled a finger at his secondary monitor, not that his listeners could see it. 'Oh no, you won't get me to kiss and tell. But there is indeed some kissing that I won't be telling you about. It was an accident, I'll have you know. I was supposed to remove a troublesome eight-legged intruder from her room and…well. The less said about tripping over someone's Doc Martens the better.' A carefully orchestrated pause. 'Okay. I'm in trouble. I know you all like hearing about Number Twelve…but now I think *I* might even like her.'

'Might?' Angela mouthed, dramatically clutching her chest.

Colin rolled his eyes at her.

She twirled her hand at him in response.

Colin quickly filled the dead air he'd let run for three costly seconds. 'And here's the thing, folks. I don't just like Number Twelve. I like *like* her. Now I sound like a teenager from the 1990s. I'm showing my age. Look, there's something about Number Twelve…I don't know. Maybe "forced proximity" is a trope for a reason. Art is supposed to imitate life, isn't it? Or maybe there was already a spark and all we needed to do was have meaningful conversations instead of exchanging terse words at the door. I guess there *is* something to be said for the old way of meeting people. In person, not sitting behind a screen. It really works.'

ok Boomer #splatzapp said more than a few Twits.

Colin bit down hard on the inside of his cheek to keep himself from laughing. His eyes instantly watered and the paper blurred in front of him, but at least he knew this part of the segment by heart. 'I think I want to take this—whatever it is—further. But how do you ask someone out in the middle of a pandemic? I've no idea.'

This time the dead air was planned, courtesy of Angela. It was just the right length.

'Anyway, here's a dubstep cover of "Love is a Battlefield",' Colin said over the top of the song's surprisingly demure intro. He kept an eye on the Radio SPLATZAPP! hashtag, which was rapidly filling up with advice on how to plan dates when you're not allowed to go anywhere. 'I really feel this one right now, folks.'

Colin muted the mic and sat back, preparing to enjoy the song he'd queued up earlier. He should have known a certain someone would interrupt his moment of Zen.

'You really *feel* it?' Angela queried. 'Have you even listened to the lyrics? I don't think they apply to us—or to the fake versions of us.'

'Sometimes a song...' Colin hesitated, casting around for an explanation that wouldn't immediately cede the point to her. '...makes you feel something completely different to the words someone's slapped over the top of the beat.'

'Then you're reacting to the dubstep beat and not Pat Benatar,' Angela pointed out with a wicked grin. 'Might as well admit it. You'll listen to anything now, not just New Wave.'

Colin shook his head, smiling. 'You won't let me win this one, will you?'

'You won't even *try*? So much for our sexy banter. I'll have no inspiration for tomorrow and your poor listeners are going to miss out.'

'The sexy banter would only work in my segment if the both of us were on the mic,' Colin told her, tapping his fingers against his desk (he definitely wasn't copying that dubstep beat, no way). 'It's not sexy if I'm quoting it like yesterday's news—not to mention pretty time-consuming. I can't go on like "she said this, I said this, she said this, and now she's looking at me with bedroom eyes and this silence is a little awkward and I'm simmering in this unresolved sexual tension". Radio is all about brevity.'

'I know exactly what you mean,' Angela said, nodding. 'In novels you can get away with cutting out entire pages just by relying on the reader to bring their own assumptions to the text. Your hero doesn't have a beard, but this other potential suitor does? Obviously the other guy is the villain. Boo, hiss!'

'So what assumption would someone be making of us right now?' Colin asked, leaning back in his chair and stowing his restless fingers inside the pockets of his jeans. 'If we were characters in a novel, that is.'

Angela's eyes perused him for a moment, making him feel very glad that the desk was covering certain parts of his anatomy. How did she do this to him with a single look? And why couldn't he stop thinking about her? It couldn't just be the 'forced proximity' thing. She had always lingered in his thoughts when they'd encountered each other on the stairs, on the stoop, outside the letterboxes...

Angela's matter-of-fact voice cut through the foggy memories he'd been slipping into. 'Any reader would know that we're obviously enjoying a mix of the "enemies to lovers" and "roommates" tropes. Or would that make it "enemies to roommates to lovers"? And let's not forget the "fake dating" thing.'

'Fake dating,' Colin repeated.

'Fake dating always leads to actual dating in the books.'

Colin rubbed his temples, suddenly fighting a headache. 'I think I'm going to have an existential crisis in a minute.'

'Colin. Relax. This is real life.'

'I think it'd make more sense if it wasn't,' Colin said.

'No, fiction has drama and complications,' Angela replied. 'I prefer this.'

Her smile unfurled something low in his abdomen. Standing became a little more problematic. Colin swiftly launched into his next segment: a round-up of the best Ask Reddits from the past twenty-four hours. Leo hadn't been wild about this segment at the start, given his preference for his DJs not providing the listeners with information they could get elsewhere, but the arguments on the #splatzapp hashtag always made it clear that Colin's audience enjoyed it—especially when DJ Coop sided with them.

Colin was off the hook for that one. At least until the listeners grew tired of it.

Now if he could just concentrate on skimming the posts in the subreddit and stop picturing Angela in that dress...

He'd see it on her later, he told himself.

T-minus nine hours and counting.

25

The buttonholes on Colin's shirt were surprisingly stiff. He'd never tried to put it on before, so perhaps it wasn't worn in yet. Or perhaps he just wasn't used to buttons. Mildly embarrassing, given his age. Red, however, was an excellent colour for a dress shirt and it gave him a rakish edge (if he did say so himself) that white alone couldn't have managed. It also went surprisingly well with one of his pairs of skinny black jeans.

Colin's fingers shook. But eventually he won the war and the button slid through.

He really could have used a friend as a sounding board, but Rob was still avoiding him. Ishani was being similarly mum with Angela, though at least the café owner had sent through a text about how she was feeling better—except for her inability to taste the instant chicken noodles her culinary-challenged brother had found in the pantry. Colin was sure Angela would never have allowed him to look at her phone if they hadn't been exchanging notes in an attempt to solve the Rob/Ishani Mystery.

Colin was tempted to hit up his fellow DJs for dating advice, but A) he'd already bothered them enough with his personal life recently and B) Danika had called a moratorium on anything Angela-related in their Zoom meetings until the weekend.

The other DJs had agreed to this, but Colin was sure a one-on-one plea for help wouldn't be refused.

The Love Doctor was currently dominating the WiFi waves and Colin could actually call Peter for live advice. Leo was keen to keep a phone system running for the show because it catered to a slew of listeners who were Peter's age. Dating advice for that generation was in short supply, no matter the medium. Radio SPLATZAPP! had cornered the market. But it wasn't unusual for younger listeners to ring in occasionally.

'Peter would just tell you to put your chin up, go out there, and be yourself,' Colin told his reflection. He'd had to use the bathroom mirror, since he preferred to keep his soundproofing up and he couldn't even remember the last time he'd seen his wardrobe doors. His appearance really hadn't been one of his top priorities—he could have delivered his show in his pyjamas if he'd wanted to. Now he had a roommate to impress.

'You can do this,' Colin assured himself. 'You're an *adult*.'

Not much a pep talk, but it'd have to do. He couldn't keep leaning on other people, couldn't keep expecting them to bolster him emotionally, couldn't keep letting them write his own fudging segments.

With a sharp nod, Colin left the bathroom to find Angela already waiting for him. She stood beside the sofa, eyeing the cushions as though they were some sort of trap and smoothing her hands over her hips and onto her thighs. Clearly she was nervous about wrinkling the dress. Bloody hell—bother, it looked good on her.

'Wow,' Colin managed. 'Speechless. Me.'

Angela smiled, her eyes filled with more sparkles than there were woven into the fabric flowing down her form. 'I've no idea how you landed your job at Radio SPLATZAPP! if I can render you speechless just by dressing up a little. Was Leo having an off day when he interviewed you or something?'

Colin swallowed, using the banter to mask how affected he was. 'Leo wasn't wearing a dress during that Skype call. Wow, I'd forgotten that Skype existed. It's all about Zoom these days. Anyway, he's not my type.'

'Hmm, good point,' Angela agreed. 'Your type is someone who refuses to hold the door open for you. Someone who makes snippy comments instead of outright asking you to stop making the mysterious thumping noises.' She walked a quick circle around the sofa, swinging her arms in an exaggerated fashion until she was laughing too hard to keep going. Gasping for air, she added, 'And apparently your type also chooses her cheese based on how cute it looks rather than how good it tastes. Swiss cheese will always be my downfall—since obviously a mouse put the holes there.'

That had been the afternoon's question-in-a-hat: favourite type of cheese.

Colin shrugged. 'Couldn't really judge you for that, since my favourite cheese comes in those plastic sheets that you can buy in bulk.'

'Oh, how I wish I'd never learned that horrifying fact about you.' Laughing, Angela indicated the coffee table with an over-the-top flourish. 'Do you like the additions? You needed something underneath the candlesticks. For aesthetics, of course. The doilies I used were handmade by Em's mother—she tried to teach me how to make them before…well. Shall we get on with this fancy dinner?'

'We shall,' Colin said.

He marched over to the door and opened it, revealing the delivery that had been waiting there for about three minutes (according to the app that Colin had only downloaded two hours ago). The box exuded waves of warmth when his fingers neared the cardboard and it smelled temptingly of the Indian restaurant down by Rob's pub.

Colin left the door slightly ajar and carried the box over to the coffee table. He set about following the instructions printed on the side. It may have taken a full minute in which he tilted his head almost upside down to read the numbered steps, but he got there in the end.

When the right tabs were pulled in the right sequence, the flaps of cardboard opened out to reveal a design on the interior: bright green grass with a chequered picnic rug in the middle. The food was stacked neatly on top of the 'rug' and somehow hadn't moved while the box was in transit, despite the gaps all around the edges.

Angela looked down at the flattened cardboard, lips twisting. 'I don't know whether to laugh or to applaud.'

'I'd say applaud,' Colin said. 'Not everyone's been able to adapt to the lockdown laws that forbid dining out and this is pretty creative. People still want their fancy dinners, not just food crammed into a rectangular container and buried underneath a handful of serviettes and disposable cutlery—damage to the environment notwithstanding.'

'So what do we do with the copper serving bowls they've delivered the food in?'

Colin smiled. 'Easy. We load them all into the box and stick it outside the door for someone to pick up later.'

'Room service!' Angela exclaimed. 'It's actual room service. I love it. So convenient.'

'And cheaper than hotel room service too,' Colin said.

Angela peered over his shoulder. 'Is there more? Or should I be shutting the door to protect our neighbours?'

'There's more,' Colin promised and went back to collect the last item, a small box containing a bottle of sparkling red wine (just below room temperature, as promised) and two glasses that still had the local second-hand store's pricing stickers stuck to the bottom of the stems. 50p each, apparently. The restaurant wasn't risking their own personalised glassware, no doubt keeping those in reserve for when they were allowed to seat customers again.

Colin wondered if the second-hand store had given them a bulk discount. He liked that idea: small businesses helping each other to survive the pandemic. It would have made a good filler for Daily Inspo. Smiling at Angela as she settled herself on the sofa, he decided that he no longer disliked that old segment as much as he had while running it. After all, it had brought her to him.

Even if he couldn't stop feeling guilty about what he'd done.

'Maybe just a tipple tonight, thanks,' Angela said, eyeing the wine bottle.

Colin checked the label and nodded fervently. 'Definitely more loaded than the Moscato. You'll get half a standard drink. I'll stick to the same, for solidarity.'

Angela gasped loudly and clutched at invisible pearls. 'Oh no! We'll be dreadfully *sober*. It'll be like an awkward dinner where one party has just served the other with divorce papers. And the mains haven't even arrived yet.'

Colin winced. He hoped she wouldn't notice it.

But of course she had. 'Colin?'

'That pretty much describes how my parents did it,' he said.

'I'm so sorry.' Angela watched him carefully. 'Unless I'm not?'

Colin began arranging the bowls on the coffee table, making sure they were evenly spaced apart—and keeping his eyes well away from Angela's. 'They got together because both their families had money and it seemed like a good idea at the time. Don't marry down if you can help it. And don't you dare leave the next generation with a single penny less than what you started with! But you kind of need passion in a marriage, don't you?'

'Um, Colin…we live in *England*.'

'Fair point.' He darted a brief grin at Angela. 'Passion might not be necessary, but you've still got to have a strong connection of some kind, with mutual goals and respect. My parents didn't have that. Heck, *I* wasn't even a shared interest. So they broke up over dinner—no fireworks, no crying, nothing. It was like they were two strangers who just happened to be sitting at the same table. I want more than that.'

She wrinkled her nose. 'More drama?'

'No, just something more…something more real.'

'Real hurts,' Angela said quietly, no doubt thinking about the ex-boyfriend. 'But it's definitely worth it. At least I hope so.'

Neither of them said anything for a few moments.

Colin cleared his throat. 'So let's sidestep that awkward topic of conversation with all the nuance of a train wreck. Lol.'

'Yes, let's,' Angela agreed, chortling. '*Lol.*'

'Sidestepping commencing in three, two, one…' Colin pointed at the bowls on the coffee table, one at a time. 'The vegetable korma from this place is a little average, but the butter chicken is something else. I'm pretty sure it's the one dish that everyone expects their local restaurant to get right…' Realising that he'd slipped into DJ Coop Mode, Colin forced himself to slow down. 'But you are definitely *not* getting the extra garlic naan.'

Angela eyed the sides they'd been supplied with. 'Wow. Three naans. Brutal. Quarantine is bad enough without having to pick who gets the extra naan. I bet people have broken up over this already.'

Unease prickled Colin's spine.

'How about I put some music on in my room and turn up the volume,' he suggested.

The next few hours passed in a pleasant haze, one made even more pleasant by questionable quantities of wine. Thankfully, there were no other topics that needed to be avoided and the Fleetwood Mac album that Colin had left on repeat provided a nice background to their companionable silences.

He only remembered to check his phone on his way back from the front door, where he'd just left the box (filled with empty dishes and glasses) for the restaurant's delivery driver, who was due back some time before midnight. Colin's phone had received multiple messages from Peter, who was wondering if anyone had heard from Graveyard Danika. She was supposed to touch base with him regarding the handover between their shows.

Hers started at eleven. And it was now half ten.

Colin stared at his phone, not sure if the heat coursing through him was alcohol-related or some sort of omen.

'Something up?' Angela asked, surprising him. He'd expected her to make some sort of snarky comment about how the phone was getting more of his attention than she was. She'd made it clear earlier in the evening what she thought of people who went on dates with their devices, rather than the people sitting opposite them.

'Not sure,' Colin said.

Zoom meeting now, DJ Sunshine abruptly commanded, the lack of personalised greeting revealing that this was a group text. *Peter you need to queue up another song!*

Colin entered the meeting as soon as the invitation appeared. The

DJs present were in their usual spots. Sunshine was stroking a soft toy that looked more alive than the cat lying across the back of Peter's chair. Danger Jones had his camera perched far enough away from him to show off a black, shimmering robe that was artistically parted to reveal an abundance of chest chair. Naturally, he hadn't neglected to put his sunglasses on. Peter remained the classiest person in attendance; he was wearing his best suit. He called it his 'uniform' and never hosted without it.

The only one missing was Graveyard Danika.

'Danika's mother was put on a ventilator this morning,' Sunshine said, her expression grave. 'She passed away an hour ago. Danika wasn't even allowed to say goodbye in person. She had to do it over the phone. There's no way the poor dear can host overnight.'

'*Shit*,' Danger said.

'I haven't been able to get a hold of Leo,' Sunshine went on. 'I called and asked the students if they could fill in, but they all have assignments due this week. Some of them also have work—retail work. It's unbelievable that we're relying on teenagers to fill frontline jobs at a time like this, but they've always been cheaper to hire, haven't they?'

Colin wondered how Sunshine had established contact with the mysterious weekend DJs. He hadn't thought anyone in their 'stable' knew the students' names, much less their phone numbers.

Colin wet his lips. 'We have to fill in for her.'

'You volunteering?' Danger asked.

'Can't you see he's on a date?' Peter waved a hand at the camera to indicate Colin's attire, apparently forgetting that he wasn't in the same room as the people he was talking to. 'He's all dressed up. Hello, Angela. I'm assuming you're there.'

'Hello,' Angela said politely.

'Are you saying a date's more important than Danika?' Danger demanded.

'Is sitting there in your dressing gown any more important?' Peter fired back.

Danger's mouth popped open. Peter had never spoken to him like that before; he'd always been a perfect, demure gentleman, no matter how strongly they had disagreed with each other.

'Settle down, you two!' Sunshine barked.

Surprisingly, they did.

'We'll do it together,' Sunshine said. 'All of us. Peter, you'll be the host, dear. If you don't know how to add us to the live stream, I'll walk you through it.'

Danger stroked his non-existent moustache. 'What will you guys even talk about?'

Colin was already on his feet and heading for his bedroom (after pitching an apologetic look at Angela). 'How to maintain our relationships during The Plague. Peter's show will give us a good jumping-off point. But let's make it about every type of relationship, not just romantic ones. We'll do a panel of sorts and run more music than usual, especially towards dawn. Everyone will be exhausted by then and we'll need to cover for Sunshine while she gets a few winks in before her show.'

'Thank you, Colin,' Sunshine said softly.

Peter frowned, the object of his disappointment no secret to anyone.

Danger Zones sighed. 'Fine. *Fine.* But I'm not getting out of my dressing gown.'

Colin seated himself at his desk and took a few minutes to slow his breathing. He could hear The Love Doctor announcing the DJstudded panel that was due to start soon, ramping it up, making it sound like this had been planned all along. Not long now.

Just before 11pm, Angela appeared in the doorway with a steaming mug of tea.

'Thank God,' Colin said.

Angela half-dropped the mug onto his desk, causing several drops to slop over the edge. 'Thank *me*. Since I'm not sure God has the time to get off his cloud and give you a shot of much-needed caffeine.'

'Thank Angela,' Colin said solemnly.

Angela snorted and left the room. Once she was gone, he snapped his headphones on and swallowed a few times to grease up his throat.

Time to do what he did best: launch into a show without a single plan behind him.

26

Day Six

Angela upended her mug and teapot on the drying rack, swept the floor, muttered under her breath, then left the kitchen. She eyed Colin's door. Still shut.

A yawn wrenched her jaw apart. Angela's mutters now contained more swear words than punctuation. Even though she hadn't been the one hosting a radio show in the wee hours, she'd had to put up with hearing voices all night; Colin had constantly circled the sofa, outlining each upcoming segment to his fellow DJs with increasing mania and volume. He hadn't even napped between Sunshine's show and his.

Thankfully, Danika had reappeared in time to start her daytime show (the handover had gone smoothly, with Danika even making wry jokes about how her show had been hijacked in her absence) or Colin might have actually passed out at the microphone.

Angela was clapping another yawn back into her mouth when her phone vibrated—a text from Ishani. She managed to drop her phone in the process of punching in her passcode and had to dive for the floor, catching it about two inches away from…well, not certain death. The carpet might be threadbare from Colin's 'exercise', but it was still a lot kinder than the tiles in the kitchen.

Wanted to say something funny, Ishani's message read. Several more lines of text popped up moments later, rapid-fire and slightly aggravated—if typed words could have a tone, that is.

Like I'd rather have The Plague a second time than see Rob Chance again

But I'd b lying

I feel like shite

Less shite than yesterday

But still shite

Angela's thumb danced over her screen before it finally connected. *Dare I ask? Wait yes I dare. I'm dying to know and nearly asked yesterday but didn't want to bother you.*

U can ask, was the swift response, followed by an emoji that was simultaneously laughing and crying.

Angela spent ten seconds trying to find the emoji that was sticking its tongue out. Weren't emojis supposed to *save* her time, not take up more of it? She quickly hit send.

I'm OK tho, Ishani assured her. *But this is a mild case?*

Bugger me

I'm flatter than Madonna's singing that time at Eurovision

Angela bit her lip, causing blood to bead as she tried and failed to curtail a smile. Ishani had said it was alright to laugh about these things and it did make Angela feel better, strangely enough. Carrying on in stoic silence and never acknowledging the problem had been 'the done thing' for generations of Tweedie women (and presumably the men as well, though Janet Tweedie maintained that they had been too useless to marry or share a name with).

But that was before now. Before Angela had needed to find some way to cope with being shut up with her own thoughts, day in and day out.

She might not be dying, but there was that dark hole she'd found herself falling into lately. She'd never been one for depressive thoughts, even with the stuff she'd gone through at high school. It was a terrifying new experience.

Random strangers on the Internet seemed to agree that it was normal to feel this way in the middle of a seemingly endless pandemic. She hoped they were right.

Rest up and get better, Angela typed back. *Or I'll kill you myself lol*

She waited. No response.

Oh God.

Shit I'm sorry that was really insensitive, Angela hurriedly sent.

Ishani put her out of her misery. *Chill Angela. It was lame but I still laughed*

Find some way to relax ok?

Continuing my Downton *marathon ttyl*

PS: Tom is a studmuffin

No disagreement there, Angela replied, smiling. *Ttyl*

She was about to slip her phone back into the pocket of her skirt when it actually started ringing. Peering at the number and recognising it, Angela considered tossing her phone out the window—but common sense prevailed. It wouldn't make her feel any better and she wasn't allowed outside to rescue the phone. Most crucially, she was in the middle of a novel on an ebook app she'd grudgingly downloaded. Her small collection of pre-loved paperbacks wasn't enough to sustain her for eight more days.

Angela steeled herself. 'Hi, Em.'

'Is it true?' Emily demanded.

Angela's mind floated through various answers to that question, none of them sensical or helpful. She finally managed to string three words together. 'Is what true?'

'That you have The Plague.'

'Ben tested positive, not me,' Angela said carefully. She felt pressure mounting against her temples and her Angela-sense was tingling. This was a trap. With bonus sharpened stakes.

'Uh huh.' Emily's monotone didn't make her feel any less anxious. 'And you're in quarantine, aren't you. Just like you're totally staying with Ben at his parents' house. It's not like you'd ever lie about something like that. Right?'

Angela swallowed. That didn't sound good.

'Right?' Emily repeated.

Angela weighed up her options. She suspected she'd already lost this fight and there was nothing to do but bite the bullet. 'Oh, Em. I never moved in with Ben. But I did come into contact with him while he was infectious. That was when I dumped him. Not because he was infectious—how could any of us have known at the time—but because you made me realise that someone was wearing pink Lycra at his place. So I confronted him.'

Okay. Time for the apology. There was still a chance their friendship could be salvaged, even if she was no longer willing to grovel. They had to meet each other as equals.

Angela drew a breath, but she didn't get the chance to start again.

'Ange. I know what you're doing.'

'What am I doing?' Angela wondered, clenching a fistful of her black skirt. She was wearing the skirt because she liked it, not because someone else liked it. Not at all.

'You're trying to make me feel sorry for you,' Emily said, the sting of accusation sharpening her words. 'And I do. A little bit. But I'm not the one who fucked up here. Why don't you just stop lying? You don't have anything else to talk about? Is that it? No. You wanted to make yourself feel better by pretending to have something I didn't! I get it now.'

Angela blinked, trying to dislodge the hot, wet sensation gathering behind her eyelids. 'But…but I'm not lying. And I'm not trying to—'

'You lied about living with Ben.'

'Because you would have made me feel like crap for failing to meet your standards!' Angela cried. 'I'm sorry I didn't tell you the truth. I am! I know I'm in the wrong there. But every time I've been honest—*really* honest—about my feelings with you, you've always found some way to knock me down or make it about yourself, even if it was unintentional. I'm sorry.'

'I'm over your drama,' Emily said. 'Don't contact me again. You're cancelled.'

Angela stared at her phone for a good two minutes before she realised that the screen had gone dark. Any chance she'd had at retrieving her friendship and her last remaining tie to Mrs Benson…was gone. For good.

She went back into the kitchen and rescued the teapot from the drying rack.

Time for something strong, dark, and unforgiving.

***

'Favourite TV series and why,' Angela read out loud, holding at arm's length the piece of paper that had emerged from the darkness inside the hat—not unlike its owner, who had only just stumbled out of his unlit room at 3pm.

Angela squinted at the mess that was Colin's handwriting, trying to decipher the second line. 'Not including anything released in the past five years. Colin, that's not fair. It's also not going to make me proclaim a sudden fondness for the original *Magnum PI*. You're lucky I didn't stop you until we'd finished the whole first disc.'

Colin looked up from his mug of tea, still bleary and unfocused despite the strength of the brew. 'Well, if you have a better topic of conversation, I'm open to it.'

'Rough night?' Angela enquired.

A thin-lipped smile. 'I should have gone to bed when Sunshine came back on. But we were all highly strung after the show. It went really well.'

'I take it Leo wasn't unhappy about the last-minute change.'

'He loved it, judging by the texts he shot our way at 4am,' Colin said. 'I'm not sure if he ever sleeps, but he didn't check his phone until then. Apparently that's when his "date night in" with his husband finished.'

'Wow,' Angela mused. 'We only made it to 11pm.'

'Did you want our date to go until 4am?'

'*Noooo!* I'm getting way too old for late nights. And so are you, judging by how smashed you look.'

'It was definitely a one-off,' Colin agreed with a laugh that segued into a yawn. 'I did feel bad mentioning Danika's situation to her listeners, even though Sunshine said we had her blessing, since it seemed like a convenient excuse in case the show fell below their usual expectations, but they were very supportive and wanted to know how they could help. They were even Tweeting about setting up a GoFundMe for funeral costs. I had no idea that Danika pulled those kinds of numbers at that time of night.'

Angela shrugged. 'Everyone has an audience, I guess, they just have to find them. But since I don't have a radio show, you're my only audience until the end of quarantine. And here's where I change the subject with all the nuance of a meteor slamming into the Earth.'

'This sounds serious.'

'It is.' Angela blew out a breath. 'Em rang me.'

'*Oooh*,' Colin said. 'I mean, oh. How interesting.'

'Colin Cooper, does something about my life amuse you?' Angela asked in a stern voice. 'I know we're running out of things to entertain ourselves with, but wow. *Wow*. This is real life, not another part in a radio serial. I'm a real person with real feelings.'

Colin nodded solemnly, but a smile threatened.

Angela rolled her eyes. It was strangely difficult to feel angry with him. 'Em wanted to check if I was lying. About the self-isolation thing.'

'Why would you lie about that?' Colin was predictably perplexed.

'To make her feel sorry for me, so she'd fork out an apology when she was owed one instead,' Angela muttered. 'I was going to apologise, you know. For my part in the big blow-up. But she was acting like I was...I don't know...trying to cheat in some sort of game. By pretending to have something she didn't. As if our friendship was some invisible tally of points and I was causing her to lose.'

'Power games,' Colin suggested. When she tilted her head towards him, curious, he continued, 'I saw it with my parents. There had to be a loser in every conversation. Compromise was a sign of weakness and the other party *never* had a good point to make. Only one person had the right opinion. It was exhausting.'

Angela sagged. 'I didn't set out to make her "lose". I didn't even know we were competing.'

'I know you didn't,' Colin assured her. 'You can be a bit of a grump and seem to enjoy coming out on top during our sessions of sexy banter, it's true, but you're not so bad when it really matters.'

'Thank you,' Angela said, her stomach settling.

He looked away, seemingly uncomfortable with the topic. 'Yeah, well. Anything else happen on the call?'

'If we were dating, I'd say she broke up with me. But this wasn't a relationship.'

'Wasn't it though?' Colin asked. 'The Love Doctor and I got into it with Danger Jones last night over the end of friendships being just as painful as breakups. Peter sided with me, even though he's from the generation that didn't cancel people. They tended to let those friends hang around like a noxious cloud, constantly wearing them down for decades. So...that's what happened. You broke up.'

Angela eyed him for a moment. 'You're getting deep again, Colin.'

'It's not my natural state,' Colin assured her with a laugh. 'When you're tired and wired, everything seems like a revelation. Did it help?'

'Maybe. Sort of.'

'You can be honest,' Colin said.

'I was! And you'd better believe it.'

'I do. You're always grumpier when you're being honest.'

'Oh well,' Angela said, once she'd stopped poking her tongue out at him—and once her cheeks had stopped feeling so warm. 'It's not like I have a pitifully small pool of friends to draw from or anything. Oh God. Colin, it's *hard* to start over as an adult.'

'I managed it, moving here from up north,' he pointed out.

'Yeah. But I'm assuming this flat of yours is bought and paid for, given the Porsche story. It wasn't that hard for you.'

'Ouch, but you're not wrong.' He shook his head, grinning. 'Okay.

Your square one is worse than mine. But I don't think you're doing too badly.'

'Even though I'm the biggest grump in Newfield?'

'I'd say you're doing extremely well for the biggest grump this side of the Channel.'

Angela settled back against the sofa, arms crossed, but was unable to muster a glare.

Colin raised an eyebrow. 'Did I win this time?'

'Do we really need to keep score?' Angela asked. 'I think we just agreed it's unhealthy to do that in a relationship.'

'I wonder if you'll still say that when you're back on your winning streak,' Colin mused.

Angela grinned. He knew her too well. Oh no. When had that happened and why didn't it bother her as much as it should? She needed to get her head out of the books, get herself away from these four walls, go for a walk…

Oh, yay. A walk. She wasn't allowed to do that anymore.

Angela huffed in annoyance.

'What's wrong?' Colin asked.

'I really, really need to go for a walk.'

Colin launched himself off the sofa and kicked his slippers across the room. Angela groaned loudly. She already knew where this was going.

'No, I am *not* walking around the sofa with you,' she said.

Smirking, he grabbed a rumpled A4 sheet of paper from underneath the coffee table and scrawled 'walk two miles' onto it. Colin stuck the paper onto the wall and winked over his shoulder at her.

Angela threw up her hands. 'Fine. But I'm getting out this skirt. Chub rub is not a fun thing to live with, even in quarantine.'

Colin looked like he wanted to ask what that meant, but wisely decided against it.

'I'll start now,' he said. 'You'll have to catch up.'

Angela, despite her better judgement, got herself into a pair of leggings in under a minute and began to chase him around the sofa.

27

Day Seven

Colin exploded into her room just before 7am, causing Angela to fly up off the mattress, her duvet hitting the wall an impressive metre away. She yanked her *Blues Brothers* nightie down her thighs and tried to think of something to say. Something that didn't involve a string of swear words.

'Oh fudge,' Colin said, then backed up and slammed the door.

Wondering if she looked as bad as she felt, Angela ran her hands through her hair. The chin-length bob resulted in fewer tangles of a morning and she'd been glad to get it cut so short, never mind her mother's horrified gasp when Angela had emerged from the hairdresser on her eighteenth birthday with a new look and the sudden realisation that she could do anything she wanted. Including move out into her own place.

Angela dropped her fingers into her lap, frowning.

Had Colin really appeared inside her room a few seconds ago, or was it some bizarre dream? A dream. It had to be a dream, of course it was.

Nope, there he was. Knocking at the door.

She ought to invite him in, since she was now awake, but what Angela really wanted to do was roll herself back up inside a cocoon of blankets. What good was being in quarantine if you couldn't take advantage of the excuse that you weren't able to go anywhere?

'Can I come in?' Colin asked in a muffled voice.

Angela grabbed her duvet, throwing it over her legs and purple knee-high socks. 'I think the horse has bolted on that one, Colin.'

'I really am sorry. My enthusiasm got the better of me.'

'I'll say.'

'So…can I come in?' he repeated, sounding plaintive.

'Sure, why not,' Angela said. When he opened door again, his hair somehow even more mussed up than usual (not that she was complaining—it was a good look on him), she continued, 'I guess we need to start adding lie-ins to The Plan. Although, I suppose not knowing when you'll be woken up of a morning can be kind of exciting when the rest of your day is already scheduled. Who needs sleep anyway? It's not like I was kept up all of Monday night or anything.'

Colin paused at the threshold, seeming to consider whether or not he wanted to start a session of banter with her. Angela had been very deliberate in leaving him an opening. And he took it. 'Rob wants to chat. I thought I'd put my phone on speaker. Unless I should go somewhere more private for this…?'

He leaned backwards, his shoulders clearing the doorjamb.

'You can take the call in here,' Angela suggested quickly. Too quickly, she knew.

'This isn't one of your novels, Angela.' Colin tutted, but he winked at her. Definitely taking the piss. 'It's real life. It's not supposed to have drama or be entertaining. But I know you. You can't help yourself. You *want* to hear about Rob and Ishani's sordid past. You'd rather eavesdrop than read one of your beaten-up books. I'll bet you anything.'

'I won't take that bet,' Angela muttered.

'I thought so,' Colin said. 'Another win for me?'

Angela slammed a hand onto her mattress. 'You get over here right now.'

He didn't need much convincing. Colin—who was clearly making an effort with a clean shirt, crisp jeans, and those new fluffy slippers—seated himself at the end of the mattress and yanked a corner of the duvet over his lap.

Colin found Rob in his contact list. He selected Rob's name. And then the wait began.

Angela realised she was holding her breath and forced it to puff out over her lips. 'Wow, we've definitely been stuck in here for too long if this is how we're getting our jollies.'

'I can think up better ways to get those jollies if you'd like,' Colin said with a waggle of his eyebrows. Angela was sure his innuendo would have inspired irritation instead of amusement barely a week ago. As it was, the answering grin was almost impossible to stifle.

'Colin!' she cried, mock-outraged. 'Not before our first date!'

Angela abruptly clapped a hand over her mouth, because she was pretty sure she was about to descend into hysterics. She was now wondering if their fancy dinner on Monday constituted a first date, and if she'd just accidentally suggested that one date was all she required before going to bed with someone.

They'd be halfway through their self-isolation tonight. Seven more days to fill. Seven more days of getting their *jollies* somehow.

Judging by the sudden darkening of his eyes, Colin was thinking along the same lines.

Nope, nope, nope, Angela told herself sternly. *Not when we're slap-bang in the middle of the 'forced proximity' trope. Can't be sure if it's real yet. And I need it to be real.*

It was a relief when Rob finally answered the phone.

'Col, mate, you really picked a bad time to get yourself locked up,' Rob complained.

Angela grumbled quietly to herself; she'd wanted him to get straight to it. But she supposed some men had to approach any discussion about their feelings in a more roundabout way.

Colin smothered what looked suspiciously like a grin. 'Why's that, Rob?'

'I just got this massive order of piña coladas for the old folks' home up near your place,' Rob said with a disgruntled sigh, as though his paying customers had done him a huge disservice. 'You know the code to get in the back gate, which they keep refusing to give me—something about murdering a bunch of gnomes with my van last time. I can't believe they're still blaming me for that. You were there as well! Anyway, I'm assuming the code still worked for you just before you went into quarantine. I have to get over there today and I'm in no mood to lift the trolley up all those steps at the front. I need to get inside the gate. And I really need another pair of hands, to be honest.'

Angela gave Colin a questioning look. What had he been doing up at a care home?

And wait, what was the story with the gnomes?

Colin seemed very determined not to look at her. 'Rob, I know you didn't just ring me to complain about my being in quarantine…'

'Yeah, true enough,' Rob conceded. 'I have a bone to pick with you, mate. You sent me straight into the den of vipers last week. To the door of that den, anyway. My *ex*, Colin. *The* ex! You know the one. I told you about her the very first night we met.'

'Oh,' Colin said. 'That one. You didn't exactly use a name.'

Angela sat up straight, needling Colin with her eyes.

Colin held up a hand to forestall the questions she was dying to hurl at him. 'Rob, I thought it was your own insecurities that ended things. It's not her fault you started getting paranoid. Way I see it, she had plenty more monogamous bones than you possessed, mate.'

'I wasn't...okay, I was a bit insecure,' Rob said, voice heavy with reluctance. 'But she didn't have to tell everyone I was a biphobe, Colin! I was young and stupid is all.'

'Doesn't mean it didn't hurt her when you assumed that her being bisexual somehow translated into her cheating on you,' Colin pointed out. 'Just man up and apologise and get on with your life. You and I both know you're not that same idiot anymore. So stop acting like it.'

A long, deep sigh on Rob's end. 'Friends are supposed to commiserate, you know.'

'Frankly, I have nothing to commiserate about,' Colin said cheerfully.

Angela returned his tentative smile with one of her own.

'Yet,' Rob added.

'Party pooper,' Colin shot back.

Rob chortled. 'Only returning the favour, mate! You needed a reality check just as badly I did. I'll text her an apology later. Someone needs to drop more groceries her way and I'm hoping that'll stop her saying passive-aggressive shit when I knock next time. Do you need anything? I'm going to end up with a giant batch of the piña colada mix. I always make too much of the stuff.'

'*Noooo*, no more alcohol,' Colin said at the same time that Angela began shaking her head furiously. 'I'm not as young as I used to be.'

'Col, age has got nothing to do with it—even my oldest customers can drink you under the table,' Rob said, a smirk painting his words. 'Catch you later.'

The call ended and Colin shoved his phone back into his pocket.

'Wow,' Angela said.

Colin looked pensive. 'Yeah. Rob was the only one who welcomed me here two years ago, so I've really hung onto him. I was drinking alone at his bar when he took pity on me. He's come a long way since then, but he's a bit stuck up his own bum sometimes.'

'At least he's improving?'

'I wouldn't have stayed friends with him otherwise,' Colin assured her. He hesitated, as if noticing the nightie for the first time. 'I guess I should let you have a lie-in.'

'The horse for *that* has bolted too.' Angela flailed her legs, knocking the duvet off him. 'Impromptu pyjama party?'

'You're the only one in pyjamas,' he pointed out.

'Pillow fight, then?'

He eyed her end of the mattress. 'You're the only one with pillows.'

'I fail to see how this is my problem,' Angela said, grinning.

'I think it's time for a tactical retreat,' Colin decided and ran for the door.

But he wasn't fast enough to avoid the pillow that bounced off his backside.

'Direct hit!' Angela howled after him.

***

Day Eight

Angela peered around the edge of the sofa, clutching a pillow to her chest while she gauged the danger of the situation. Her phone remained on the floor beside her knee. It was on speaker, obviously, since she needed both hands free in order to survive Pillow Fight #1 (according to today's to-do list). Her head cleared the corner—and Colin's missile immediately slammed into her face. Angela tumbled backwards.

'I take it you're losing,' Ishani's voice said, full of exactly zero surprise.

Angela bit down hard on a grumpy retort and threw her pillow across the room. She then scuttled to the other end of the sofa, hooking her foot around her phone and moving it closer in the process. Alright, maybe she shouldn't have been bragging on the phone to Ishani about her pillow-fighting abilities last night. Especially since Colin had been within earshot at the time.

'I'm sure it's just a momentary setback!' Colin called, parroting Angela from earlier, when she'd realised that he'd ordered an entire box of pillows. Expedited shipping.

Bernard had aided and abetted Colin by bringing them up from the ground floor, where the courier had insisted on leaving them. Signatures and close-contact deliveries were a thing of the past now. As was compassion, evidently, since Bernard had looked inside the box and outright laughed as he told Angela through the door that Colin meant business.

'But I'm on Team Angela!' Bernard had promised, which raised all sorts of questions about his recent intake of pop culture. Maybe the lack of cricket was to blame.

'You better be on Team Angela,' she whispered into her phone.

Ishani's laugh was still hoarse, but it was noticeably improving.

'Not a chance. The odds Rob offered on you were too long for me to bite.'

Angela hissed and ducked as another of Colin's missiles grazed her hair. For someone who claimed to be a novice, he was scarily good at this. She swiped the pillow and sent it back. His laughter told her that she'd missed. Again.

'Are you still mad at Rob?' Angela asked distractedly. 'I know what happened. He deserves every bit of ire you can throw his way. He was an utter lout.'

'Lout is such a polite word,' Ishani mused.

'Bastard!' Angela bit out and rolled as another pillow went flying her way. She barely avoided it. Colin's chuckle only incensed her further.

But now she had more ammunition, thanks to him.

'Yeah, that's more like it, that was my name for Rob until yesterday.' Ishani kept up her side of the conversation, completely unfazed. 'He actually apologised. Was even respectful when I turned him down after he suggested we make a second go of it.'

'What! He made a pass at you!?' Angela exclaimed, hurling the pillow at Colin. He tried to contort himself into a safe position behind the coffee table, but her aim was true this time. The throw connected.

This left her with exactly zero pillows.

Oh shit.

'Well, I am pretty hot,' Ishani said with a snort. 'And he did back off, which I didn't expect from him. Not even sure I know this version of Rob Chance. No more bitching and moaning or mooching about like an incel. Complete and utter alien, I tell you.'

Angela grabbed her phone and dived for the safety of the kitchen, which she was allowed to use as a pit stop once every five minutes. She collapsed onto the floor well shy of the saloon doors. Rubbing her sore elbow, Angela gasped out, 'Or maybe Rob's matured? Stranger things have happened.'

'Ha!' Ishani snorted. 'I wouldn't go that far. Alien it is.'

Colin's next shot took out Angela's phone. She tried to save it from the floor, in case it got stepped on, but accidentally swiped the red button on the screen, hanging up on Ishani.

Angela growled. This meant war. Well, more war anyway.

She rolled and rolled towards the nearest pillow, this one shaped like a boomerang instead of a rectangle. She was so sure she'd make it—until she collided with Colin's ankles. He wasn't wearing any slippers, because apparently this was classed as 'exercise', but he *was* wearing a cheeky grin that suggested he knew exactly who the winner of this engagement was going to be.

Angela fled, rolling in the other direction.

He immediately gave chase, though his triumphant laugh was cut short when he tripped on one of the pillows he'd lobbed across the room earlier. He went down hard.

'Bother, that hurt!' Colin said, swearing like a little old lady. The wall closest to him thudded angrily, followed by real expletives being shouted by the next-door neighbour. Colin shot them one-fingered salute, which they couldn't see, and shouted, 'Sorry!'

Angela attempted to tumble back out of range, but ended up plastered against the front door.

She wasn't allowed out into the corridor for six more days.

Nowhere to go. No escape.

Colin approached her, unhurried and similarly unarmed. There was no point in continuing the war when he was the clear victor. The gloating would start any second now.

Angela was surprised when he dropped onto his hands and knees to look her over. 'Are you hurt?'

'Not physically.' Angela sighed. 'Just my pride, my dignity, my social standing…'

She trailed off as he sidled up from her feet, until his face was in line with hers and his elbows were braced on either side of her. His warmth seeped through her clothes, her skin, her soul; she wondered if she could actually absorb him. This definitely wasn't a tactic to keep her from grabbing another pillow. If Colin tried to say it was, she knew he'd be lying.

That stupid, sexy smirk of his made an appearance. 'So, did I win this one?'

Angela arched an eyebrow. 'What do you think?'

Not really an answer, if she was honest, and more of a way to buy time, to figure out what to do and what to think, because her heart felt like it was about to explode out of her ribcage.

Oh. Oh *no*.

This was a compromising position if ever she'd seen one.

And she rather liked it.

'This wouldn't happen to be a good time for a kiss, would it?' Colin asked.

'If this was a romance novel, absolutely,' Angela replied, embarrassed to hear that her voice seemed to have dropped an octave.

She waited for her phone to ring, for a message to come through, for Ishani to save her from this ridiculous situation. But her phone remained stubbornly silent and the tension in the room was growing thicker by the second.

'So…' she said nervously. 'Are we going to kiss?'

'But this is real life, not a novel,' Colin teased.

'Colin!'

He slowly bent his head down to hers, his breath playing along her lips—she had moistened them with her tongue at some point, though she had no idea when or why. That mystery was rendered unimportant the moment he kissed her. It was chaste, far too brief, almost like a question, and he drew back to meet her eyes with his, waiting for her answer.

Angela was more than willing to give it to him.

Her fingers trailed along his clean-shaven jaw and then down his neck, to where cotton met skin. He was wearing the *Rio* shirt. Her favourite. That inconsequential detail struck her as utterly perfect.

Colin was still poised above her. He wasn't moving, just drinking her in, like she was the oasis he'd always been searching for, lost among an endless sea of sand for countless aeons. Oh wow. Poetic much?

She really needed to stop thinking. She wanted to enjoy this.

Angela hooked her hand around the nape of his neck and pulled him back down.

He dutifully followed and delivered a deeper, slower kiss that caused her heart to pump even harder. Angela closed her eyes, inhaling his cedar scent, devouring the taste of the chai tea he'd had earlier. The kiss never seemed to end. Eternity had come to a small flat in Newfield.

It was beautiful. It was everything.

And it felt like a promise, that what they had brewing between them would only get stronger with each steeping.

28

Day Nine

Colin's mouth was moving and he knew the words he was supposed to be saying, but he couldn't seem to hear them. His secondary monitor rapidly blurred as new comments appeared in the hashtag, his tens of thousands of listeners desperate to know more, desperate to *hear* more.

He couldn't blame them. His and Angela's alter egos were awkwardly avoiding each other after a night of passion, which could only be referred to in PG terms (to please Leo, of course) but Angela had left just the right amount of gaps in the story for people to fill in themselves (blush-inducing fanart had started appearing, which pleased Leo even more).

Colin couldn't help but wonder when Angela had come up with this particular gem. Before or after? Before or after their earth-shattering kiss?

And did it in any way inspire today's segment?

Colin wet his lips. His listeners weren't complaining about him spouting gibberish, so he should be alright for now. He just needed to stick to the bullet points. He could do that. This little performance had nothing to do with the 'real life' that Angela insisted on them having out of earshot of the Radio SPLATZAPP! hordes—they hadn't done the horizontal tango for one, and they weren't avoiding or dancing around each other like their radio counterparts were.

Heck, he'd even kissed her goodnight at her door.

It was supposed to have been a chaste peck, but the kiss had somehow turned into something deliciously slow and long. He'd been tempted to ask if he could come in for the good old Netflix and chill. It wasn't like she needed permission from her roommate.

Then again…there was Wills, the most judgemental toy Colin had ever laid eyes on. Not that he'd admit to backing off because he was worried about the opinion of a *stuffed bat*.

'So there you have it.' Colin tuned back in when he realised he was reaching the end of Angela's bullet points. 'It's a complete and utter disaster, without recovery, and she's definitely going to find some way to move out now. Which means this segment is over. For good. And I'm never going to talk—or think—about Number Twelve ever again. I swear.'

His listeners rightly called him out on that.

Grinning, Colin checked the time and saw that he had fifteen seconds left to play with. 'I mean it. I do.' He let the pause build, just long enough that it supplied tension instead of dead air. 'Okay, fine. Watch this space. Not that anything is going to happen in said space. In the meantime, you can listen to some Harry Styles. Why did no one tell me he'd belted out something as epic as "Sign of the Times"?'

Would u have listened tho old timer #splatzapp was one swift answer.

Colin couldn't argue with that. If Angela hadn't stepped in and updated his music tastes…his listeners would have kept complaining and Leo would have fired him.

Angela had really turned his life around—and turned it upside down at the same time.

It was her fault he'd opened a Spotify account and definitely her fault that he had moved on from simple covers to songs with lyrics that weren't any older than the spotless new hand towel hanging up in the bathroom (courtesy of a deep dive in the linen cupboard). The previous towel had been so ratty that Angela had taken it upon herself to hang his shirts on the railing as a not-so subtle hint.

At least she hadn't threatened the *Rio* shirt.

Probably because she couldn't keep her hands off him when he wore it.

'I ship it too,' Colin muttered under his breath as he scrolled through his Twitter feed. '*I ship it*' was a popular comment among his listeners these days. 'But why are some of you so obsessed with our star signs?'

Come to think of it, he had no idea when Angela's birthday was.

He stood and walked over to his door, kicking it open. Just as he'd predicted, Angela was scribbling away on the sofa, a steaming mug of tea in front of her.

She glanced up at him. 'What have your listeners done this time?'

'Why would this have anything to do with them?' Colin asked before he could stop himself, drawn right into her trap. He couldn't think of anywhere else he'd rather be.

'Colin,' Angela said flatly. 'Your arms are swaying as if you want to deck someone.'

'Something else might be annoying me,' he tried, but it was moot. She knew him too well.

'What happened?' she pressed.

Colin quickly fastened his arms to his sides—where they stayed for about two seconds before going right back to swaying.

'They're trying to guess our star signs,' he told her.

Angela pursed her lips. 'That's not a bad idea for a segment.'

'Horoscopes? No way. I can't use that rubbish in my show. That's Peter's thing.'

'Colin.' Angela set aside her notebook and pushed her glasses back up her nose with one finger. 'People don't want surprises in a time that's full to the brim with them—and those haven't been very good surprises, I might add. This year's been an utter train wreck.'

'What's that got to do with horoscopes?' Colin demanded. 'Wait. Is this a trope thing?'

'Certain star signs are more compatible than others,' Angela explained. 'I can use this as a way to show that our two lovers are destined for each other. Your listeners will eat it up, because it's like comfort food. It'll reassure them. There are no surprises coming. Just the HEA—or HFN, depending on whether or not you want a sequel. So yes, it's a "trope thing".'

'HEA? HFN?' he repeated.

Angela smiled. 'Happily Ever After. Happily For Now.'

'Oh.' Colin paused, then grinned. 'No sequels, thanks. I like the sound of the HEA.'

'I thought you might. So what are you?'

'What...' Colin trailed off, confused.

'What's your star sign?' she asked patiently.

'Sagittarius. I think. Yeah, that's me. Sagittarius.'

'Perfect,' Angela said, swiping her fingers across her phone. 'I'm a Taurus. According to the Internet, we're either very well-suited or a terrible, terrible match. Okay. We'll have our counterparts on opposite sides of the argument. It's time they found something to talk about, since they'll have been avoiding each other for almost two days post-coitus by the next show. I'll start sketching out some ideas now.'

Angela set her phone down and flipped to a fresh page in her notebook. Her pen whisked across the paper as she sank into her work, completely oblivious to the effect her words had had on him. Colin knew he shouldn't be thinking about pre- or post-coitus, or anything in between, but his stupid brain had gone there in a heartbeat.

'Right,' he said in a strangled voice and edged away from her. He knew he didn't have long before he was needed on the mic, because the sponsor ads had started and there weren't any songs queued up after them. Colin only made it halfway to his room before he abruptly spun back around. 'Wait. You're a Taurus.'

Her pen never wavered. 'Yes, I believe we've just established that.'

'Angela, I don't have time for sexy banter, I'm back on in a minute,' Colin said tightly. 'Your birthday. Did it happen already?'

He didn't have much left of Taurus to play with. He was hoping she wasn't a mid-April baby or he'd have missed it. Judging by the fact that she actually set her pen down and arched a playful eyebrow at him, he was suddenly sure that he hadn't.

'No,' Angela said, confirming his suspicions. 'It's on the last day before we're out of quarantine. No wild parties in this day and age, unfortunately. Not that I did those in the first place. You kind of need friends for that and I haven't had any decent ones until recently. Why do you ask? Are you going to *plan* something?'

'I just might,' Colin told her and shut his door.

It occurred to him, as he sat down and grabbed his headphones, that he might have bounced all the way back to his chair.

***

Day Ten

'It's alarming to be thinking this so early on in our relationship, but I'm starting to feel like I could have her as my roommate for the rest of my life,' Colin said, twirling his fingers through the cord of his headphones. 'Today the question we pulled out of the hat got us sharing our favourite dinosaur movies and she said hers was *We're Back! A Dinosaur's Story*. I've never met anyone else who knew about that one, let alone loved it. We're scarily compatible, her dislike of *Magnum PI* notwithstanding.'

His listeners, in varying states of exhaustion and annoyance, did not stay silent for long.

'Compatible—is this about horoscopes?' Peter asked tiredly.

'What! No!' Colin said, exiting the tabs in his browser window with the finesse of a teenager lurking on Pornhub. It was a good thing the camera on his phone was aimed at him instead of his computer monitors. He *was* looking up horoscopes.

The Love Doctor's eyes narrowed. 'That's a relief. Because, Colin, you need a damn good excuse for expecting us to join a Zoom meeting on a Saturday evening.'

'How about the fact that we're friends?' Colin tried. 'Not just work colleagues?'

Sunshine beamed, apparently flattered. Although, this might have more to do with the fact that for once she wasn't trying to corral her brood of grandchildren, though no explanation had been forthcoming when Danger had suspiciously asked her what had happened to them.

'*Friends*,' Danger repeated, once more in the dressing gown. There was vague chatter in the background; he was in the middle of a Humphrey Bogart marathon. Colin had never heard of Humphrey

Bogart fighting an octopus, but Danger had held the camera up to his laptop to prove that such a scene did exist. 'Friends...yeah, alright. I could use a few of those, especially Lefties. Need to make sure people know I have balanced opinions around me.'

'Around you but not in your own head, hmm?' Peter said.

Colin was sure Danger would have retorted if he hadn't seen the cat behind Peter yawn widely. Colin was shocked to see it move himself.

'It's nice to have adult friends in a time like this,' Sunshine added. 'All of my conversations these days are about who should be on solids, and who knows how to use the potty but is pretending they can't so they can poo their pants while watching *Frozen*. Again.'

Danger's whole face twisted.

'Perhaps a moratorium on poop?' Peter suggested and darted a look up at his cat. 'I myself am tired of that subject.'

Sunshine's camera winked off.

'I am sorry, Sunshine,' Peter said hurriedly.

Her disembodied voice was quick to reassure him. 'No, no, it's fine. But my grandson is a bit camera-shy and he wants to come in for a goodnight kiss before Pop puts him down. Mr Sunshine's back home. He quit his job as a lorry driver and isolated himself for fourteen days, to make sure he wasn't bringing any nasties with him. So lovely to have him around again.'

Colin smiled into his mug of tea. The piping-hot caffeine was exactly what he needed to clear his head while skimming the bullet points Angela had written for Monday's show. Horoscopes were silly, but he liked what she'd done with the concept. And he was looking up star signs for *research*, to make sure his ad-libbing was smoother. No other reason. Definitely not to see if their relationship was headed for a fiery explosion.

'Angela made that tea for you, didn't she?' Danger accused.

Colin didn't bother to deny it.

'She has you so whipped,' Danger said, eyeing Colin's mug. 'I don't know why you haven't told Leo this thing has gone from fiction to fact, since Leo would stop badgering you to make it sound more authentic.'

'Shh,' Sunshine's voice said.

'What?' Danger demanded. 'As Danika is so fond of reminding me, Leo won't hear us just because we mention his name. He's not Bloody Mary. But I can bring it up myself at the next meeting, if Col lacks the balls.'

Sunshine turned her camera back on and gave Danger a very pointed look. She continued to swipe her fingers over the iPad in front of her, excelling at some brightly-coloured game that looked like it was designed for her grandchildren (except Colin was fairly certain it had microtransactions that made it unsafe for little fingers).

'Danger,' Sunshine said calmly. 'If Leo gets wind of Colin and Angela *actually* dating, he will be a certified nightmare. He'll make a whole song and dance out of it and advertise Colin's show as somewhere that people can make genuine love connections. Colin does not have the experience for something like that.'

Peter cleared his throat. 'And my reputation might take something of a hit. Love connections are supposed to fall under my jurisdiction.'

'You're all idiots,' Danika said, suddenly appearing. Her screen had been dark for days but she'd still responded to every Zoom invitation, which suggested that she had been listening to all of their meetings, professional or otherwise. Colin had hoped she would say something at some point.

Apparently his predicament was what she'd been waiting for.

Danika eyed her camera, as if daring them to ask how she was.

Behind her was a painting that depicted the sun set against space, but there were petals surrounding it instead of rays of light. It was the best piece of hers Colin had ever seen.

He hadn't realised how much they'd all missed her, how unbalanced their conversations had been without her presence—until now.

'The main issue,' Danika said, once she was certain she wouldn't be interrupted, 'is that Angela wants this thing with Colin to be kept off the air. To make it more *real*. I think that's the gist of it, anyway. It's hard to remember all of Colin's rambling, isn't it? I already know what's going to happen, though. Leo will push for more authenticity, our Col will cave, and the segment will suddenly be about his real relationship, not the fake one.'

'I wouldn't do that to her,' Colin protested.

'You absolutely would if you thought your job was in danger. Or are you going to argue with a grieving daughter?'

Colin wasn't sure if she was joking or not. He held his tongue.

'I thought so,' Danika said with a triumphant nod of her head. 'Look, who gives a toss about Leo? Angela is the one who makes you happy. So make her happy. Geez, Col. It really is that simple. We'll keep your secret from Leo. But you've got to do your part too.'

'Radio silence, then,' Peter confirmed.

'But does it even matter when she'll leave him the moment he tells her why he invited her to stay in the first place?' Danger asked.

Danika pursed her lips for several long moments.

'It matters,' she decided. 'Because it shows growth on Colin's part. She might not forgive him for using her as Daily Inspo, but his actions since then will prove to her that he's changed and deserves a second chance. You are worth sticking around for, right, Col?'

Colin's stomach clenched. 'Yes! I want to make her happy.'

Danger tilted his sunglasses down to peer at Colin in disbelief. '*Riiight.* Even if it means losing your job?'

'Yes, of course!' Peter exclaimed.

'I wasn't asking you!' Danger told The Love Doctor. 'You know Leo's riding him hard about the segment not sounding real enough. He'll cave and incorporate bits of his own domestic bliss next week just to get Leo off his back. You just watch!'

Colin supposed he should have said goodbye before abruptly disconnecting from the meeting.

He was sure they'd got the wrong idea about why he did it.

29

Day Eleven

Angela stared up at the blanket hanging dangerously close to her nose. She wasn't in bed and she wasn't trying to sleep. Nope, this was part of The Plan.

'What else were we going to do with all those pillows?' Colin asked from beside her.

They were lying on their backs inside the pillow-and-blanket fort that had resulted from the morning's scheduled activity. They'd fallen into a regular pattern of Colin coming up with silly ideas the night before and both of them enacting those ideas during the day. Angela was happy to go along with it all. Fourteen days of self-isolation would have been too much for her otherwise—boredom aside, she wasn't sure she'd have written quite so much of her book's first draft without these scheduled breaks.

'This was an excellent idea,' Angela said, then grinned wickedly at her companion. 'Although, if you wanted to have a snog, you really didn't need to go to this much trouble. All you had to do was ask.'

Colin swiped his bare wrist in front of him. 'Would you look at the time! We need to pull a question out of the hat.'

'Did you seriously bring that in with you?' Angela asked, watching as he retrieved the hat from behind the nearest column of pillows.

'It's three o'clock,' he defended. 'We always do this at three o'clock.'

'So you're willing to stick to The Plan if it means missing out on something else?'

Colin visibly swallowed. 'I'm trying very hard not to think about something else.'

Oh. *Oh.*

'And I'd much rather wait until we're no longer locked in here together before we do...' Colin glanced aside at her. '...something else.'

'No disagreement here,' Angela said, trying to ignore the traitorous spark that had set up shop between her thighs. 'Go on, then. Hit me with a question or a discussion topic. I can't imagine there are many of them left in there.'

'You'd think that, given my predilection for winging it, but I deliberately wrote too many of them so I wouldn't be able to guess what was left.' Colin reached into the hat and pinched a piece of paper between his fingers. His eyes flicked over the words. 'Pick two people, one alive and one dead, that you wouldn't mind being stuck with right now.'

'What exactly is this supposed to reveal about our personalities?' Angela wondered. 'Did you google "worst questions to ask on a work retreat" or something?'

Colin gave her a look. She made a poor attempt at stifling her laugh.

Ducking the pillow he lobbed at her, Angela decided to humour him.

'Dead, it'd be Mrs Benson for sure—Em's mum,' she said. 'I could really use her advice. Alive? Tough one. I want to say Ishani, but our friendship is really new and I'm sure I would have said or done something by now to permanently aggravate her. Relationships can die horribly in close quarters such as these.'

'Yes, yes they can,' Colin said, sounding a fraction nervous.

'Colin, we've survived eleven days so far,' Angela said, shunting her shoulder against his. 'Let's not give up now. So, alive? It'd be you, cheesy as it sounds. Your turn.'

Her cheeks felt so warm they had to be irradiated and her stomach seemed to be stuffed full of bees. A comfortable *something* was growing between them. She definitely liked whatever it was, but she was afraid to get used to it. What would happen after Day Fourteen? Would they still be able to stand the sight of each other?

'Let me guess,' Angela said, interrupting her thoughts before they flew past quarantine and into a hazy, distant future. 'Your dead guest would be a frontman who was popular in the 1980s. But which one? My bet's on Freddie Mercury. Not quite New Wave, but…'

'Definitely my first choice,' Colin agreed.

'And living?'

Colin cleared his throat, no doubt sensing the trap. 'There really is only one answer, isn't there.'

'Yep,' Angela said with a laugh.

'Well then. Myself.'

'What!' she exclaimed. 'Take this seriously, please. Like I did.'

'I'm alive, aren't I?' he mused.

'Your clone isn't, though! Ughh, Colin!' She grabbed the nearest pillow and whacked him, causing the column she'd taken it from to list alarmingly. Some of the blanket caved in and she made a big show of lowering herself closer to the carpet to avoid it. But it was obvious that she didn't need to brace herself on Colin's chest. Or move her lips quite so near his, which were clearly forming some sort of rebuttal.

She kissed him. That seemed to settle the matter.

'Alright, alright,' he said with a long, drawn-out sigh. 'You. I'd want to be stuck in here with you.'

'Even if there's not going to be any funny business?' she asked.

Colin's eyes gleamed. 'Well, if we just stick to snogging…that shouldn't be too dangerous, should it? So long as it doesn't become *something else*.'

'That a challenge?'

'It might be.'

Several minutes later, they emerged from the fort with stupid grins on their faces. Only one of them, however, bore a more obvious piece of evidence. Angela burst out laughing when she saw the love bite she'd left on Colin. He wasted no time in dashing off to the bathroom to confirm his suspicions in the mirror.

'My hair isn't long enough to cover this,' he complained when he returned.

'Who's going to see it?' Angela asked.

'Quarantine is over in three days! I might be lucky for it to have faded by then, but…no. This can't happen again.'

'Oh? It can't?'

Colin's lips compressed into a thin, thin line. 'That is another trap and I refuse to answer.'

'Suit yourself,' Angela said and shot a quick look at the piece of paper Blu-Tacked to the wall. 'It seems I have to do some solid work on my book while you clean the toilet and then get tea ready. I hope you've procured something better than a ploughman's disaster, like last night.'

'Ploughman's lunch,' Colin corrected.

'No, Colin. *That* was a disaster involving unappetising leftovers. But...' Angela tipped her head to the side, considering. 'I will admit that the Shreddies provided an adequate crunch in lieu of actual crackers. Tonight's plan for dinner must be pretty good. That's the only excuse I can think of for yesterday's paltry offering.'

Colin grinned. 'You'll just have to wait and see.'

***

'Didn't want you to miss tonight's disaster,' Colin said from her doorway three hours later.

'Oh God, my back,' Angela groaned.

She slowly straightened out of the awkward position she'd adopted while writing on unlined A4 sheets pressed against the front cover of her notebook (now extremely full). Arrayed in front of her were pages and pages of notes, some of them opening lines and many of them the final scene of the novel that had made so much more sense in her head before she had tried to transfer it onto paper.

Colin held out a bowl with two slabs of bread—crusty end pieces, both of them—hanging off the edge. He looked apologetic, though not about the food as she soon discovered. 'Sorry. I really should have let you use my desk. Or you could order one in.' When she hesitated, he added, 'I won't stop you. I'd rather avoid your trademark grumpiness if I can help it, not that I don't find it strangely attractive at times. A back that doesn't ache will make you a much more pleasant roommate, don't you think?'

Oh. That was…a lot for her to unpack.

If he wanted to bring in furniture for her, did that mean this wasn't a temporary arrangement anymore? That was practically commitment, wasn't it? And commitment meant that the snogging wouldn't take long to graduate into something else. Oh God. When was the last time she'd had her IUD replaced? She cast her mind back a couple of years and exhaled lengthily. Whew. She was still good.

Angela tried to ignore the sudden flutter of anticipation. 'A desk? We'll see. What culinary delight do you have for me this time?'

'One of my best,' Colin assured her, which wasn't worrying. Not at all. 'I found a tin of diced tomatoes so I put them on the stove with some curry powder. I even managed to scrape just enough butter out of the container for the bread.'

'I'm not sure if that's a stroke of genius or incredibly lazy,' Angela told him.

Colin shrugged. '¿Por que no los dos?'

'Hand it over and I'll decide. Have you had yours already or do you want to join me in this world-class restaurant?'

'If there's a free table,' Colin said.

'I don't have any tables. Or even a chair, which I'll need if a desk is forthcoming.' Angela gestured vaguely around the room. 'You'll have to pull up a piece of carpet.'

'I don't even rate a spot on the mattress?'

'Not with those slippers you don't! Didn't you only just start wearing those less than a week ago? How do they smell so bad already?'

He kicked them off so vigorously they hit the wardrobe, causing the mirrored doors to rattle. Angela fell sideways off the mattress, clutching her midsection and gasping for breath. It wasn't even that funny, but the expression on his *face*.

'I'm really glad I'm not renting,' Colin said after a moment.

'Have you ever caused so much damage that you lost your deposit?' Angela asked, genuinely curious. 'Wait, what am I saying. You've probably never rented in your entire life.'

He tsked. 'Assume at your peril. I might add that question to the hat, actually.'

'Oh no you don't. You are *not* going to find out about my sordid rental history. I'm good. No need to add that question.'

'I can't imagine you lost your deposit in a particularly creative way,' Colin said.

Ughh. He was right. But Angela thought it would be nice to have some mystery floating about her.

'Sit down and eat,' she commanded.

Smirking, probably because he knew he'd won that round, Colin deposited the bowl into her hands and retrieved another from the kitchen before joining her on the mattress. Both of them sat up against the wall, their knees touching, eating their dinner together in silence.

Angela contemplated her furniture options while she shovelled diced tomatoes into her mouth. She was still skint, but she'd managed to scrape together a few quid since her benefits weren't currently being eaten up by rent or utilities. She could afford an IKEA desk and chair set, something cheap but hopefully serviceable. And then she'd change the dirty beige curtains, maybe find some blue fabric covered in stars. She might even buy a matching duvet. Add in some tasteful storage baskets...

Angela's breath caught. She was making plans and she knew what that meant. She wanted to stay. Permanently. But how was she supposed to mention this? She couldn't assume that he'd agree to it.

'So if I'm allowed a desk, does that mean I'll also get a wardrobe?'

she asked in what she hoped was an offhand way. Totally not asking for a commitment of any kind.

Colin's eyes darted to the mirrored doors. 'Hmm. Yes. All in good time.'

'What on Earth have you got stashed in there anyway?' Angela demanded, wishing she wasn't quite so annoyed but unable to help it. It was entirely possible that her hint had flown right over his gravity-defying hair. 'Drugs?'

'No! Not drugs.'

But he didn't expand on that. Just looked very hard at the window, as if he could teleport himself onto the grass outside if he concentrated hard enough.

Angela swallowed another mouthful of tomato-soaked bread and waited for the curry powder to kick in. There it was. His improvised dinner was actually kind of genius, but she'd never tell him that. Not while he was keeping secrets from her. He didn't deserve the compliment.

'Looking forward to your birthday on Wednesday?' Colin asked.

'That's an abrupt change of topic.'

'Yes, it is,' he agreed, still staring out the window.

Angela had a feeling she wouldn't win this one. She'd just have to accept that he didn't trust or know her well enough to gift her this nugget of information.

Wow. She didn't really know him either, did she?

Shredded pieces of paper with questions written on them hadn't solved that.

'So?' Colin prompted, looking adorably hopeful, especially with his hair in its usual state of disarray. Did he even own a comb? She doubted it. And yet somehow, against her better judgement, she didn't mind. Her fingers itched to slide through his hair—like they'd done this morning, when he'd pressed up behind her while she was stacking their bowls in the drying rack. It had been impossible to stop herself reaching back to touch him. Then he'd turned her around into a kiss that had swiftly wiped clean the memories of her soggy, unappealing cereal…

Angela realised that he was waiting for an answer. Apparently catching on to her confusion, Colin clarified, 'Are you excited about my plans for your birthday?'

Oh. He wasn't asking her if she knew him. Well, that was a relief. She didn't have to lie.

'A little,' Angela admitted. 'I feel a bit like a kid the week before Christmas.'

'I guess the Santa suit had a bigger impression on you than I realised. I can wear it on Wednesday, if you'd like?' Colin added a suggestive wink.

Angela shuddered and set aside her bowl. 'Argh. Please don't sully my childhood in that manner. By the way, that change of topic wasn't as smooth as you think. Stop looking so smug! I guess the secret of the wardrobe can wait. I trust that's it not something illegal and/or creepy. But Colin? If it's a portal to Narnia, I'll be very annoyed that you kept it from me. That previous grumpiness will be nothing compared to what I'll hit you with.'

Colin's face went ashen.

'It does go to Narnia, I bloody knew it,' Angela said.

Just as she'd hoped, the tension between them immediately dissipated. He even smiled. 'You got me. It's a portal to Narnia. Don't trust any strangers who pop out of it and offer you Turkish Delight. Now, there aren't any activities pencilled in for tonight, but…'

Angela indicated the piles of paper beside her. 'I think I might actually work. I'm trying to outline my way through the mid-novel slump and I want to get it done before I go to bed or I won't sleep. At all.'

'I won't intrude any longer then. But I'll pop my head in later to say goodnight.'

Colin leaned over and snagged her bowl, his lips darting across hers.

'Just a bit of inspiration for your book,' he said, throwing her yet another wink as he jumped off the floor.

Angela tried not to check out his backside in those skinny jeans of his.

She didn't try very hard.

30

Day Twelve

All of the paper was missing. And so was the Blu Tack.

Colin peered down into his mug of tea, which was stone cold from being left out on the kitchen bench all night. It was herbal tea, a citrus type, so he could be forgiven for reattempting it. He wondered if he should wait for Angela to bring him something hot and caffeinated. His usual Zoom meeting was due to start any minute.

Maybe she was still asleep. He couldn't expect her to make him tea every morning.

Colin looked around the living room again. This time he saw the tiny scrap of paper stuck to the wall. Impossibly neat handwriting proclaimed The Plan for the day: *Angela is busy working. Colin can do what he wants.*

Mutely, Colin went back into the kitchen and made an entire pot of tea, using that insanely strong brew she kept in a tin on the bench.

He knocked on her door after he'd tested the tea and found it appropriately bitter.

'What?' Angela demanded.

'I made you tea,' Colin said.

A big sigh. 'Thank God and thank Colin. Leave it outside the door and I'll rescue it in a minute.'

'It comes with a kiss if you rescue it now,' Colin baited, feeling a touch ridiculous—but only until the door opened and a hand yanked him in.

***

Day Thirteen

'Oh my God,' Angela groaned. 'What year is it?'

'Still the Year of the Plague, unfortunately,' Colin supplied.

Angela slapped the carpet around her until she found her glasses and grimaced when she saw the smudges her fingers had left on the lenses. She hoped to be able to locate her phone just as easily. No such luck. But at least she'd finally figured out where she was. For some reason, she had passed out on the living room floor, though it seemed she had made herself comfortable inside a nest of pillows at some point. Empty mugs formed a trail towards the saloon doors—and Colin's slippered feet.

Angela rubbed her forehead. 'Ughh. You'd think that if I felt this awful, I'd have slept long enough for the pandemic to have passed us by. What's the time anyway?'

'Nearly time for my show,' Colin said.

Angela bolted upright. 'Oh God. I did the segment, didn't I?'

He kept his expression solemn, clearly building up the suspense, and laughed when she threw him an impatient scowl. 'Yes, you slid it under my door last night and said not to disturb you, especially since you'd already wasted enough time writing for me when you had your own writing to do.'

'That was a bit rude of me,' Angela mused. 'I must have been really tired. Not that being completely awake has ever stopped me being rude before—isn't that what you were about to say?'

Colin hovered there at the saloon doors, looking torn.

'What?' Angela asked.

'The serial is getting in the way of you finishing your book,' he said.

'Don't worry, I'll keep typing up those bullet points for you,' Angela promised, trying not to feel too hurt when she saw the relief flash across his face. She wasn't sure why it bothered her so much. She knew what he expected from her. 'I can't believe we made it to the end of quarantine without killing each other.'

Colin slid her that easy smirk. 'There's still tomorrow to get through.'

'Argh. My birthday. You'd better make it a good one, Colin, because it's hard to get excited at my ripe old age. Thirty-one is practically over the hill.'

'I'll do my best,' he said. 'But I should warn you, I'm more than over the hill myself.'

'I always did have a thing for older men,' Angela said with a laugh.

***

Day Fourteen

It was midnight when the realisation hit him, like a punch to the gut.

Colin was out of his room in four strides, but forced himself to slow down just shy of Angela's door. All he could hear was silence.

He carefully turned the knob and inched the door open, pausing halfway to take in the scene in front of him. It looked like a tornado had blasted through her room when he hadn't been paying attention. Colin almost laughed.

Angela, the epicentre of the carnage, was curled up on her side with the duvet twisted around her ankles. Piles of paper were scattered around her, all of it covered in her tiny handwriting. That wasn't unexpected. She preferred to use a pen instead of a keyboard. Colin was fairly certain she hadn't swapped to using her laptop, because the printer was in the living room and it hadn't run all evening. He hadn't heard it spit anything out in the past day, now that he thought about it.

She always printed the next day's bullet points for him.

Either she hadn't remembered to print the segment…or she hadn't written it all.

'Fudge,' Colin muttered and closed the door.

There were only two options. Wake Angela—or write the segment himself.

It was past midnight. Her birthday.

Nodding, decision made, he made some tea and retreated to his room. How hard could it be?

Colin grimaced, immediately wishing he hadn't thought that.

***

'Colin, I trust you are ready for today's show,' Leo said after Colin had yawned for the third time in as many minutes.

'Absolutely,' Colin replied, his eyes roaming over the piece of paper he'd printed off just after 4am. His head ached and his nose tingled, but he was fairly certain he wasn't sick. Both he and Angela had been stuck inside for two weeks with no symptoms whatsoever. He was just tired. So, so, *so* very tired.

'This is the last week you'll be running that segment,' Leo told him, expression stern. 'It's gone on long enough. We need to keep your show fresh, Colin, so end the serial on Friday and be done with it.'

Or else was the usual unspoken refrain.

'Will do,' Colin muttered, feeling an uncomfortable jerk in his navel.

Having to conjure up an entirely new segment by next week was a frankly terrifying prospect and he had no idea how he was going to do it. Angela was definitely too busy to keep helping him with his show.

Leo either didn't notice or chose to ignore Colin's panic. Knowing his boss, it was probably the latter.

Leo quit the meeting, leaving Colin at the mercy of his friends. He was relieved to see that Danika had stuck around. When she had first appeared, she'd mentioned that the livestream of her mother's memorial service had been about as reliable as her mother's cooking. No one had been brave enough to ask her to clarify that statement.

'What are you going to do next week, dear?' Sunshine asked Colin.

He shrugged. 'Not sure. I'll think of something.'

'You won't have your ghostwriter after today!' Danger crowed. 'She'll leave your sorry arse the moment you tell her the truth! You're royally screwed.'

Colin crossed his arms and leaned back in his chair, letting them see just how completely and utterly unbothered he was. 'I managed to write today's part of the serial all by myself, thank you very much. I'm sure I can handle whatever next week has to throw at me.'

'*You* wrote something in advance?' Danika gave her camera a sideways glance, her suspicion as heavy as her eyeliner. 'You're not much of a writer, Col. It's obvious when you fly off into a tangent instead of sticking to Angela's bullet points. Not to the listeners or Leo, maybe, but *we* notice.'

Peter stroked his chin, looking troubled. 'We should reserve judgement until we hear what he's come up with.'

Colin made sure to experience 'technical difficulties' before they could ask too many questions—anxiety had already turned his stomach into a washing machine. He definitely didn't need them adding to the turbulent load.

Colin popped out of his room a couple of times after that, to use the lavatory and to brew up some tea. A quick peek on both occasions confirmed that Angela was still asleep (and still comfortably snug under the duvet, which he'd needed to pull back over her several times during the night).

He hoped she wouldn't sleep through to lunchtime again. He had something planned.

Thanks to Bernard, Colin now had enough flour, eggs, and milk to whip up some pancakes. The whole production wouldn't be quite as fun if she wasn't there to witness it. He wanted everything to be perfect. Okay, so he lacked any syrup. He hoped that butter and jam would suffice. If not, he was sure he could convince her with a kiss. Or two. Or three…

'I'm worried about you, love,' DJ Sunshine said while they waited for her last song to finish before the handover.

'Why's that?' Colin asked. 'I'm obviously plague-free. Not unwell at all.'

Her cheerful disposition vanished in the blink of an eye, Stern Grandmother Mode activated in its place. 'That's not what I meant and you know it.'

'I'm sure I'm fine!'

'And that itself is concerning,' Sunshine said, then sighed. 'I have to sign off in nine seconds. Please don't do something you'll regret, Colin.' Her voice immediately brightened as the song began to fade out. 'I wish I was walking on sunshine up here in Whitby, but it's a bit dreary this morning. Not to worry. I can see plenty of people enjoying themselves on the beach anyway. Never let a tiny cloud stop you, my dears—and here is DJ Coop, who I know you've been hanging out for! His rambles have become a little saucy of late, haven't they?'

Colin smiled. 'It's nice to be wanted. Thanks, Sunshine, it is indeed time for The Late Morning Rambles. Now. I know why everyone's listening today. I know, I know. But to be honest, I feel a little weird about baring my soul to all of you every day. This is terribly personal.'

The hashtag filled with sympathetic comments. His listeners thought he deserved a bit of privacy. Too bad they didn't really care so long as he gave them the goods. And he had no choice but to deliver said goods.

'So, Number Twelve,' Colin mused. 'What can I say about her?'

That you love her most ardently lol #splatzapp, someone suggested.

Well, they weren't wrong.

'I'd better come right out and say it,' Colin said, taking his time, stirring the pot and inviting more snarky comments.

'I'm in love with Danger' #splatzapp, another listener jested.

'Sorry, folks. Danger and I would kill each other if we lived in the same confined space, so you can quit those fantasies.' Colin laughed shortly. 'Look, this is serious, it really is. I love Number Twelve. I really love her. It hit me when we were lying inside a silly pillow-and-blanket fort that we built. No time to argue which is better right now—pillow or blanket forts. Because everyone knows that forts made of both are the best, right?'

That incited a frantic war on Twitter, just as he'd intended.

'But enough about that.' Colin refrained from sighing too deeply; Leo would have his guts for garters if he allowed that much feedback on the microphone. 'So Number Twelve and I have been doing this thing where we pull a question out of a hat everyday, to get to know each other. We've got to pass the time somehow, since we both ended up in legitimate quarantine, which I think I forgot to mention—'

OMG that's why she hasn't bailed yet #splatzapp, a listener exclaimed immediately.

This next part Colin had written out word for word, though it wouldn't sound like it—he'd memorised every line until he was sure he could glide through the segment without revealing that he was reading off the printout in front of him. It was tempting to make pre-writing his segments part of his routine.

'*No*, being forced to stay indoors with Number Twelve for two weeks did not make me fall in love with her,' Colin griped around the grin he couldn't quite temper. 'Maybe it sped things up. I don't know. Anyway, the question we pulled out of the hat the other day was "who would you rather be stuck with in quarantine, alive *and* dead?" So maybe I chose Freddie Mercury for the dead option. But alive? Definitely her. Always her. For the rest of my life. Her.'

His Twitter feed exploded.

Maybe they could hear the truth in his words. Maybe they just didn't care, so long as it gave them the warm and fuzzies. Ha. Leo couldn't take him to task for a lack of authenticity today. Not when his listeners were so worked up. If Colin couldn't think up a new segment good enough to keep him from being fired next week, then at least he was going to go out with a bang. And what a bang it was.

'I love her and I'm going to tell her today,' Colin declared, meaning it. 'Because it's her birthday and I want to make it special. But there's a roadblock. A rather large one, actually.'

I KNEW IT he's in love with Danger, crowed someone in the hashtag—repeatedly.

Colin couldn't help but picture Captain Picard performing a facepalm. He quietly copied the gesture. 'I'm not sure how many of you have been following the Number Twelve saga from day one, but this all started because I wanted to do a good deed. I was running a segment called Daily Inspo and I had to fill it. If I failed to do that, my boss said he would have to make an unpleasant decision about my show. Maybe he meant I'd lose my job. Maybe he meant something more dire. Some inventive new form of punishment. I wouldn't put it past him.'

Some good-natured commentary followed this on social media, mostly from those listeners with cantankerous bosses of their own.

'Anyway,' Colin went on, 'I was staring out my window one morning when I saw Number Twelve on the footpath. She was clearly upset about something, so I decided to go out and check on her. That's worthy of a pat on the back, right? But my boss wanted me to find something big for Daily Inspo, something better than just asking someone if they're okay. Never mind that checking on other people is important right now, but I digress. So where was I going to get that elusive good deed?

'I needn't have worried. Turns out Number Twelve was being evicted. "Great!" I thought. "I'll ask her to move in. This will score

281

me major brownie points." But I didn't expect to want her to stay forever. Or that I'd want to put a ring on it.'

OMG OMG OMG #splatzapp seemed to be the general consensus.

'Have I asked her yet?' Colin echoed the Tweets that immediately followed. 'No. Should I ask her this early on in the game? Probably not. Will I ask her? It's just a matter of time. Frankly, we need to ride out a bit more of this lockdown and make sure we *really* know each other…but it may as well be written in the stars, the cards, and whatever else you want to use to divine the future. This Sagittarius and that Taurus are meant to be.'

The excited chatter on the feed buoyed him, even as it turned into a discussion about his listeners' favourite relationships in other mediums. He and Number Twelve ranked up there with Booth and Bones, apparently. His life was like a TV show to them. Fictional and scripted.

No wonder Angela had wanted to keep their real romance separate. This was kind of creepy.

'But back to that roadblock I mentioned,' Colin reminded his listeners before they could get too carried away. 'Number Twelve thinks I offered to let her stay out of the goodness of my heart. That's not true. I want her to look at me and get exactly what she sees, so it's not a secret I can go on keeping. Not if I want to move forward with our relationship. And I don't want to keep living with this bellyache I get whenever I think she might not want the real me, the slightly selfish me. I have to tell her. Wish me luck.'

Some of his listeners thought he was doomed.

Colin was afraid they were right. But he took courage from the Tweets that praised his honesty. Angela had told him, one night over dinner, that heroes in romance novels with secrets always kept them too long, usually to the detriment of their relationships.

He was hoping to avoid that. She didn't want *drama*.

'I'll update you tomorrow,' Colin said cheerfully. 'Now here's some Freddie Mercury. I'm allowed to play this, folks. He's never gone out of style.'

None of his listeners disagreed with him. Colin smiled and leaned back in his chair.

And then the smile slid right off his lips.

Angela was standing in the doorway, the knob still clenched inside her fist. He had no idea how long she'd been standing there, or how much she'd heard, but the look on her face was downright scary. It definitely wasn't an ecstatic grin.

Colin swallowed.

He wasn't prepared to face the music, but he didn't have a choice.

31

Angela woke with a bang, not a whimper.

Her frantic thrashing caused the duvet to wrap around her like a shroud and her vision gained multiple white spots as she tried to extract herself. Lungs—spasming. Heart—pounding a million times a minute. What the hell was going on? Oh God. The Scourge of the Twenty-First Century. She had it.

Angela groaned and rubbed her eyes with the heels of her palms.

This couldn't be late onset. It couldn't be. Nope, she definitely didn't need to lose her freedom on the last day of quarantine.

Sure, her mouth was dry, but that was because she hadn't had enough non-caffeinated water the night before, right? And the wooziness had to be exhaustion. But what about the boulder-sized dread sitting in her stomach?

For a moment, Angela wondered if she should get tested, but then she realised that what she was feeling was less akin to physical illness and more like the sinking sensation she'd had on a regular basis back in high school. The one that always appeared after she'd woken up from a blissful sleep—only to remember that she hadn't finished an assignment due by her first class.

Oh shit. The segment.

Angela slapped the floor as she rolled off the mattress in the direction of her phone—she was lucky it was sitting on top of a pile of paper instead of buried underneath it. Angela stared down at the screen, eyes burning as she tried to make sense of what she was seeing.

8:59am was the heart-wrenching time displayed in front of her.

'Oh God,' she whispered.

One minute was definitely not enough time to plot out and write the next part of the serial.

'Why didn't you wake me?' Angela growled under her breath.

She hurried out into the living room as soon as she'd managed to throw on her peach-coloured jumper—fresh underwear would have to wait. Even if that decision was followed by instant, unignorable itchiness.

Angela ran to Colin's door, her mind a jumble of words, some of them angry and most of them apologetic—and then drew up short. She could hear his voice, muffled a little by the soundproofing but still discernibly fluid, as it always was whenever he stepped into DJ Coop's shoes.

He was already on the air.

Angela hovered there for several moments, knowing that bursting in right now was something that Leo would look very, very unfavourably upon. She'd never heard of a radio show being interrupted by a roommate before, and the sudden visions of her going viral and becoming the soundtrack to a million comedic TikToks sent shudders rippling through her.

Colin had to have planned something. He was getting better at that.

Sinking down onto the sofa and plugging in her earphones, Angela located the Radio SPLATZAPP! app on her phone's home screen. In an instant, the wall between her and Colin faded away, his words so clear they may as well have been in the same room as each other.

His opening line? Perfect.

She couldn't have written it better herself.

Angela's shoulders slumped as she expelled a relieved sigh. If Colin was capable of doing this on his own, then she didn't have to help him anymore. She could focus on her own stuff.

The smile didn't even make it onto her face before everything went wrong.

Her feet belonged to someone else as they took her back to his door; she watched in a detached way as her hand grabbed the doorknob and twisted it, nowhere near as satisfying as twisting his bloody head off his shoulders. Okay, not as satisfying but a lot less gross.

It took him a while to notice she was there.

'Angela…' That was it. That was all he said.

'Lost for words all of a sudden, DJ Coop?' Angela demanded. She wished she wasn't distracted by the thought that she really ought to have put on a fresh pair of knickers for this encounter. 'That's strange. Couldn't shut you up before now, could we?'

Colin stood from his chair.

Angela took two very large steps back.

He dutifully stayed right where he was—and this time he seemed to have found his voice. 'I'm so sorry. It's been eating me alive.'

'Oh goodie,' Angela bit out. 'At least there's that. Can't have been eating at you for very long, though. Overnight maybe, but definitely not long at all.'

Colin frowned, his hand clenched around the band of his padded headphones. 'No, Angela. Not just overnight. This whole time I've been in agony—ever since that morning I offered you my spare room. I did it for a selfish reason. At the time I thought I'd be okay with it, but then I got to know you and love you and I just...I shouldn't have done it.'

Angela glared at him through a hot, fuzzy veil. This must be what other writers referred to as 'a red film', though it was noticeably less red and a lot more tear-filled.

'Colin, I don't care about that,' she said truthfully. 'I really couldn't give a rat's arse why you offered to let me stay. If you'd told me at the beginning, then I still would have accepted because I really, *really* didn't want to move back in with my mother. You were always going to be the safer option. The safer option! Ha!'

She could tell he still had no idea what was bothering her.

The bunching of his eyebrows, the slack mouth, the blank eyes—she knew him well enough to know what he was feeling behind that infuriating face. But it seemed he didn't know her at all.

She waved away the questions he tried to ask her. They weren't relevant. He wasn't listening, just like he hadn't listened to her when this ill-advised lockdown romance had started. 'Let me refresh your memory, since you seem to be having so much trouble remembering the details. What was the one thing I didn't want? For anything about our real relationship to make it into the segment. Nothing from our so-called courting was to be used. Not even as inspiration. And you knew that! My feelings didn't even factor into your decision, did they? It's all about Colin Cooper and his stupid job and his stupid boss and his stupid listeners! So long as they're happy! Well, I hope it was worth it.'

'You were sleeping,' Colin said, rather feebly she thought.

'Then you should have woken me!' Angela cried.

'But...'

288

'But nothing!' she charged on. She was done, *done*, with letting people wring her up like a sponge whenever they needed something from her. Especially since they had no trouble tossing her away once she was no longer useful to them. 'I know it's about time you took over and started writing your own segments, I get it, but at least come up with something fictional. Don't use me, don't use *us*. I wanted this kept private, Colin.

'And now it's not.'

His silence was deafening. And very telling.

She spun back towards her bedroom, the door springing aside like a matador's red flag as she charged it. The suitcase was still mostly packed, because she'd been living out of it since moving in with Colin, but there was a small explosion of paper all over the floor. That wouldn't take long to bundle up, though. And just how heavy was the mattress and bedding anyway? She could totally hurl them down the stairs, or maybe someone would take pity on her. Hopefully someone who wasn't Bernard and who had a strong, young back.

Wait, she was on Day Fourteen of quarantine.

Shit. She still had to wait for tomorrow.

Colin must have finally unfrozen because she looked back to see him filling the doorway, regret creasing his expression and making him look slightly constipated. Before today she'd probably have used the words 'dashingly remorseful'. His attractive qualities weren't nearly enough to make up for this blunder, however.

If it *had* been a blunder.

'Don't you have a show to run?' Angela demanded.

'I'm not replacing you,' was the non sequitur he used.

Angela stared at him. Was she feeling replaced? Maybe, just a little, but that was so far from the main issue here.

'No one can replace you.' His earlier reticence was apparently forgotten. 'I think it's pretty obvious that I'm no good at planning. Or writing fiction.'

Angela saw no reason to keep the waspish comments locked away, as they had been, because he definitely deserved all the ire he had coming. 'Or apologies.'

'Or apologies,' he agreed. 'I'm so sorry. I wanted your birthday to be special.'

'At least that's one thing you wanted to keep special,' Angela muttered.

Colin's gaze fell on her, heavy and stifling. 'What does that mean?'

'I didn't say anything.'

'Yes you did. I'm pretty well-versed in Angela Speak by now and I know when you've lobbed something passive aggressive my way, even if I haven't heard it properly.'

Angela clenched her fists until her nails bit into her palms. 'Nothing. It means nothing. Just like your opinion of me, apparently. You keep so many bloody secrets and never think I'm worthy enough to know them. Why am I even upset? It was so obvious. This is textbook behaviour for an unsuitable love interest. I should have listened to those alarm bells in my head, but of course I didn't. Makes me wonder what other secrets you're hiding.'

With that, she turned to the wardrobe and wrenched one of the doors open.

He didn't try to stop her; she could see his static reflection standing there on the sliding door she hadn't touched. And then her gaze was stolen by the unbelievable sight in front of her.

Rolls and rolls of *toilet paper*.

Practically the same as rolls and rolls of tenners.

'Unbelievable,' Angela said, fury fanning each breath. 'Un-fucking-believable. I've been living out of my suitcase and daydreaming that one day I'll finally find somewhere that feels like home. I was coveting the hell out of this wardrobe. But I was never going to have that small luxury, was I? I never had a permanent place here. *This* is what's more important to you. Your stash of toilet paper. Do you realise that before I moved in with you, I had to use serviettes because I ran out? Because all the shops ran out? Even the loos at the McDonald's got burgled!'

She turned her chin over her shoulder, meeting the gaze belonging to the real Colin. He'd already opened his mouth, but she didn't want to hear it. Nope. It would be easier if he didn't give her a sensical explanation for having that much toilet paper—not that she was expecting him to have one.

The anger made her feel better. Less stupid.

Less likely to let him reel her back in with more secrets and lies and sweet nothings.

Angela jerked her eyes back to his reflection. 'And here you are, sitting on hundreds of bog rolls. I wonder if you felt guilty when Bernard and Loraine were out. Most of us in Newfield were out at one stage. Selfish bloody hoarders. And you're one of them. You made people use whatever they had on hand. Do you know how many stressed pensioners I saw at the Sainsbury's? Hell, even the local care homes ended up nothing!'

Colin wet his lips. 'I know what this looks like...'

'Oh, do you?'

'In my defence,' he said, 'it was an accident. And that's not what I—'

His pants buzzed angrily. Colin ripped his phone out of his pocket.

'Danger?' he muttered and shook his head. 'Not taking this. Not now.'

But his phone didn't quit. It started vibrating so hard it sounded like a wasps' nest, maybe even in danger of exploding. Colin looked back down at the screen. His eyes widened.

'Oh fudge, the song ran out and nothing's playing,' he babbled. 'Fudge! Angela—we're not done here, okay?'

Colin turned and ran back into his room, the door banging shut behind him.

'I think we are,' Angela said to the neatly-stacked rolls of toilet paper.

She grabbed half a dozen of them and shoved them into her suitcase—she might as well get herself sorted just in case there was another run on toilet paper. She'd seen her fellow humans do some crazy stuff since the pandemic had begun, but the toilet paper hoarding (and the ensuing shortage) was one of the most selfish things she'd seen so far. The sewers were trashed, according to the local paper, all filled up with foreign objects.

'What am I supposed to do now?' Angela asked Wills, who was perched on a throne constructed out of pillows. Wills hadn't complained about his new position. Or said anything, really.

'I can't—I won't—stay here,' Angela went on. 'Not with that tosser. When push comes to shove, he'll always choose his show over anything else. *Anyone* else. So where do I go?'

The one-eyed bat said nothing, though his meaning was clear.

'No, I can't!'

Wills remained unmoving on the subject.

Angela huffed out a sigh, but she still dialled the number that she'd told herself she would never dial again.

Of course it took barely two rings for her mother picked up.

'What do you need, darling?' Janet Tweedie asked, her voice like a bottle of vintage red wine. Leo would have salivated over it.

'Can't I just ring to say hi?' Angela tried.

'Please, darling. You never call unless you need something. It does make me feel like the oily rag, since you'd so obviously prefer to talk to someone else, but what can I do except wait for you to remember I exist?' A sniff, but a well-practiced one. 'If I wasn't such a concerned mother…'

Angela rolled her eyes. *Concerned about your reputation as a mother, more like.*

'Well, yes, that is true,' her mother agreed. 'But one mustn't admit that in polite company, you know.'

Angela grimaced. She must have said that out loud.

Fortunately, her impolite honesty hadn't caused the world to end. Janet Tweedie might have struck back with a vague barb about her daughter not being 'polite company', but she hadn't sounded as offended as Angela had feared she would.

'Our relationship's always been transactional, hasn't it?' Angela wondered.

'Yes, darling.' Her mother's ensuing sigh was gusty enough that Angela thought she'd left the window open for a moment. 'Oh, that's a relief. We understand each other at last. I've been trying to step delicately around this issue for years, you know.'

Angela smiled mirthlessly. A relief for one of them, maybe. 'I need a place to stay.'

'Lost your job, did you?'

'Yes.'

'I told you there was no point working in London. All those long days commuting and for what? They'd just as soon toss you out as promote you. Best not to get your hopes up and stay in Newfield, like a sensible girl.'

Angela's knuckles ached as she gripped the phone tighter. 'So can I stay?'

The *chink* of a wine bottle skimming the rim of a glass answered her. 'Of course, darling. How could a mother possibly leave her child homeless during a pandemic? It wouldn't look good, would it?'

It had always been about appearances with Janet Tweedie. And now she'd finally admitted it. Rather than feeling vindicated, Angela felt sick to her stomach.

'Actually, I don't think I will move in with you,' she said. 'I couldn't think of anything worse. For either of us. We would side-eye and side-snipe at each other until we both died of polite resentment.'

Her mother didn't even try to disagree. 'Do you need money, darling? Two months of rent ought to be useful right about now.'

'Yes. It would be incredibly useful.'

'I thought as much. Let me know how much and I'll deposit it into your account.'

When her phone was dark and silent in her hand, Angela realised that she'd just had the easiest conversation with her mother in her entire life—and for once Angela hadn't bothered to grit her teeth and thank her mother for her insincere help. Angela had swerved far away from 'the done thing'. She didn't even feel guilty about it. She felt...*liberated.*

Time to pull some other strings.

'Hey,' Angela said as soon as her second call was answered, her fingers crossed behind her back. 'I feel really dirty doing this, but here goes. I need to ask you a favour. I don't want to interfere with your healing process or anything, so you can shoot me down without any hard feelings.'

'I just got a negative result from another test, one I did yesterday,' Ishani told her. 'Still feel a bit shit, but nothing that'll stop me walking to the letterbox. That's about all I can manage, mind. What's up?'

Angela drew a breath and held it. 'The done thing' would have been to bemoan her current situation to the point of exhaustion without actually coming right out and asking for help—a good friend and/or neighbour would feel compelled to offer her a place to stay. But Angela was done with doing 'the done thing'.

'You don't hoard toilet paper, do you?' Angela asked.

'What! No. Only tossers do that.'

'Exactly,' Angela said and didn't hesitate before asking her next question.

Thank God Ishani said yes.

32

The Day After

'I've lost her,' Colin said to the empty room.

The chai tea in the mug he was holding would go cold before she ever heard his proper apology. The one she deserved. The one that his fellow DJs had refused to help him with. He wouldn't have been surprised if they'd stopped talking to him entirely after yesterday's dead-air debacle. Five whole minutes! It was unprofessional and had cost them tens of thousands of listeners, according to the numbers. Even Graveyard Danika had lost some.

Leo had been apoplectic, especially as Colin couldn't give him a good reason why it had happened. But Leo hadn't done worse than yell at him, because Danika had unexpectedly threatened to quit if Colin was ejected from the line-up.

Leo had shut up after that.

Once their boss had left the Zoom meeting, Danika had added, 'This is your mess, Colin. You clean it up. A broken heart only gets you so much sympathy from us.'

Colin supposed he shouldn't have expected Angela to stick around after their government-imposed quarantine was over. Things hadn't looked promising at 6:30am in the kitchen, when she had avoided eye contact and kept munching her way through the last of the cereal (the milk had gone off yesterday, but Colin had tested it and knew it was still edible—Angela's sour expression had more to do with his presence than anything else).

He hadn't seen her since. Hadn't even stuck his head out of his room. He'd been too afraid to show himself, in case she duly ripped him to shreds again.

Now he wished he'd said something. *Anything.*

Instead he'd retreated behind a closed door, like a coward. The shame burning inside his ribcage had been compounded by the lack of preparation he'd done for the serial. He'd flubbed his way through the segment, glad it was Thursday and that he only had one day left of this painful charade. His listeners were still asking why he had sounded 'like a robot'. Colin was doing his best to ignore them.

His counterpart would get that Happily Ever After tomorrow.

He wouldn't.

And while Colin had been spewing out words that were supposed to build up to a romantic proposal scene, Angela had obviously enlisted someone to help her move out.

Where had she gone? Her mother's. That had been her only option before he'd run down those stairs and tossed a grenade into the middle of both of their lives. Crap. He had no idea where her mother lived, so he couldn't perform some overly romantic gesture, like walk a thousand miles and fall down at her door, or hold up a boombox outside her window.

Colin glanced down at his phone. Text messages. Heaps of them. When had he set his phone to silent instead of vibrate? Had Angela said goodbye? Had she changed her mind or was she—

His heart sank.

Rob. All of them were from Rob.

Wanker

Utter wanker

Helped Angela move out while u were too busy yakking away to notice

No response huh

And u gave me shit for the thing with Ishani

Ok I deserved that shit

But you deserve this shit too

Colin slowly sipped the tea he'd made for Angela. Rob was right. Wait, how had Angela got his mate's number anyway?

Ishani.

Angela would have done anything to avoid moving in with her mother. Anything.

Rob had said in passing that Ishani owned a three-bedder on Saddler Street, something about it being the most Newfield house in Newfield. All the houses up that way were identical post-war affairs. Hard to tell them apart—unless more than one of them was known to have a tiny TARDIS out the front. Ishani's choice of letterbox had caused something of a stir among her neighbours, according to Rob.

Okay. So Colin might know where to find Angela, if he looked long and hard enough.

Did that change things?

Unfortunately, no.

***

'What am I going to do?' Colin bemoaned the next night, completely at a loss and vibrating his way through his eighth mug of tea. He'd been wired all day, ever since he'd had to lie on radio and say that he and Number Twelve were starting their lives together.

His listeners had instantly known that something was up.

'I have decided against airing your song request,' Peter told him. Colin had rung the number for The Love Doctor's show and so their conversation was verbal only, but he could easily picture the frown behind those dulcet tones. 'Really, Colin? "Un-Break My Heart" by Toni Braxton?'

Colin knocked back a mouthful of tea and grimaced. These dregs weren't as bitter as he'd hoped they'd be. Just weak and disappointing.

'Not on-brand for me, is it?' Colin mused. 'A mid-1990s ballad.'

'Colin—'

'No, no, you're right, Peter. I'll go with "Walking on Broken Glass" by Annie Lennox. Still 90s, but early enough that it carries a hint of New Wave. That'll do.'

'Absolutely not!'

'Why not?'

'Are you drunk?' Peter demanded.

Colin eyed his empty mug. 'Nope.'

'I see. I'll have to explain my reservations to you.' Peter sighed. 'And in under forty seconds, since I have a proper request to announce then. Colin, you have picked songs which ask the other party to do the hard work and pick up the pieces. You're the one responsible for the breakage, my boy. This attitude of yours leads me to believe that you're not ready for any second chances. I highly doubt Angela is listening to my show anyway. Now go get some sleep—and drink some water. Just water! You'll thank me in the morning.'

Peter hung up without ceremony.

Colin moved his fusty tongue about in his mouth. Peter had a good point. Not about the songs, obviously, what a fudging wanker.

Just how dehydrated was he anyway?

***

Colin woke up with a hangover. That didn't make much sense.

Neither did the handwritten scribbles on the paper scattered in front of him. He lifted his head with a groan, nearly knocking over a nearby glass of water with his nose in the process. He realised that he'd fallen asleep at his desk.

There was no sign of alcohol or any other explanation for why he felt like he'd gone on a bender with Rob. But he did have vague memories of drinking mug after mug of tea.

Radio SPLATZAPP! had apparently been his background noise of choice during his late-night brainstorming, because the app was still open on his phone. Currently, one of Leo's Saturday students was giving a step-by-step tutorial on how to make face masks, using only a pair of scissors and an old sock. Angela had a few of those types of masks, didn't she? He could pop out into the living room and ask her if she'd consider helping him make some.

Brilliant. Just what he needed. Another reminder that he'd lost her.

Colin sorted through the paper smothering his desk, cheering up when he noticed two very promising words: 'segment ideassssss!!!'.

He scanned the space underneath the oversized heading, seeing the same line repeated over and over again, which made him think of Jack Nicholson's character in *The Shining*. Creepy. But all work and no play had yielded a stroke of genius.

'Second Chance Songs,' Colin mused out loud. The next few

sentences his eyes found were squished onto the very bottom of the page. 'But don't mention why you're doing it or who you're doing it for. Prove that you can keep your private life private. And you should listen to more covers.'

Well, there it was. A new segment *and* a way to fix the mess he'd made. Colin was well aware that he didn't deserve Angela's forgiveness, but he had to at least try.

Even if she didn't listen.

***

'Fuck him,' Ishani said helpfully.

Angela peered over the rim of her porcelain cup, its matching saucer placed well away from the edge of the coffee table in front of her. The tea set they were using bore asymmetrical silver shapes dotted sporadically on top of a pale blue background. She'd been horrified when Ishani had told her that each cup and saucer cost a hundred pounds. Something about a fancy Edinburgh-based designer.

Ishani had assured Angela that she owned 'five different tea sets just in case, don't worry, eat a biscuit before you have a fainting spell'.

Everyone had their vices. Angela's vices tended to be rent money, groceries, and the occasional cheap romance novel from the second-hand bookshop—sensible expenses, all of them. Not that she'd ever mention this out loud to someone who was letting her stay for free.

'I think the point is to *not* fu…uh, sleep with him,' Angela said.

Ishani shrugged. 'Not quite what I meant, but hey, if it helps you get over him, then by all means jump in the sack. When the lockdown lifts, of course.'

Angela swirled the tea in her cup. The inky liquid had absorbed every lashing of milk she'd tried to throw at it. The tea remained as dark as her soul. Maybe that was being a little melodramatic. Maybe she should consider trying her hand at poetry.

Or maybe she should find a new hobby that didn't involve listening to Colin's older shows, including the one which mentioned that he'd invited his miserable neighbour to stay in his flat. He hadn't sounded evil in that particular segment, not as Ishani had proclaimed (while twirling an invisible moustache), just desperate.

Angela was sure she'd never wanted the weekend to be over and done with before.

'Weekend plans,' Ishani declared. 'We need some or we'll murder each other.'

'You read my mind,' Angela said quickly.

Ishani swivelled on her satin-covered cushion to pin Angela with a look that would have made Wills very proud. 'And we're obviously not trying to kill time until Monday morning. When Colin's next show is on.'

'Is it that obvious?'

'Angela. The astronauts orbiting Earth can see it—and maybe even the grey aliens on their way past to planets that actually contain intelligent life. And by intelligent life, I mean a species that doesn't think that mask ordinances are a conspiracy to turn everyone into "sheeple", instead of an attempt to save lives.' Ishani's lips twitched. 'Not to worry. We'll wean you off him. No need to go cold turkey. Speaking of which, I'm glad I got off the fags before I got hit with this thing. Not sure I'd have recovered so fast otherwise.'

Angela grimaced. 'I'm so, so sorry about that.'

'Hey, I might not have got it from your gross ex-boyfriend, remember. And it's not all bad. I found out that the openers at the café, the ones who start in the morning, can mysteriously get on with it and not call in with a hangover when their boss is at death's door. And now I know who the most responsible employees are.'

'That's a surprisingly positive outlook,' Angela said.

Ishani's nonchalant expression faded into something undefinable as she peered down into her empty cup. 'There's worse that can be positive.'

Angela wasn't going to argue with that one. 'Fair enough. Okay. Weekend plans?'

'Definitely not exercising,' Ishani said with a shudder. 'The neighbours won't keep quiet about my old "filthy, filthy habit" if they see me huffing and puffing.'

'I think I'll trim the hydrangeas,' Angela mused.

Ishani blinked at her. 'How did you know they needed it?'

'I may have seen two older gents out the front, shaking their heads and pointing at the hedge in your back garden. It's just *barely* visible from the footpath.'

'Bert and Ernie,' Ishani grumbled.

'What? Those are their real names?'

Ishani chortled and set her cup down with a loud, careless clatter. 'No, but it fits, doesn't it? Right. You get the shears and I'll get a book. My brother's raiding with some of his video game buddies later, so it's going to be hella noisy when he starts slaughtering avatars. Usually I'd go topless to really grind Bert and Ernie's gears, but I have a guest over...so I suppose I should be decent. Just this once.'

Angela hacked away at the overgrown hydrangeas for a good half hour, but couldn't stop thinking about bloody Colin Cooper and his bloody show. The exercise was supposed to distract her, damn it. Argh. It didn't help that Ishani was reading a romance novel (something about tattooed bad boys)—she had already burned through every K-drama that Netflix had to offer.

Romance novels. Now there was something reliable.

Predictable. Safe.

Angela already had the characters, the opening and closing chapters, a comprehensive outline and, thanks to He-Who-Must-Not-Be-Named, the knowledge that she could in fact create a believable romance. Now that she no longer had the serial to write for, she could focus on her own work. She wanted to finish her book, not just start it.

At least her characters could have a happy ending.

33

There it was again. That awful, leaden feeling in her stomach.

Wait, why was she even awake? Angela could have sworn she'd only just put her head down on this glorious mound of pillows—courtesy of Ishani's enviable stash, which had been put to good use in a free-for-all pillow fight involving Angela, Ishani, and Ishani's brother, Rayaan, on Sunday afternoon (after all the tea sets had been packed away, naturally).

Argh. Someone was knocking on the door.

That explained a few things.

'Sod off, Colin!' Angela growled, then clapped a hand over her eyes. The intruder had ignored her and marched inside to snap open the shades, admitting painful rays of light.

'Nope, not Colin,' Ishani said with a merciless grin. 'A lot more queer and lot less of a pillock. But if you want to trade me in for an inferior roommate, I can get Rob to take your stuff back to Colin's later. Rob feels so bad about what when down between us that he'd do just about anything I asked of him.' A thoughtful pause. 'Too bad I can't bring myself to take advantage of The Ex. It really isn't fair that he looks so much like David Tennant. Honestly. And he knows it. He's practically weaponised it.'

Angela tilted her head to the side, appraising Ishani. 'So is this you waking me up in time for Colin's show, or do I need to provide you with reasons for and against getting back with Rob?'

'No way!' Ishani's eyes went wide with horror. 'No! Just because I've shagged crazy—and enjoyed it, I have to say—doesn't mean I'm going back for seconds.'

Angela nodded emphatically, which she decided was the safest response.

Ishani threw a towel at her. 'Get in the shower. Get dressed. And brush your teeth, woman. Being in a funk is no excuse to let these things slide.'

'Yes, Mum.'

'You take that back! I'm much better than your mum and you know it.'

***

'This feels a bit 1940s,' Angela observed from her armchair.

Sitting across from her on a sofa which had ornate wooden spirals arching over the top of the mint-green upholstery, Ishani and Rayaan continued to sip from their delicate cups, the matching saucers carefully balanced in their palms. A Bluetooth-enabled speaker, shaped like an old wooden console radio and recently moved downstairs from Rayaan's bedroom (aka gaming dungeon), had pride of place at the front of the living room. Angela was using the speaker to stream Radio SPLATZAPP! off her phone.

'We weren't going to let you suffer all by yourself,' Ishani told her.

'And what else am I 'sposed to do?' Rayaan added. 'All my mates are still asleep because they're in the US. Need me some quality entertainment right now.'

'Bled Netflix dry during quarantine, did you?' Angela asked with a smile.

Rayaan nodded miserably.

Fortunately, he hadn't tested positive for the virus. But he had told Angela that he'd been stressed out enough as it was, since he'd spent days waiting for the symptoms to show up. Being stuck inside with his sister had not been as bad as Rayaan had expected. He and Ishani had needed to schedule who was using the kitchen at any given time, in order to lessen his exposure, but at least they hadn't needed to share a bathroom. There had been plenty of space for the siblings to avoid each other. Rayaan had admitted that they had a lot of experience with that anyway.

Angela immediately perked up when Sunshine began the handover between the shows in the usual chipper way, then shook her head, annoyed with herself for feeling like she had a connection to a DJ, someone whose true persona was hidden behind a glib performance. The DJs at Radio SPLATZAPP! weren't her friends any more than Colin was her...something.

Whatever he was to her, his voice still made her heart jump when she heard it.

'Thanks, Sunshine, try to send some of that good weather down this way, will you?' Colin said cheerfully. In the background, quiet enough to form an undercurrent to his words instead of overwhelming them, were upbeat strings.

It wasn't unusual for a DJ to speak over the start or the end of a song—Angela knew that from listening to Radio SPLATZAPP! for weeks on end—and it also wasn't unheard of for a song to be played during a segment. But this song. She *knew* this song. It was on her Spotify playlist, the one titled 'Modern Beats That Annoy Colin Cooper'. She'd inflicted it on Colin more than once. Argh! Why couldn't she remember the name of the song?

The music faded out before any lyrics could make an appearance.

Colin filled the void it left behind. 'Welcome to The Late Morning Rambles. So I know you were all hoping for some salacious new serial, but you'll have to swallow your disappointment. I know, I know, you frantically got out of bed and brushed your teeth, all in preparation for whatever exciting tidbit I had to throw your way. Well, I'm hoping you'll fall in love with my latest segment. This is Second Chance Songs—'

'That's a bit on the nose,' Ishani observed. 'Especially since he just used "Second Chances" by Imagine Dragons as his backing track. May as well hoist a neon sign declaring: "Trying to get my roommate back. Wish me luck."'

Rayaan nodded and sipped at his tea.

Angela didn't add anything to Ishani's running commentary; she was too busying white-knuckling her phone as she watched the Tweets appearing in the relevant hashtag. Most people posting there were delving deeper and deeper into conspiracy territory, so sure that the lacklustre finale on Friday (followed by this banal Second Chance Song segment) was due to a Big Bad Breakup. Complete strangers desperately wanted to help DJ Coop win back 'Number Twelve'.

It was the only thing that got me thru the day #splatzapp, someone wailed.

Why wont he tell us wats up? #splatzapp someone else demanded.

Angela realised she was holding her breath and forced it to putter out over her bottom lip. Of course. It was all for his listeners. Always for them. Any minute now, he would announce that this 'second chance' thing was all about winning her back.

But he surprised her.

'—and this time every weekday, we'll listen to one of those retro songs my boss hates so much,' Colin explained, laughter chasing his words. 'And then we'll compare it to a new version, a cover, giving the lyrics a second chance. Yes, it's a little lame, but give it a chance. A second chance, if you will.'

'Ha,' Ishani said.

Colin didn't miss a beat and probably wouldn't have done so even if he'd been in the room with them. 'We'll start with one of my old favourites. "I Ran (So Far Away)" by A Flock of Seagulls. I've picked the shorter radio edit—sorry about that—but next up is Darude's take on it, so you might be able to finish that cup of tea before you hear from me again. See you on the other side. And don't hold back. Let me know what you *really* think.'

Clearly a joke, Angela thought, since nearly every listener on the hashtag was doing just that. But instead of discussing the songs, they were preoccupied with *her*.

They were making assumptions. Working themselves into a frenzy.

But still he denied them.

At exactly half nine, when Colin began running through 'The Less Dire Headlines' (another new segment that was meant to remind people that good things still happened out there, in an increasingly scary world), Ishani called an end to their streaming party and Angela closed the Radio SPLATZAPP! app.

'It's clearly aimed at you,' Ishani said.

Angela felt her cheeks contort as her face failed to choose between a grimace and a hopeful smile. 'Yes. But you should see them baying for blood on Twitter. He's going to have to give in to the sharks and feed them something. And he will. As for me?' Angela stood up and made a show of dusting herself off, as if she had dismissed him from her thoughts (ha, she wished) along with any specks. 'I'm retiring to my room. Enjoy your tea.'

Ishani and Rayaan lifted their teacups in a twin salute.

Laughing, Angela left them to it and set up camp at the desk that had come with the guest room. Definitely not from IKEA. Solid. Stable. And it had a perfectly reliable patch of sunshine, courtesy of a south-facing window.

Colin was a distraction. It was time to focus on her own project.

The words flowed out of her, fast and furious. She'd conquered and cleared the dreaded mid-novel slump, so things were finally moving again. It was tempting to rewrite the ending (for the tenth time!), since she knew that scene like the back of her eyelids. It would be so easy.

But Angela wasn't sure she wanted things to end. Not just yet.

***

'Colin,' boomed a voice that seesawed between ominous and exasperated.

Colin leaned back in his chair, leg resting on his opposite knee and a mug of tea perched near his lips. 'A call *after* midday, Leo? I'm honoured.'

'"Honoured" is not what you're going to be when I'm done with you,' Leo all but snarled. 'Your listeners deserve more than this—more closure, more answers, more engagement from you. And you are ignoring all of them. Radio does not exist in a void, Colin.

We have to appease your target audience, keep them coming back for every show, if we want the sponsors to continue paying us for their timeslots.'

'You're the one who told me I needed a new segment, Leo.'

Colin supposed he shouldn't have chosen that moment to tip his mug back at the exact angle as used by Kermit the Frog in that tea meme. Leo's face went through several interesting shades of red and purple before settling on a fantastic puce. 'You were supposed to end the serial in a way that satisfied everyone.'

'You never said that. You just told me to end it.'

'I also never ask you to be professional, but it's a given.'

'Ignoring my listeners hasn't resulted in the world ending—any more than it is already,' Colin added thoughtfully.

'Would you like to rephrase that apology, Colin?'

Yikes. He'd taken it a *little* too far this time.

Colin quickly sat up. 'Leo, have you noticed how many people are lurking in the Radio SPLATZAPP! hashtag at the moment? And how many of them are making fanart and fanfiction and coming up with theories about what I'm not saying? Nothing I write or say will ever be good enough for the most dedicated followers. Let them fill in the gaps themselves. And anyway, I bet there's been a surge of activity in my archived shows since the serial ended. People love hunting for clues.'

Colin's phone felt like it was overheating from his boss' ire—that or it was out of warranty and about to explode.

'He's right, you know,' someone off screen said to Leo.

Leo opened his mouth, only to disappear when his phone was snatched away from him. A new face filled the screen: Leo's husband. Colin knew it was too dangerous to relax, despite the 'chaotic artist' aesthetic the man had going for him.

Moving towards a window that showed the startlingly empty streets of London beneath him, Leo's husband said, 'Hello, Colin. I'm Bran. Big fan of your show, by the way. I've run the numbers, since I'm pretty much Leo's entire behind-the-scenes staff, and you're right. Your refusal to engage with your listeners has resulted in a massive increase in hits on older recordings. As I'm sure you know, we insert newer ads into those as the season dictates. Which means the sponsors more than happy with what they're paying us at the moment.'

Colin fought the urge to slump in relief. He wasn't out of the woods yet.

'That won't last long,' Leo said sullenly, still somewhere near the phone. 'What is Colin going to do when the initial surge in popularity dies down? This is one of those times when a second wave is highly desired.'

Colin felt the blood drain out of his face. He did *not* want to be thinking about a fresh resurgence of the virus. The lockdown had been going on long enough, thanks.

Bran pursed his lips. 'What's your plan, Colin?'

Plan. That word was his nemesis.

Making plans was a sure way to get your heart stomped.

Leo huffed. 'Colin never plans anything. It is both his best and worst feature.'

'Thanks,' Colin said breezily. 'But there is a plan this time and it involves running a segment called "Second Chance Songs". Originals and covers, side by side, served up on a platter of judgement. I was thinking of tricking people with a double feature of Dolly Parton and Whitney Houston, but I get that the cover itself is ancient these days…'

'That segment won't appease your listeners for long,' Bran warned.

314

'Leo is right. You'll need to regain your momentum. What's the deal? Really, Colin.'

Colin blew out a breath. Leo he'd never say anything to, because his boss didn't seem to have a sympathetic bone in his body. But Bran seemed different. He and Leo were complete opposites, which was probably one of those tropes Angela liked to read about.

'I can't mention Angela on air,' Colin said. 'I really messed up. I used our private life as inspiration for the serial one morning when she didn't have the time to write it for me—and the only thing she asked me to do was to keep our real relationship out of the show, keep it fictional only. But I was too obsessed with keeping this job (I don't actually need the cash, I just really love doing this) that I didn't listen. I put myself before her. So I'm…using this segment to prove that I can keep Angela out of my show.'

His phone's screen blurred violently. Leo's face appeared again. 'Colin. This is the perfect thing to tell your listeners.'

'No, not worth it,' Colin said flatly.

'If you don't use it, if your numbers tank—'

'It won't matter, because he doesn't care,' Bran commented. 'He's found someone who's more important to him than his job or his sanity. And that's lovely, Colin, it really is. But how do you know she's listening?'

Colin forced a smile that scraped across his teeth. 'No idea.'

'You're willing to lose your job over this?'

'Absolutely,' Colin said.

'I'm going to replace you with one of the weekend students,' Leo threatened.

Colin repeated the Kermit tea-tilt, then injected more confidence than he felt into his words. 'Go ahead, if you need to. I might move back into podcasting. What's love without a little risk?'

Leo visibly shuddered.

'Surely you've taken a risk here and there,' Colin said.

'I never jump into anything unless I'm absolutely certain,' Leo retorted.

Bran cleared his throat. 'Ahem, I wasn't a safe bet.'

'That's what you think.' Leo's stern expression morphed into a playful grin, which looked completely alien on him. 'Very well, Colin. Have fun with your show. While you can.'

The call disconnected.

'Fun,' Colin repeated. 'I'm wearing my heart on my sleeve—no, cutting it into pieces and dishing it up a plate. And for what?' He sighed. 'How on Earth did I fall in love with her this hard and this fast? Was it the "forced proximity" thing?'

He was pretty sure he didn't want an answer to that.

And now he was going to listen to a few more covers on Spotify, because he intended to see this plan through. No matter the outcome.

34

'You owe us a progress report,' Danger Jones said.

Colin eyed his fellow DJ's black silk dressing gown, the usual sunglasses, the fedora tipped at an angle (a new but unsurprising addition to Danger's wardrobe)—and knew better than to comment on Danger's appearance. But he did say, 'Good evening, Danger. Good evening, Peter. How was your Wednesday? It's been so long since we spoke. A whole twelve hours. I'm amazed that you think anything might have changed in that time.'

Peter lifted his chin imperiously. 'Can't we check on your mental wellbeing?'

'Sure. But I suspect that's not why I was invited to this private little Zoom meeting.'

'What else are we going to do?' Danger huffed. 'There's nothing on the telly anymore. And there won't be for *months*, because no one's filming anything right now. Pussies. They just need to temperature-check people before they enter the set, right? And why bother with masks since they don't actually do anything? It's all a smokescreen, for the government's secret plan to control us.'

Peter levelled a stern frown at the camera. 'Danger. I can see that mask hanging on the doorknob behind you.'

Danger suddenly disappeared from the meeting.

'All hot air, that fellow,' Peter said.

Colin shook his head. 'Nope, I am not going to be taken in by the Nice Guy™/Actual Nice Guy routine. Forget it. I won't tell you anything I didn't tell him.'

'I can help, Colin. I *am* The Love Doctor.'

'Which is a self-appointed title. Unless you've got a degree I don't know about?'

'Actually, it's a Diploma in Love Studies from the Love Institute based in Devon,' Peter replied, completely straight-faced.

Colin eyed him, unsure if he was serious or not.

Peter's smile seemed to indicate that he wasn't. 'You have things well in hand, then?'

'I think so. Angela might not even be listening—or maybe she did and immediately closed the app—but I'll live. And I'm definitely not wearing a fedora any time soon.'

Peter pulled a face. 'If you do, I'll be very disappointed in you.'

Colin thought he would relish having time to himself after Peter also left the meeting, but the silence crowded in around him. He had to get out of there. His feet took him down to the basement, where he should have done his washing, but he soon realised that he'd left the bag of dirty clothes in his bedroom.

The thought of going back upstairs, to his empty flat, was unbearable. He chose to stand aimlessly on the grass outside instead. Fresh air. The freedom to leave. He should have missed this. He'd had other things on his mind.

'Colin, are you trying to block our view?' Bernard called from his patio. The lattice fence was not so high that it could conceal the pot of tea that Bernard was sharing with Loraine in the morning sunshine, which seemed to have some power behind it for once.

Colin lifted his hand in a half-hearted wave. 'No. I'm just being here.'

'You could always "just be here" somewhere else,' Bernard suggested. 'We deserve a bit of peace and quiet in our old age.'

Loraine leaned heavily on the walker parked beside her, to better angle her stern glare at her husband. 'Bernard! Don't be rude. Clearly Colin is need of some company.'

'And here I thought you'd have an issue with me calling us old.'

Loraine sniffed. 'Some things are so obvious they don't need to be stated.'

'Like how Colin clearly needs some company?' Bernard teased.

'Perhaps not everyone deserves my company,' Loraine said tartly. 'Others are incapable of offering a kind ear because they would rather joke and clown about. *Others* can go inside if they so wish.'

Bernard held up his hands, conceding defeat. His cheeky grin faded when he studied Colin a bit more closely. 'You alright there, Colin? We saw Angela move out the other day—unless she was finally getting rid of that old mattress. I have my doubts, however. Number Six put it out twelve months ago and Angela snagged it, quick as lightning. She was very attached to that ratty thing. Probably because it was less ratty that her previous mattress.'

'We're good listeners, Colin,' Loraine promised.

'Even if we do enjoy the sound of our own voices a little too much.' Bernard chuckled. 'Myself, I don't mind listening to this bit of crumpet.'

Loraine, rather than whipping out a stinging remark, muttered something under her breath that sounded a lot like 'not when someone's *listening*, Bernard'.

Colin watched them for a moment, perplexed. 'How do you do it?'

'Do what?' Bernard asked.

'Stay in a relationship. It starts out so well, so easy. But then you hit one speed bump and...' Colin threw up his hands, miming an explosion. 'How do you recover from that? Aside from saying sorry, which isn't an instant fix. What comes next?'

'We never go to bed angry,' Loraine said.

'Yes, dear, but that only worked in our day,' Bernard pointed out. 'We couldn't afford to leave or arrange alternate accommodation when we got tired of each other, could we? We had to sit down and work things out. The young ones of today aren't forced to do that, they have more options. What happened, Colin?'

Colin did his best to explain the situation. He could see they didn't really get it—or at least, they didn't understand his side of things, or why he'd gone against Angela's wishes (it wasn't like he'd planned to do that). He'd had good intentions.

'Oh dear,' Loraine said. 'We all know what the road to Hell is paved with.'

'Probably lava,' Bernard remarked.

She slapped his knee; a playful gesture that didn't match the glower she sported.

Bernard somehow managed to keep a straight face, though Colin could see the cracks of mirth forming. 'Could have been worse. You did apologise, didn't you, Colin?'

'That might have worked if she hadn't found my stash of toilet paper,' Colin said.

'Your what now?' Bernard spluttered.

Loraine nodded sagely. 'Oh, I see. Hoarding is not an attractive quality in a romantic partner at the moment, and justifiably so. I did notice that the toilet paper was never on the receipt you gave us when you brought back our groceries.'

Bernard's stare moved between Colin and his wife. 'It wasn't?'

'You never read the receipt, do you? You're as bad as the young ones sometimes.' Loraine eyed Colin. 'You're the toilet paper Santa, aren't you?'

'The *what?*' Bernard exclaimed.

Loraine tilted a triumphant grin at her husband, scarily similar to what Colin had seen on Angela's face whenever she got the upper hand in one of their banter sessions. My schoolfriend, Dorothy, told me all about it the last time she phoned. She lives up at one of the care homes.'

'Christ, that old bag is still alive?'

'Bernard! Watch your language.' An exasperated huff. 'And do let me finish. The care homes near us all ran out of toilet paper. They weren't sure what they were going to do—there was even talk of using baby wipes and emptying the dustbins more often. It would have been very unsanitary. But then someone started showing up several times a week dressed in a Santa suit, dropping off toilet paper. Dorothy told me the deliveries had stopped lately and I noticed that this was when Colin went into quarantine.'

'That's what gave me away?' Colin asked with a laugh.

'Oh no, dear. I've seen you sneaking out at night, all dressed up and carrying a rubbish bag over your shoulder. It was rather obvious what you were up to.'

Bernard still looked very lost.

'I'm a night owl, Bernard,' Loraine told him. 'You'd snore your way through anything, even a bomb landing on top of you. I have to entertain myself somehow in the wee hours, so I like to watch the foot traffic at night—what there is of it—since that's when you'll see the most interesting sorts out and about. It's hard to miss Santa Claus.'

Bernard seemed to have finally recovered from his stupor. 'Then why didn't you explain any of this to Angela, Colin?'

'That would be unchristian,' Loraine said primly. 'Good deeds must not be advertised.'

'You were being a good Christian boy?' Bernard sounded sceptical.

Time to be honest.

'Nothing so selfless, I'm afraid,' Colin said. 'I was very embarrassed about the mess I'd got myself into by accidentally over-ordering toilet paper—it was back when you couldn't get the stuff anywhere. I was only able to find some on a wholesale site and managed to buy a whole pallet instead of just one packet! Anyway, it gave me something to use in the "good deed" segment on my radio show. By making it about some anonymous guy in a suit, I could please my boss by pretending to do research for my show—mind you, he started wanting me to do those big deeds myself, not just mundane ones like fetching your groceries. I felt so bad about using you two that way. I only mentioned you once, if that helps.'

'You kept visiting us after that one time,' Bernard pointed out.

Colin shoved his hands into his pockets. 'I'm not close to my family, so I'm pretty lonely sometimes. You're the best grandparents I could ever ask for. Or randomly find, that is.'

Loraine patted her eyes with a tissue, blaming 'allergies'.

Bernard and Colin mutually agreed (with silent nods) that it was best not to correct her.

'Anyway, I had a selfish motivation for introducing myself, but I'm glad I met you two,' Colin said. 'The Santa thing? It doesn't give me the warm and fuzzies. It's just incredibly embarrassing. If I'd been caught…no, I'd rather not think about that.'

'But it would have endeared you to many Newfielders,' Bernard said.

Colin sighed. 'No, I'd just be the same disappointing son who always makes poor decisions, like accidentally spending his wealth on toilet paper instead of wisely investing it. Oh.'

Wow. Had it really taken him this long to realise it? Angela was always on about 'the done thing' and worrying how she looked to other people, but he'd assumed he was above it all. That he didn't care, because he was hidden away with a microphone, where no one could see him. He'd deliberately moved half a country away from his parents…but he was still acting as if they lived down the street. As if he had something to prove.

'Well, I guess I finally understand that hang-up,' Colin said with a shrug.

'Then what's stopping you getting caught now?'

Colin narrowed his eyes at Bernard. The older man had developed a grin that kept getting wider by the second.

'No,' Colin said.

'Why not?' Loraine asked.

It was very tempting to say 'because!' and stomp the ground like a petulant child.

'Colin,' Bernard said gently. 'Love makes fools of us all. It's a shame the current laws won't let you go over to her new address so you can beg her forgiveness and make a fool of yourself there. I would in your shoes. But this is what you've got to work with. Get caught, Colin. Make a grand gesture.'

'*No*,' Colin said again.

'You might as well,' Bernard told him. 'What have you got to lose?'

'My job,' Colin muttered. 'Which I'm already risking anyway.'

Bernard was unstoppable. 'Well then. A bit of dignity isn't all that much in the grand scheme of things, is it?'

Colin stomped back upstairs, channelling Angela at her grumpiest. He wasn't going to do it. There was a fine attached to wandering around for no reason, especially at night. Exercise was allowed during the lockdown, sure. But a Santa suit wasn't exactly exercise gear.

He spent two hours brooding in his chair. Then he donned the suit.

One last time.

***

Angela was awake long before Ishani threw open the bedroom door with gusto, a steaming teacup in her hand and the local paper rolled up under one arm. The past few editions had misprinted The Bean and Gone's website in the adverts and Ishani was now checking every single page to make sure the editor got it right. She wanted her customers to make their orders on a dedicated site instead of through a third party app, which ate into Ishani's profits.

They had a routine in the mornings now: Ishani would grumble about the paper, Angela would humour her, then they'd go their separate ways—Ishani to annoy her neighbours with some new stunt involving topiary or toplessness (sometimes both) and Angela to write her novel with Colin's show on in the background.

His voice was infuriatingly soothing. It made her feel like they were back on his sofa, sitting knee to knee and drinking chai tea out of mugs that probably should have been rinsed two days ago. She was still waiting for him to reveal to his listeners the real reason he'd created Second Chance Songs. But all week he had kept his silence.

His listeners were constantly asking each other what might have happened. Some even suspected that 'the whole Number Twelve thing' had been entirely fictional.

Angela had laughed out loud upon seeing those comments trending in the hashtag.

Turning away from her desk, where her alarmingly large collection of notes was stacked in chronological order, Angela smiled at Ishani and indicated the teacup. 'What'll I be having this time? Please don't say pu-erh. I'm sure it's lovely to some people, but my palate obviously isn't dignified enough for it. I *am* down for whatever black tea you gave me yesterday, since I managed to write ten thousand words between dawn and dusk. I didn't expect that. Or maybe it's more to do with me improving than the quantity of caffeine consumed...'

Ishani held out the newspaper, letting gravity unroll it in her hand. 'You might want to read the cover story.'

'Of *The Newfield Times*?' Angela asked, bemused. 'Can't imagine it'd be that interesting. Unless they're going to complain about another toilet paper shortage.'

'Don't look so disappointed; it is about toilet paper,' Ishani assured her, now smirking. 'But this one's also gone viral on the Internet. And I have a feeling you're going to hear about it on that phone of yours soon.'

In the background, Angela could distantly hear DJ Sunshine handing over the reins to DJ Coop. They were probably making the usual remarks about the weather in Whitby and Dover. No need to pay attention until Colin got into his first segment.

Angela's eyebrows knitted together. 'Ishani, what do you mea...'

Ishani tossed the newspaper into her lap. The front page bore a giant-sized photo, one that filled the page and showed Colin in that hideous Santa suit of his, though the beard had been pulled down to his chin. There was barely enough room at the top for the shouty headline: *Father Bog Roll Caught!*

'Oh my God,' Angela said.

'Thanks for telling everyone, Sunshine,' Colin was saying through the poxy speaker on her phone. 'It's not like I was going to use that topic to fill some time during my show later! But yes, it's true. Last night I was arrested while wearing a Santa suit. Roaming around at night like a proper creeper.'

'Proper creeper is right,' Ishani said. 'Did you know about this?'

Angela slumped in the chair, one hand clapped over her mouth, the other braced on the desk in front of her. She'd lost the ability to speak.

'I wasn't strictly exercising,' Colin went on cheerfully, 'but I didn't get slapped with a fine for breaking the lockdown laws, because the local boys in blue decided that I was providing care. Which is allowed, by the way. The local paper is calling me Father Bog Roll and I guess if the shoe fits...look, those care homes ran out of toilet paper and I'd accidentally bought a thousand rolls. Seemed like an obvious solution to me.'

Ishani laughed outright. 'Sure. *Accidentally* bought them. Hoarded and couldn't find a way to discreetly sell them with a huge mark-up, more likely.'

'I think I actually believe him,' Angela said.

Ishani gave her an incredulous look.

Angela poked her tongue out at her friend.

Oblivious to this showdown, DJ Coop continued with his show. 'It was too embarrassing to admit that I had a toilet paper problem. People would have got the wrong idea. I'm not a hoarder, just incredibly bad at checking my receipts *and* my privilege. Anyway, I got some advice from a neighbour who said I should let myself get caught. Why? Same reason I started this segment—and that's a reason you'll never be privy to. Moving right along. Today's double feature is "In the Air Tonight". Drum solos are cool and all, but have you ever added heavy metal and Millennial angst?'

Angela turned the volume down on her phone and stared out the window, at the achingly blue sky.

'Grand gesture,' she murmured.

'What was that?' Ishani asked.

'It's a grand gesture,' Angela explained, pen pressed against her bottom lip. 'To make up for all the crap the romantic lead has put the heroine through.'

Ishani clicked her tongue against her teeth, unimpressed. 'Didn't you say you wanted something more real? Less fictional?'

'Yes, I suppose I did say that.' Angela flattened the newspaper onto her desk and studied the photo of Colin posed between the policemen, his sexy grin on display. 'He wanted to apologise and explain himself, without using me on his show or getting into my personal space. It's…it's kind of romantic, actually. Life imitating art.'

'Romantic?' Ishani repeated dubiously. 'So, what, you're going to forgive him? Just like a character in one of your books? You don't have to, you know. Grand gestures are plot devices—you don't need to do anything about them in real life.'

Angela closed the Radio SPLATZAPP! app. 'I think I need to be alone for a while.'

'Okay, but if you need to be talked out of making a monumentally stupid decision, you know where to find me.'

Angela lobbed a pillow at Ishani. 'Go away! I've got work to do.'

'All work and no brooding about a certain DJ. Got it.'

Ishani dodged the next squishy projectile Angela sent her way and left the room, still laughing.

35

'Got busted on purpose, did you?'

'It worked, didn't it?' Colin retorted.

Rob gave him a sideways glance and took a long draw from a supersized coffee cup which proudly bore The Bean and Gone logo, the words spelled out in cartoonified coffee beans. Colin was holding a cup of tea that felt a lot colder than it ought to be, considering he'd only just bought it.

Ishani wasn't there yet and nor was Angela, but Colin had already received no less than seven scowls from the barista on duty.

He was clearly persona non grata right now.

'Can't argue with you there,' Rob conceded. 'Ishani and Angela keep randomly laughing about it, which means they're less likely to murder you when they show up. Now remember, I'm not here for you, mate. I'm Angela's backup. The bodyguard. So don't get fresh and I won't have to stop pretending to exercise in a circle around the café.'

'Got it,' Colin said.

He stood there awkwardly after Rob had left his side, drinking his tepid, flavoured water in silence and wondering how long Angela was going to make him wait.

'Hey, aren't you Father Bog Roll?' one of the customers in the nearby queue asked.

Colin nearly spat out a mouthful of tea. 'Yes. Yes, I am. I also host a show on Radio SPLATZAPP!, but I guess the toilet roll thing is going to be my legacy.'

'Neat!' The woman scrambled through her handbag and pulled out a pen, only to frown at it. She sighed. The pen disappeared. 'I'd ask for an autograph, but yeah...don't want to spread any germs. Just in case.'

'You can ask me in a few months,' Colin offered.

'You a regular?'

'I'm hoping I don't get blacklisted,' Colin said under his breath, though Ishani hadn't threatened to do that to him. Yet. He would dutifully stay away if he had to. This was Angela's safe space and he didn't want her to lose it.

And there she was, making her way down the hill with Ishani at her side.

Angela was clad in the soft peach jumper and that long black skirt, exactly what she had been wearing when he'd invited her into his flat and, unknowingly, right into his heart. There was no room in there for anyone else and he'd be a fool to pretend otherwise. Colin took a quick shot of his cold tea.

'Here goes everything,' he said.

Ishani split off to go around to the back of the café, heading for a service entrance. She gave Colin a look that would have flattened him if her eyes were packing lasers instead of mere judgement. Ishani would give no quarter.

But he wasn't here for her.

'Hello,' Angela said as she walked past him to join the queue. Colin tossed his cup into a nearby bin and lined up behind her. It was impossible to read her expression, since all he could see was the back of her head, but she was nervously knotting her hands at her sides when she spoke again. 'Grand gesture. That's a trope.'

'It is,' Colin agreed. 'I'm now the laughing-stock of Newfield and my parents will be livid when they get wind of it, but I thought it was better a idea than walking a boombox over to Ishani's place.'

'Because the cops would actually have fined you for that one?'

Colin suppressed a shudder. 'No. Lockdown laws aside, I have a feeling that randomly showing up like that wouldn't do me any favours. You know, it's weird. I used to enjoy those grand gestures in the movies. The ones with public settings and the big speech that embarrasses the person you're trying to apologise to.'

A laugh escaped her. 'There's that. I hope you're not trying to "win" me back.'

'Nope. Definitely the wrong century for that. I'll respect whatever decision you make.'

'Well, Colin, I think you just won a round of sexy banter,' Angela said, tossing a grin over her shoulder.

He ignored the hopeful jerk in his navel. 'Anyway, I could keep trying to get your attention with new and inventive methods, but I've run out of secrets to spring on you. I promise. And I managed to keep my lips sealed when Leo tried to bully me into giving the listeners what they wanted. He hasn't fired me yet, so that's something.'

Angela turned around, no doubt to make sure that he saw her rolling her eyes at him. 'You defeated the Big Bad Boss for me. Swoon.'

At least she hadn't tried to take a chunk out of him.

'I'll order for both of us, if you like,' she offered. 'You had the sourest look on your face when you took that last mouthful of tea. I can't imagine you've been getting any decent drinks here lately.'

'That'd be great,' Colin said. 'And some exercise in the park would be even greater.'

Angela froze, a strange shadow flitting through her eyes. Then her face smoothed out again. 'Angling for more time alone with me?'

Colin sighed. 'Rob can come too.'

'I think we'll be fine by ourselves, Colin.'

Colin's chest spasmed. He hoped he wouldn't mess this up.

A few minutes later, they were walking back up the hill, two metres strictly maintained between them. Colin had never been to this particular park, but Rob had assured him it wasn't popular and there wouldn't be too many witnesses if things went horribly wrong. Rob had a questionable sense of humour sometimes. Hopefully this was not one of those times.

Colin needn't have worried. The park fit the bill perfectly: abandoned benches, a stray dog sniffing suspiciously at a patch of grass—and completely empty, since parks were no longer places where people were allowed linger.

Angela paused at a particular bench (Colin slowed his steps, wondering if he'd misread her intention to follow the rules), but then she smiled and kept walking.

Always two metres ahead of him.

The distance between them was almost solid in nature; Colin lifted a hand and stretched it out towards her, but felt an invisible pressure push back against his palm. He slipped his hand into his pocket. This was absolute torture.

'I messed up,' Colin said.

'That you did,' Angela replied. 'I wish I'd known about your Father

Bog Roll alter ego sooner, mostly because I'd have used up a whole day of quarantine laughing so hard I wouldn't have been able to think clearly, let alone feel bored. I'm sorry I got so mad about the wardrobe reveal. It was really just an excuse to pile on and I should have let you explain.'

Colin took a sip of his tea. Piping hot, which oddly made him feel more optimistic about his chances. 'There I was, pleased with myself for having done a good deed by letting you have a lie-in on your birthday...but you were right. I was doing it to make my listeners happy, not you. But I'm willing to make you happy, if you'll allow me.'

'And getting yourself arrested by the police was the first step in your "make Angela happy" plan?' Angela asked, bemused.

'You know, this made a lot more sense the other night.'

'I bet it did. So.' Angela drew a breath. 'Were you serious about what you said?'

'Which bit?' Colin said, fumbling through his memories. 'I've said a lot of things, some of which I probably shouldn't have.'

'You being in love with me. Unless you shouldn't have said that?'

'Wasn't a good time for it,' Colin admitted.

Angela laughed and nodded. 'Definitely not. Maybe you'd like to try again?'

'Alright then.' Colin cleared his throat and almost adopted DJ Coop's well-oiled voice, then dropped that urge. Fast. It was easier to be the DJ, with confidence on standby and a microphone that no one else got to touch, but that wasn't the real him. 'I love you, Angela Tweedie. I love how you look in that skirt, I love how you can out-talk this DJ, I love your taste in tea, and I love spending time with you so much that I'd gladly follow you around this park all day, even if you never said a word to me. And I especially loved living with you.'

'Did you write this speech in advance?' Angela asked, a smile warming her words.

Colin wriggled his hands about in his pockets. 'I thought this was important enough to merit some planning. Something a bit more sophisticated than my previous plans, like March's "crap, I need to dump all this toilet paper—oh look, a Santa suit from that themed party at Rob's pub last Christmas".'

'So that's why you have the suit!'

'I fill it out well, don't I?'

Angela raked her eyes over him, lips pursed. 'I prefer the jeans and band shirts. You wore the *Rio* shirt today? Just for me? You shouldn't have.'

'I absolutely should have,' Colin said. 'And I bought five more like it, just in case.'

'Bold of you to assume you'll need them,' she teased.

'So.' Colin swallowed. 'Will I? Need them, that is.'

Angela shot a nervous look around the park. Apparently satisfied that no one was hiding behind the bushes and no police cars were passing by, she gave up any pretence of exercising and turned to face him. 'I didn't plan a speech. Which is…really unlike me. But while plans work perfectly in fiction, I've never had them work for me *at all* in real life. Therefore, I'm just going to wing it.'

'We've been a terrible influence on each other,' Colin said.

'Terrible or brilliant, who can say,' Angela said with a snort. 'But I wouldn't change any of it. Okay, maybe the bit where you ruined my birthday.'

Colin grimaced. 'Fudge. I really did ruin it.'

'I'll have more of them, so just do better next time,' Angela told him.

'Right. I'll definitely need the *Rio* shirts for those days.'

'Yes, you will. Just so you know, I love you too, Colin Cooper.' Angela shook her head, as if she couldn't quite believe what she was saying. 'You bring out the best and the worst in me. And I like that. Oddly enough. Hmm, maybe the "enemies to lovers" trope isn't as far-fetched as I used to think it was.'

Colin looked down at the stretch of pavement dividing them. 'I'd really love to kiss you right now.'

'Two metres feels like two miles,' Angela sighed.

'We shouldn't break the rules and kiss.'

'No, we definitely shouldn't.'

They stood there, staring at each other for what felt like an age. Colin studied her lips, tempted to lick and linger on each corner, to pull her into his arms, to get her scent all over his *Rio* shirt. He wanted to touch her. He wanted to take her home and kiss every inch of her, until neither of them had the energy to get out of bed. But Colin was fairly certain he wouldn't get away with calling it 'exercise'. He'd been lucky to avoid the fine once already.

'Okay, how is this standing here and not touching each other the sexiest thing I've ever done?' Angela mused.

Colin burst out laughing. 'I was just thinking the same thing.'

'Really? Because I can assure you the rest of my thoughts were definitely not PG.'

'Neither were mine.'

Angela's lips curled into a smirk. 'Oh good, we're on the same page then.'

'So you'll move back in?' Colin asked hopefully.

Angela hesitated.

Oh crap, he thought. He'd moved too fast. He didn't want to lose her. Not again.

'Forced proximity,' Angela said.

'What about it?'

'Things between us went too hard and fast because of forced proximity,' Angela explained, beginning to walk again. Colin kept pace with her on the grass this time, the required distance still between them, but at least this way he could see her face. 'It might work in fiction, but this is real life. I want this to last. So I want to take it slow.'

'This does make dating a bit harder,' Colin said. 'Especially now.'

Angela didn't look concerned. 'I'm sure you'll come up with some grand plan that solves our "dating during a lockdown" problem.'

'And if that plan ends with you moving back in after lockdown…?'

'I don't see a problem with that. So long as your plan involves me getting my own wardrobe.'

Colin couldn't hide the grin after that, nor when he returned to Grace Park, where Loraine and Bernard were waiting on their patio. He didn't say a word, but they took one look at him and toasted him with their cups of tea.

Colin marched upstairs and got busy with planning several weeks' worth of socially-distant dates.

***

Five Weeks Later

'Did you see the news?' Ishani asked from her sun lounger, which she'd moved into the front garden. The better to display her new bikini, of course. Ishani and Rayaan had a bet running on when a neighbour would actually stop to lecture her instead of walking past repeatedly, huffing and shaking their heads as they did so.

'We're allowed to form social support bubbles now,' Ishani went on. 'I think it's a good thing, allowing families to meet up again and be there for each other, and it's better to be cautious and make contained bubbles instead of letting everyone mingle all at once. Since your DJ's living alone in a single household, he's allowed to glom onto our bubble. Which means you can visit him. If that's what floats your boat.'

Angela smoothed her hands down the sides of her skirt. 'Why do you think I'm dressed up? We've exercised together so much it's getting a bit boring, though I can now confidently walk to Dover and back in under an hour, so that's something.'

'Should I expect you back—ever?' Ishani asked.

'I'll have to come by and get my things,' Angela pointed out.

'So you're moving out then?'

Angela just grinned and hurried up the footpath. It didn't take very long to reach Grace Park. She waved at The Bennets, who were enjoying tea in the sunshine—with two of their grandchildren sitting beside them on dining chairs that had been dragged out of their studio.

'He's waiting upstairs!' Bernard called.

Angela raced inside. She wasn't going to wait around for the lockout laws to tighten again.

This polite Regency romance she and Colin had going actually had its benefits. It had helped to slow things down. Alright, maybe their phone calls had been a little too sexy for Regency times. But still.

The door was already open before she finished walking up the stairs.

'Hi,' Colin said.

'Really?' Angela remarked. 'You said the other day you were going to go for variety this time and yet you got another Duran Duran shirt. And it's...*The Wedding Album*? Just what are you trying to say with that?'

Colin's face blanched. 'Not what it looks like! I just thought...well, new day, new shirt. And I've really, really missed having you here, by the way. I could always take the shirt off once you come inside, if that will make it up to you...?'

'Colin! I thought we could discuss how we're going to split the utilities.'

'You got a job?'

'That's what you're leading with?' Angela rolled her eyes. 'Fine. Yes. The local library hadn't a clue how to set up an ebook lending system and I offered to do it for them. For a contractual fee, of course. I'm going to have an actual job with them as well. Part-time, so I can still write my books. I'll be working from home until they reopen. Anyway, I'm more than happy to move in, but I'd really like to pay my way this time.'

Colin cleared his throat. 'So should we wait until you're moved back in, or...?'

Angela kicked the door shut, sidled up to him, and slid her arms around his neck. 'I am not waiting another minute, Colin Cooper.'

***

Angela was wearing one of Colin's many *Rio* shirts when his phone buzzed the next morning. Yawning, she fished it out and unlocked the screen (Colin's passcode was, embarrassingly, 1234) to discover a very angry text message from Leo. Throwing Colin a baleful look, because he was still peacefully asleep, Angela located the Zoom invitation in Colin's inbox and joined his usual 6am meeting.

Silence and stunned expressions greeted her.

'Colin's a little busy,' Angela said mildly. 'But I'm pretty sure he has all of his segments planned for later. And no, I definitely won't be in any of them.'

'I see our Col finally made a smart decision,' Danika commented.

Sunshine smiled broadly, Peter began to dab at his eyes, and as for Danger—Angela had expected a suggestive or offensive comment from him, but all he did was mutter about how he really needed to change his branding.

'I'll let it slide, just this once,' Leo said stiffly. 'Tell Colin to be on time tomorrow or he needs to start looking for a new job.'

That dealt with, Angela slid the phone back under Colin's pillow and curled up beside him. She didn't know when the lockdown would end (that depended on the pandemic, unfortunately), or if she'd ever get the Happily Ever After that pervaded the romance novels she loved.

But she was more than happy with her Happily For Now.

About the Author

Alyce Caswell lives in Sydney, Australia with zero cats, one husband, and one son. When she isn't drinking her way through a giant pot of tea, Alyce is a keen reader of Highlander romance novels and a Christmas movie addict. Before all this, however, she was a radio DJ. Alyce joined her local community radio station in high school and was producing her own show by the age of fifteen. She may have hung up her headphones since then, but she hasn't lost her love of New Wave music.

You can contact her via e-mail (alycecaswell@outlook.com) or on Twitter (@alycecaswell).